THE EYESPELL EXPERIMENT

THE EYESPELL EXPERIMENT

▼

Eyespell, Earth, and the Emergence of Mystic Management

John P. Cicero, Ph.D.

Writer's Showcase
San Jose New York Lincoln Shanghai

The Eyespell Experiment
Eyespell, Earth, and the Emergence of Mystic Management

Writer's Showcase
an imprint of iUniverse.com, Inc.

For information address:
iUniverse.com, Inc.
5220 S 16th, Ste. 200
Lincoln, NE 68512
www.iuniverse.com

ISBN: 0-595-17367-5

Printed in the United States of America

To my wife, Christina Jo, and my son, Michael Christian.

CONTENTS

FOREWORD

I was certain that *The Eyespell Experiment: Eyespell, Earth, and the Emergence of Mystic Management* was a work of fiction, actually science fiction with elements of truth running through it. My intention was to integrate my thirty-year management discipline as a college professor with a bent for writing and a concern for business ethics in this new millennium. I did not want to write just another business textbook. *Eyespell* is now finished and I am not so certain about what I have written with regard to its fictional and non-fictional aspects.

Late one afternoon about a year ago I happened upon a book tucked away on an out-of-the-way rack at the local Barnes and Noble Booksellers. It had a somewhat intriguing title, *From Elsewhere: The Subculture of Those Who Claim To Be of Non-Earthly Origins.* I had never heard of the author, Scott Mandelker, Ph.D., nor had I ever considered the subject of extraterrestrials seriously. In fact, somewhere around the launch the first Apollo moon flight in 1969 I met Adrian Clark a NASA engineer working at Huntsville Space Flight Center. He was promoting his book *Cosmic Mysteries of the Universe.* He proposed lots of other worldly theories including much biblical reference and the concept that dinosaurs were seeded on the earth by aliens. I dismissed him as basically nuts and hoped he was a better engineer than philosopher. *From Elsewhere* sparked memories of this earlier alien encounter.

The whole subject of extraterrestrials as fact versus fiction makes me reasonably uncomfortable. Something possessed me to read Mandelker's book anyway. I did so with relative detachment until almost the end and then it hit me like the proverbial "ton of bricks;" the character in my book, supposedly a fictional account of an extraterrestrial accidentally stranded on the Earth, exactly fit Mandelker's profile of extraterrestrials, specifically those he calls "Wanderers"! Worse yet, many of the characteristics of my fictional world, Eyespell, fit Mandelker's description of "other densities" almost exactly! Understand, I knew nothing of these things while writing *Eyespell*. I immediately contacted Scott Mandelker and he agreed to read my manuscript. He liked it and wasn't even slightly surprised at its consistency with what he had written in his non-fictional account of extraterrestrials. I think that upset me even more and the manuscript has been sitting in my computer…until now.

There is something archetypical about what's written here. At least parts of *Eyespell* must come from what Jung describes as the collective unconscious. Even the manner in which it was written struck me as strange. I had no outline and did not have a clear vision of Eyespell until I found myself writing about it. I didn't know where the manuscript was going until it got there and then one day it seemed finished. And that's what's important about *Eyespell*: it was written. I hope you will take it one step further and read it and then the final step and act on it. To paraphrase His Holiness The Dalai Lama, to recognize compassion is not enough, one must act compassionately. And that is what a Mystic Management ultimately recommends, acting compassionately in a world of swirling changes, a world where the long-term, sustainability, and the constant harvest appear to be impossible to maintain. I sincerely hope you enjoy reading *The Eyespell Experiment*. Whether it is fact or fiction is up to you.

John P. Cicero
Northern, California
October 16, 2000

ACKNOWLEDGEMENTS

As this work progresses toward final publication I am sure there will be many people who deserve thanks. However, first and foremost there will always be my wife and editor Christina. Without her diligent and loving effort there would be no book. She molded the manuscript into a story that flowed from beginning to end. Mostly she asked me questions about Eyespell; insisting on more information. When I would show my frustration at her picky inquiries her standard retort was: "Well then, who should I ask about Eyespell?"

I would also like to thank Jennifer Braaten, a colleague when I taught at the College of Boca Raton, now Lynn University. For a brief period Jennifer and I worked on this manuscript together and then abandoned the idea in favor of doing something more constructive. There lingers, however, disconnected bits and pieces of Jennifer's input particularly in the passages referred to as "Phillip's old manuscript." Jennifer was also instrumental in naming the six tenets of Mystic Management.

Patrick Hardy is the inspiration behind "Used Water Works" and part of the vision for the future of Earth portrayed toward the end of the book. Patrick was a student at Shasta College. He loved Eyespell and has always thought I know much more than I do. He called his vision Chimanuka.

There are several people who have been kind enough to read the manuscript in its various stages of development and offer feedback. Three people immediately come to mind, Tienne Beaulieu, Carolyn Warnemuende, and Lew Schmitt. Tien wanted to go to Eyespell and gave me the confidence that it was as neat a place as I thought. Carolyn offered much specific input fearing our friendship might never be the same. And she was right—it's better. Lew read the book at least twice, once in its infancy and once when I thought it was completed. As a connoisseur of science fiction I think he said something like: "I have read far worse." From Lew this was all the encouragement I needed to be sure that someday this work would make its way into print.

Of course there are many others along the way who have been the inspiration for *Eyespell* in all its aspects, the good, the bad and the other worldly.

CHAPTER I

▼

THE RETURN TO EYESPELL (EYESPELL)

His head hurt so badly that he couldn't tell if the pounding at his temples was causing double vision or if there were, in fact, two suns in the desert sky. Antonio remembered being hideously depressed, even suicidal. He also remembered being in his dingy rented room in a small Northern California town. He knew it hadn't rained all month, and it was getting hotter by the day in preparation for another summer of drought.

Antonio was a young man of twenty and his life was in as much a drought as the parched lands of the Central Valley. He thought that as the lack of rainfall reduced the flowing Sacramento to a mere trickle, maybe his life-blood too could be dried to a mere trickle and he would just die. He could become a symbol of the hopelessness of the youth of his time and place. He could just wither and die in a walnut grove. They would find him with his back against the grafted stump of a walnut tree, his hands palms down in the dry dirt, and his face blank, totally expressionless, devoid of emotion. The authorities would determine that the cause of death involved no violence, no drugs, just a giving up; sort of like dying of a broken heart over an empty life.

Antonio had spent a great deal of his time thinking about this potential death scenario and the message it would convey. At this exact moment, however, he was preoccupied with how he came to be in this unworldly desert and, as he rubbed his grayish eyes with his cool, tanned fingers, he determined that there were, indeed, two suns. One shone directly over-head in the familiar yellow noontime zenith; the other was due north, hanging low on the horizon, and a brilliant blue. At some level, he was also aware that this desert was comfortably cool for what appeared to be high noon. His six-foot-three-inch frame tensed as he realized he stood stark naked with muscles rippling where, just moments before, there were only the meagerest of biceps barely covering the bony frame of an under-nourished field worker.

Antonio was sure he wasn't dreaming. He was not afraid and he was not depressed. He felt wonderfully at home and alive in this foreign place and unfamiliar body. Suicide was the furthest thing from his mind, even though he clearly remembered the deed and the circumstances that led up to it.

Antonio was the eldest of four children born to Hernando and Maria Gomez. He was American by birth and Mexican by heritage. He was born in Santa Maria, California. His parents were working the tidy strawberry fields west of town. Those were good times with high hopes. Hernando and Maria saw their future as bright and endless like the often-visited flower fields of nearby Lompoc. Hernando was promoted to field foreman and then Maria died with the birth of their fourth child. Antonio was sent to live with cousins further north and inland. The flowered fields faded to endless days of hot summers and drafty winters. Antonio was the child of poor relatives. While welcome in his uncle's house, he was last on every-body's emotional and physical necessity lists. There was only so much to go around and Antonio typically got what was left over.

Under the strange suns Antonio reflected on his past. For some, his type of situation sparks courage and an undaunted need to achieve great things, especially great wealth. For others, the situation is less dramatic. The will to survive, often cloaked in the will to do God's will, allows one to go on and seek some pseudo-peacefulness in the single hope of achieving heaven as a final reward. And for still others, others like Antonio, the spirit breaks and one moves further and further into the grips of an unbearable hopelessness. This discomforting reminiscence was broken by the sound of a man's voice.

"You would think that you could come up with something more creative than fading out against an old walnut tree."

The voice came from behind Antonio and belonged to Leo, an elderly man dressed in baggy white shorts, a blue and lavender polo shirt, and sandals. He sported a shortly cropped gray-white beard and badly balding head with some longer gray-white strands along the edges. Antonio was too startled to be embarrassed by his nakedness as he instinctively slipped into the clothes the man tossed him. Oddly, everything fit…perfectly.

"You're the first one back," the man said as he pivoted on the white sand and casually motioned over his shoulder for Antonio to follow.

Antonio, sprinting and almost breathless, glided alongside Leo and asked: "First one back? What's that supposed to mean? I am really freaked out. I feel like me, but I sure don't look like me…and this place, a cool desert with two suns, I don't think so."

Leo laughed and said: "It must be weird, but you can sense everything is okay. This place feels familiar and you feel like you've known me for a long time. Am I right?"

"Yes, but how did you know?"

"It will all become clear with a little time in this place. For now just enjoy."

"Is this place heaven?"

Leo again laughed, this time shaking his head back and forth. "No, son, this is not heaven. In all the universe this may be the most beautiful place, but it is not heaven and I surely am not God. Somewhere above all of this beauty there exists a heaven, a creator, the life force. If you were in the presence of such there would be no questions, no confusion. You would simply be and you would simply know. Let's go to meet the others."

"What others?"

"Like I said, you are the first one back." The twinkle in Leo's eye shone like a third sun in Antonio's consciousness as they moved in unison across the sand.

* * * * * * * *

Melissa was wandering along a Boca Raton, Florida, beach trying to decide what to get high on. She accidentally dropped a twenty-dollar bill in the sand and could not be bothered to chase it as a mild ocean breeze gently caressed her golden hair and flew the money into the sea. As she felt her hair play around her neck and bare shoulders, she didn't need a mirror to remind her that she was the epitome of "hot." And, she was rich and smart just to rub it in.

She was going to be twenty in a few days and seemed strangely obsessed with how to die. Melissa was depressed. She often thought of just walking into oblivion, walking into the Devil's Triangle Ocean. Now that would be a death scenario with a message, she mused: "Beauty, brains, and wealth were not enough to save Melissa Commings from the ravaging hopelessness of so many youth of her time. The body was found washed up on the beach, white-crusted with salt, ghost-like and expressionless."

Melissa's death would not go unnoticed. She was the only child of Samuel Commings, world class cardiologist, and Gloria Stein-Commings, world class bitch. Her father's position and her mother's abrasiveness always made anything Melissa did as either much better or much worse than it really was. Melissa Commings was society page stuff. She was often subject matter for the *Boca Raton News*, or the *Palm Beach Post*, and sometimes even the *Miami*

Herald. Living under the shadows of her parents had turned Melissa cold, and left her skating downhill through life at breakneck speed with no hope of recovery. For Melissa, an early death was just a matter of time and place.

The blue sun almost directly overhead startled Melissa even more than her nakedness. She didn't remember getting high or having sex, and, certainly, she had never hallucinated before. The sand was whiter and the humidity lower, and, although it was not possible, it looked as though another more familiar yellow sun was setting in the west.

A neatly-folded stack of clothing caught her eye as she looked behind her where the ocean used to be. "Get dressed and follow the footprints in the sand," was neatly inscribed on a piece of metallic-like paper that did not move with the wind. Footprints led straight over the dunes and toward the folded mountains that were not there in her recollection of just moments before.

Melissa was sure this was not a dream. She was not afraid and she was very aware that she no longer felt depressed. With each step forward, the footprints behind her disappeared like invisible ink into parchment. When she looked up from her footprint-following task, she met the friendly gazes of a neat white-bearded elderly man and the good-looking, tall, young man at his side. Leo just smiled and motioned her to follow.

Not being at all shy Melissa edged her way between Antonio and Leo and said: "Okay guys, what's the deal? Is this some sort of virtual reality game or something?"

Antonio quickly replied: "Or something is more like it. I know this sounds like a terrible line but I feel as though I know you."

"Well maybe you do. Are you from around here?"

"I don't exactly know where here is."

"You sound serious. This isn't a game?"

"This isn't a game, and we're not in heaven. By the way I'm Antonio and this is Leo, and Leo isn't God. I feel better than I've felt in my whole life and I feel like I know you. That's everything I know and Leo's not talking."

"You are serious. Well Mr. Leo, what's the deal?"

Leo's enormous twinkle caught Melissa as he smiled and said: "No deal, young lady, you're finally home where you belong."

Antonio and Melissa exclaimed in unison: "Home?"

"Yes home. You were both part of a grand experiment and now you're back. Enough chat, we need to catch up with the next member of your team." Leo bent his head slightly forward and led them swiftly over the dunes. For the moment Antonio and Melissa felt content to follow immersed in their own thoughts.

* * * * * * * *

Nancy had always vaguely remembered that she was supposed to die at twenty, but she couldn't remember why. It didn't particularly bother her though. She was quite used to not remembering. She remembered only scattered blotches of her past. At barely eighteen she had awakened one day in a hospital bed in a small Southwest town outside of Phoenix. She had been found stumbling out of the Superstition Mountain area, she and her family apparently victims of the Superstition's curse. The Superstition Mountains have an uncanny propensity for just swallowing up folks. In this case, her parents were found brutally murdered in their camping trailer. Fingerprints and the effects found around the campsite identified the surviving family member as Nancy Mellon. She took the authorities at their word, never having had any recollection of the incident, just bits and pieces of a life that may have come before. As sole heiress to the Mellon estate of $42,416.84, Nancy set out on her own. She remained a recluse, lived simply and communicated primarily with her meditative world.

Hers was a spiritual path and she was very much in touch with those she perceived to be her spirit guides or angels, especially a being named Kathryn. On her twentieth birthday, encouraged by Kathryn, Nancy simply leapt off the top of a mesa somewhere in New Mexico. She had complete confidence that she would not die. Therefore, when she awakened naked under the two suns, she was neither surprised nor betrayed by this confidence. She was very much alive. She did, however, feel ever so slightly depressed. She did what she always did in times of uneasiness, she stilled her mind and began to meditate.

This meditation was like no other she had ever experienced. She seemed to connect almost instantly with what seemed like an entire planet! The experience was outrageous while familiar, and deafening while quiet. Most interesting, however, was the feeling of connectedness to the physical planet itself! This was a dimension Nancy had never experienced. At some point in her meditation Nancy sensed three figures coming toward her, an elderly gentleman, a tall young man, and a very attractive young woman. Her mind went out to greet them. It was a feeling of old and deep friendship renewed. It was curious, however, that for the first time in recent memory Nancy did not sense the presence of Kathryn during meditation.

Nancy finished her unusual and powerful meditation and was startled to discover that Leo and the others were still there in her reality. She absent-mindedly dressed in clothing obviously there for her and joined them, puzzled and still ever so slightly depressed. She found it curious that such a magnificent meditation had failed to heal her.

Leo extended his arms in a welcoming hug and said: "Welcome home."

Nancy tactfully shrunk from his grasp and addressed the three of them. "Who are you people?"

A bit flustered Leo said: "I'm Leo, this is Melissa, and this is Antonio."

"I'm Nancy and what do you mean 'welcome home'?"

Antonio piped in and said: "It's a big mystery to all of us except Leo, of course. Melissa and I are also recent arrivals. Although we don't know much about this place, it sure feels good. I'm sorry we sort of sneaked up on you. Anyway, won't you join us?"

"I don't seem to have much choice, and you're right, it does feel pretty good here."

"Let's go then," said Leo. As they moved on he had an uncomfortable feeling about Nancy. He mumbled to himself: "When was the last time an Eyespellian was denied a hug?"

* * * * * * * *

As it turns out, Kathryn was neither a spirit guide nor an angel. She was an Eyespellian and like all Eyespellians had a highly developed telepathic sense. Kathryn used this ability to deceive Nancy into thinking that ordinary telepathic probings between the two of them were communications from a higher being.

This became necessary when a telepathy link between Kathryn and Nancy bled into Nancy's semi-conscious awareness. The result of such bleed-through would be premature exposure of details of Eyespell and the Eyespell Experiment. Any concrete knowledge of Eyespell on Nancy's part prior to her re-entry was deemed a great risk. While still in Earth-fusion the telepathy bleed might accelerate and reverse mind-set polarities causing Nancy's premature re-entry to Eyespell. It was hypothesized that this would generate severe Earth-plane vibrational leakage. The havoc such vibrational leakage could wreak on Eyespell was the single greatest perceived danger of the Eyespell Experiment.

Kathryn felt very poorly about deceiving Nancy. Such deception, however, was imperative in order to cover her own identity as Kathryn Song, Earth overseer of the Eyespell Experiment. Nancy's belief in spirit guides made this deception easy. A telepathy probe is often hard to distinguish from one's own inner thoughts. Therefore, whenever Nancy became aware of Kathryn's presence in her thoughts, especially during meditation, she was tricked into perceiving her as a spirit guide. In this way Kathryn's Eyespellian identity remained hidden. What was so difficult about this was that Eyespellians simply do not lie, ever. This was an unwelcome first.

* * * * * * * *

By the time he was twelve Pete was an alcoholic. By thirteen he had donned his Raider's Cap, carried a baseball bat, and was loose on the streets only by virtue of his young chronological age and the already over-crowded conditions of the county facilities for "troubled" minors. Pete was a born leader, and had he not thrown himself in front of a N.Y.C. commuter train on his twentieth birthday, he surely would have achieved a place of stature among gang lords.

Peter Capalinni was first generation American. His parents, Carmen and Angelina, had moved from Sicily to the Bronx for a better life just before his birth in 1972. And a better life it apparently was. The Italian Rooster, the family owned restaurant, was one of the best hole-in-the-wall eating places for sixty blocks around. It was one of those places just waiting to be discovered by the famous as the best off-the-beaten-path place to eat. If the neighborhood hadn't turned so bad so fast, it just might have happened. Angelina's southern fried chicken and homemade cheese ravioli were some of the best there were. On Sunday afternoons, papa Carmen kept the clientele amused with a small organ-grinder-style accordion. What papa and mama Capalinni didn't know was that the only reason the Italian Rooster managed to stay open for business at all, was that son Peter and his gang patrolled the surrounding fifteen blocks with steel and gunpowder. Pete kept the illusion of business-as-usual alive for his parents. He even brought home decent report cards over the years, after making his teachers "offers they couldn't refuse."

When Pete awoke on Eyespell, his first thought was that he must have gone to heaven in spite of himself. He felt wonderful and was too elated to question either his nakedness or the four beautiful moons of Eyespell shining in the clear night sky. He was so intrigued by his newfound surroundings that it was several minutes before he saw Leo standing there, smiling broadly and gesturing for him to get dressed and follow.

"You are the fourth one back, and the fourth one of our children I have greeted this day," Leo said.

"Say what?"

"It's not important, just enjoy yourself."

Leo felt good about Pete. Within a couple of minutes they joined up with the others. Pete's presence added something dynamic and very Eyespellian to the group. Even Nancy warmed up offering Pete both her hands in a gesture of comfortable familiarity.

Out of nowhere Pete said: "It's so great to be home! Whoops, I can tell by your expressions that you think I'm nuts. Well, maybe, but I don't think so. This just feels too right and too familiar. And all of you are old friends, very old friends. And you, Leo, you are, as always, in the middle of things."

Leo smiled broader than ever and regained whatever composure had been eroded by Nancy's earlier behavior. "Well Pete, I see you're right out front leading the group as usual. Welcome home!"

As the four followed him, Leo thought he should get in touch with Kathryn to see if there had been any linkage with the fifth and last Eyespellian scheduled to return. His concern over the whereabouts of the last to return was outwardly disguised by his expression and white beard.

* * * * * * * *

Kathryn the Overseer was trying to decide if she should leave Earth now or take the riskier approach of waiting until the last possible re-entry window. She longed for Eyespell's blue sun. It had been twenty years since she had been caressed by the blue sun that visually transformed the Eyespellian landscape into a serene, pastel paradise. If one ignored the two suns and four moons, from outer space Eyespell looked a lot like Earth only pink instead of blue. Even though the chemical composition of Eyespell's atmosphere was almost identical to Earth's, the air was somehow different and more exhilarating to the breath. Moreover, something akin to Earth's ozone layer neutralized any harmful radiation enhancing the atmosphere's refreshing and people-friendly essence. Kathryn sighed audibly and took a long and deep imagined drink of her home planet.

Some of her concerns dissipated and others were heightened as her line of thinking shifted from when to return to Eyespell to why, in the first place, she had been opposed to the Earth-based project involving Antonio and the others. She stretched back on the over-sized floor pillows. Her flowing pitch-black hair against a white pillow offered a startling contrast to her pastel-appointed apartment. Such contrast might be a microcosm of Earth and of Eyespell. Her hair, though beautiful, seemed full of danger, as if it might absorb the rest of her, along with her pastel surroundings, in its sheer blackness. It was a visual cue portending the subtle yet potentially disastrous leakage of one thing into another. Kathryn was too busy with her thoughts about the Eyespell Experiment to notice the cosmic clairvoyance reflected in her surroundings.

She had objected to the Eyespell Experiment from its very inception. From across the galaxies Eyespell had been listening and watching Earth's social progress for some time. The parallels between the planets went far beyond similar atmospheres. Earthlings were very much like ancient Eyespellians in their attitudes, beliefs, and potential for fostering a world society both technologically and spiritually imposing. Earthlings even looked like Eyespellians. The difference was that early in its development Eyespell was set on a path of enlightenment with more than a little help from the Cosmos. The Life Force had shone brightly on Eyespell and guided her peoples toward harmony in all things and all thoughts. This Divine Direction left Eyespell harmonious within herself, with a charge to replace discord with harmony wherever discord was encountered. Throughout recent history, from the shores of her pastel desert sands, Eyespell has extended the positive vibration of the planet and its peoples to all she encountered in need of healing energy. A primary dictum, however, had always been to heal from a distance…to literally shed light and love from a distance using only the telepathic and spiritual powers developed from early times.

The Eyespell Experiment was different. Due to the connectedness Eyespellians felt with the Earth, for the first time, they proposed to deal with a healing up close and personal. The Eyespell Experiment actually proposed manifesting five participants and one observer directly on the Earth-plane for twenty Earth years. Kathryn's primary objection to the experiment had been the nagging fear that the re-entry process might be unsuccessful. There could either be problems with getting all the participants back or, worse yet, difficulty in neutralizing the Earth-plane vibrations picked up by the participants and potentially brought to Eyespell. The damage to Eyespell from such Earth-plane vibrational leakage could be irreparable and once unleashed on the planet, geometric in its progression.

In spite of such risk, the governing Elders of Eyespell had been insistent upon gaining a better understanding of the Earth and the evolution of its peoples. From an Eyespellian perspective, and even from an objective Earth perspective for that matter, much of Earth's social "progress" made little or no sense. Although of similar potential as Eyespell Earth did not seem to be getting the Divine Guidance Eyespell had received, or wasn't listening. For example, the very thought of developing an economic system in total opposition to the environmental perpetuity of a planet, and ultimately its peoples, seemed insane on any collectively conscious level. How the desire for economic profit could supersede a species' instinct for survival was at best mystifying to Eyespellians. They had no parallel experience. The Eyespellian management philosophy was based on long-term benefits and sustainability. The management of all things focused on a moral philosophy based in a compassion which respected the dignity of every living thing. The concept of life was inclusive of all things in the Eyespellian environment, including the physical planet itself. This philosophy called Mystic Management evolved and expanded from six primary tenets: Collaborative Creativity, Ego Empowerment, Gentle Generosity, Karmic Kindness, Inclusive Integrity, and Systems Sensitivity.

With regard to the Eyespell Experiment, observation, research, and even telepathy across the vastness of space separating Earth and Eyespell were somewhat limited. While it was easy enough to access communication modalities including the Internet, this information lacked feeling. These data were from secondary sources; there was no direct Eyespell/Earth connection. Telepathy links with Earth were fraught with what might be best described as mental static. One could not be sure with whom one had connected or, for that matter, whether the connection was only with Earth without outside interference. Eyespell was essentially eavesdropping on the Earth. However, even this imperfect eavesdropping had produced a number of conclusions essential to the conception and direction of what would ultimately be called the Eyespell Experiment.

It was immediately apparent that direct physical contact with the Earth, while possible, had to be balanced against the risks. This, again, was Kathryn's concern. But, it was more complicated than even the re-entry issues. Open physical contact with Earthlings would most assuredly be perceived as an alien invasion or, perhaps, an economic opportunity. And, of course, anything economic would most likely be distorted to fit what Eyespellian researchers came to call the Species Elimination Model (SEM). There had to be direct contact although it be cloaked in order to mesh with Earth consciousness.

An obscure trend gleaned from newspaper articles picked up over the Internet gave researchers an idea. One of the most severe symptoms of Earth's fragmented social evolution appeared to be the high suicide rate among teenagers and young adults, primarily those living in affluent countries. After careful consideration of the data gathered, the Elders agreed upon an experiment whereby five Eyespellians would "fuse" with the Earth-youth experience in the culturally diverse and affluent United States of America. They anticipated that such a fusing would offer the direct, yet unobserved, link with Earth necessary for Eyespell's collection of primary and unfiltered data. The participants would actually live Earth lives for twenty years and then commit suicide within hours of each other. The idea was that five suicides of young people within a short time would get peoples' attention, starting the populace on a search for reasons and solutions. This outer search would hopefully lead to inner search and a new identity with community and community building. The hope was that this would ultimately culminate in a philosophy akin to the Mystic Management. Success of the Eyespell Experiment would allow for the possibility of open and non-threatening direct intervention at some later date even to the point of teaching the Mystic Management philosophy to a receptive Earth. The exciting prospect of helping this similar planet blinded Eyespell to the magnitude of the risks.

Potential participants for the Eyespell Experiment were meticulously screened and re-screened to determine their ability to avoid incidences of severe and sustained Earth-plane vibrational leakage upon their return to Eyespell. While this screening process reduced the possibility of such leakage the overall risk could not be entirely eliminated given that such an experiment had never been attempted, and there are always unknowns. This is why Kathryn had questioned and was uncomfortable with the safety aspect of the project. To assuage her perceived over-concern, she was officially appointed the Earth-based Project Overseer. Kathryn took on her role with a sense of foreboding and, from her Earth location, maintained close yet unobserved scrutiny of the five subjects for the twenty-Earth years' duration of the Eyespell Experiment. In the end her concern was justified, one Eyespellian was missing.

CHAPTER 2

▼

REFLECTIONS ON MYSTIC MANAGEMENT (EARTH)

Koy Sosa was a good reporter. This day she had hopes of becoming an even better one. "Finally," she thought, "I'm going to do something different. I'm actually going to interview real human beings instead of reporting the dry financial news. I'm going to interview Phillip and Christian Hansen, the dynamic father and son duo who are capturing the management scene on a global level, and with something called, of all things, Mystic Management. I remember that when I first heard the term I thought it sounded a bit hokey, but corporations all over the world are listening and CEOs are taking decisive and positive action based on Phillip and Christian's high-minded ideals and espoused management principles. While my love for statistics and my propensity for being incredibly accurate got me my reporting job in the first place, they've also kept me from expanding my horizons. I have felt terribly limited. I'm glad I gave good-old-editor Dave a piece of my mind the other day. He evidently understood my concerns and is giving me a chance to get out of my rut. Let me see, I've got a news clip on Mystic Management somewhere in this mess. Ah here it is."

> At the Hyatt Hotel in Irvine, California, more than one hundred corporate chief executive officers from more than twenty countries gathered today to begin a three-day workshop on Mystic Management. The workshop leaders are noted psychologist Phillip Hansen and his son Christian Hansen, CEO of Used Water Works, Inc., the company making history in Owens Valley, California.
>
> The workshop is not about productivity, continuous quality, customer service, technology, coping with change, or increased profits. The workshop is about community building, humanizing the corporate environment, self-esteem, sustainability, and a vision of "prophets not profits." The crux of the discussion revolves around the six tenets of what the Hansens call Mystic Management. They speak of Collaborative Creativity, Ego Empowerment, Gentle Generosity, Karmic Kindness, Inclusive Integrity, and Systems Sensitivity.
>
> With so many high-powered CEOs listening we may be on the verge of a new blueprint for business and world economics based on compassion instead of dollars. Expect to hear a lot more from this dynamic father and son duo.

Koy shouted to herself, "Yes, you'll be hearing a lot more from them and from me, Koy Sosa, star reporter!" She giggled in childlike excitement. Her bright red dress danced around her slim waist and ebony calves as she bounded out of her apartment toward the elevator. She was meeting the Hansens in exactly twenty minutes at biker-approved, executive-approved, and student-approved Dinosaur's Barbecue in downtown

Syracuse, New York. After lunch she planned to accompany them to the university where they were delivering a lecture to students and faculty.

"Dynamic duo is right," she thought. "Imagine, four CEO seminars last month, seven lectures this month, and agreeing to an interview with a virtually unknown reporter. And lunch at Dinosaur's. Life is good."

Koy arrived at the restaurant exactly on time and had no trouble spotting Phillip and Christian. "They look just like they described themselves," Koy said to herself. "Well, of course they look like themselves. God, you must be nervous." She approached the two men hand extended, "Hi, I'm Koy Sosa. It's truly a pleasure to meet you."

They had barely exchanged amenities and Koy got right to work. "I brought this news clip about your seminar in Irvine last month. While it mentions the six tenets of the Mystic Management, it doesn't tell me anything about them. Perhaps defining the principles would be a good starting place?"

Both men shook their heads in agreement, genuinely tickled by her enthusiasm. They took an instant liking to her.

Koy, armed with her steno pad, got right to work. "I guess starting with the first principle of Mystic Management makes sense. What do you mean by Collaborative Creativity?"

Phillip began, "I'm glad you're planning to attend the lecture this afternoon. I think you'll probably get more detail than you want. But, I agree that basic definitions are in order at this point. By the way, we're smiling because we have good feelings about you; your positive attitude says it all. You can be sure that we'll give you all the time and information you need to feel totally comfortable with Mystic Management."

Koy smiled back confessing, "This is my first interview of this type. I've spent my whole career, all two years of it, reporting financial statistics. Thanks for making me feel comfortable. You know, I'm not such a dunce that I haven't read up on Mystic Management before getting here. What I'm looking for, though, is the principles in your own words, personally, from you to me. I've got the facts; I can probably quote you more statistics on Mystic

Management than you'd want to know. For example, how many seminars, who the participants were, where they were from, the company represented, and so on and so on. I really want to hear it from you. Maybe I can give Mystic Management a new twist, something really special."

Christian leaned forward and said, "There is absolutely no doubt you will make it special and we appreciate that. So, Dad, what is Collaborative Creativity in a sentence?"

Phillip responded without hesitation. "I see it as the ability to listen to and respect all ideas, remaining open to using at least one new idea in some form in every decision scenario. It is placing a value on creativity for its own sake."

"That's two sentences," said Christian.

"And I like both of them," responded Koy. "How about a couple more, this time on Ego Empowerment."

"That's my personal favorite," said Christian. "It's allowing people to achieve goals without beating it out of them. I tell you where I'm trying to go and let you figure out how to best get there. It's a fundamental team concept. The trick is to let go of the parenting attitude, the 'I know how to do it best' attitude, the 'mine is the only way' attitude, and probably a hundred other counter productive attitudes. This one takes a big chunk of positive self-esteem to pull off. Interestingly this is a principle that women are innately better at. By nature or certainly by socialization women are more process oriented. They really believe it's 'how you play the game that counts.' Of course, when I say 'they' I mean that big group in the middle of the bell curve. There are always exceptions. For example, dad and I are very good at this one and you've probably noticed that we're both men."

"You're really cheating," said Koy. "That's at least half-a-dozen sentences."

"He's like that," chimed in Phillip.

"So, who's going to take a crack at Gentle Generosity, and under two pages please," Koy enthusiastically interjected.

"I've got this one in a nutshell," said Phillip. "It's going the extra step to encourage; it's being compassionate. Compassion is a cornerstone of Mystic Management. Without it the rest makes no sense."

"I can appreciate that," said Koy. "It's taking the time to work with unknown reporters perhaps. And, Karmic Kindness?"

Christian and Phillip put arms on each other's shoulders and orated in unison, "What goes around comes around, and kindness is the better way: compassion, compassion, compassion."

"You've got my vote," laughed Koy. "Okay, two more to go. We can do it. Who's going to field Inclusive Integrity?"

"Two words," said Phillip. "Value diversity."

"And before you ask," volunteered Christian, "Systems Sensitivity means that all of the above are related to each other and to things as they are now and as they can be in the future. How's that for a mouthful?"

"Thank you," said Koy. "Now I can spend the rest of my day expanding, understanding, and hopefully giving some journalistic life to the Mystic Management principles. I'll buy lunch and see you at the university or 'on the hill' as we locals say. One last thing; how did you come up with Mystic Management; how was it born?"

With a definitely mischievous gleam in his eye Phillip said softly, "You mean where was Mystic Management born, not how, but that's a long story for another day."

Before Koy could pursue the issue, Phillip and Christian had slipped out of the booth and were almost out the door waving over their shoulders. She could hear over the crowd, "See you on the hill."

She paid the check mumbling to herself, "What's the big mystery? I would think one place is as good as another for an idea to be born." As she turned to leave, the sun shone through the window, its rays momentarily catching a pink tinted glass tip-jar next to the cash register, turning Dinosaur's slightly smoke-hazed interior a beautiful pink. Koy was startled by the brief other-world sensation and shook herself as if out of a sleep as she walked toward the door and headed for the university.

Koy found the afternoon lecture enjoyable and enlightening. Both Phillip and Christian proved to be top-notch speakers. Each presented in turn scenarios exemplifying the six principles of Mystic Management. Father and son played off each other brilliantly, mixing roles of professor, straight man, executive, and counselor as if blending the perfect mental meal. The conceptual plate was tasty and intellectually filling. Koy managed to stuff both her head and her tape recorder with the Hansens' delicacies. She began her transcribing task about the same time Phillip and Christian's plane lifted into the sky above North Syracuse.

"Well Dad, do you think we gave Koy an earful today?"

"She got a lot more than she bargained for," was Phillip's immediate response. "When she begins to transcribe the tapes she'll discover there's more feeling and perception than hard facts. Her experience as a statistical business reporter is about to be challenged. She's not used to sorting abstract concepts especially when they're grounded more in faith than fact. I wish I could be a fly on the wall as she tries to make perfect sense out of our managerial artscape. Somehow she'll do it though, I sensed it from the moment we met her."

"I couldn't agree more," added Christian.

Father and son gave each other a gentle high-five and settled into the task of plane-riding home.

* * * * *

Arms waving in the air and her black hair trying to jump over her ears, Koy exclaimed, "I can't believe it! I listened to this Mystic Management lecture just this afternoon. It made perfect sense at the time. Now, as I listen to these tapes, I'm not so sure what's fact and what's wishful thinking. Transcribing this verbatim would be useless. It would end up sounding too theoretical, too pie-in-the-sky, too ivory tower even for the 'ivory tower.' I think I need to listen carefully to these tapes, to capture the essence of what's being said, and to get back in touch with what I was feeling in that lecture hall. I'm sure of one thing, the Hansens elicited trust and belief from me. There's no rational way to account for that especially given my penchant for the facts, the numbers. I am a 'show me' reporter. Reporting statistics is, indeed, a whole lot more straightforward."

Koy spent the next several hours listening to the tapes and the next several days writing about what she had heard and felt. Her article came out as a special insert in the *Syracuse Herald-Journal* about two weeks after her encounter with Phillip and Christian.

* * * * *

REFLECTIONS ON MYSTIC MANAGEMENT
by
Koy Sosa

It had all the appearances of a normal Syracuse day for this reporter as I headed for Dinosaur's Barbecue to meet with Phillip and Christian Hansen, proponents of what they call Mystic Management. By the time we had barely started lunch I sensed the day would be anything but normal. By the time late afternoon came and the lecture on the hill was over I sensed the whole world would soon be anything but normal. Phillip, noted psychologist and author, and his son Christian, CEO of Used Water Works, are advocates for a management philosophy that can only be dreamed of in this competitive and ever-changing global business environment. It would be fair to say that a spirituality underlies Mystic Management. It is compassionate, a quality sorely lacking in what most of us have experienced as "business." The Hansens are uncompromising in their ideals, saying: "Should we hold generally accepted business practices as sacred and become further immersed in the post *Future Shock* clutter or should we hold high ideals as sacred in the hope of rising out of the clutter." Their high ideals take the form of the six primary tenets of Mystic Management: (1) Collaborative Creativity; (2) Ego Empowerment; (3) Gentle Generosity; (4) Karmic Kindness; (5) Inclusive Integrity; and (6) Systems Sensitivity.

Some 225 students and faculty from various disciplines attended the lecture. Phillip opened the discussion of Collaborative Creativity with a bit of reverse psychology stating: "While creativity may be good for the arts, it's definitely bad for business. I'm sure we agree that the last thing anybody wants is creative assembly line workers for example. I suspect each product would be a little different, a few would work as planned, now and then one would work exceptionally well, and many would fail altogether. This would be all too wishy-washy for achieving effective and efficient resource management. Random excellence is not a sought after commodity. And of course this makes perfect sense. Who'd risk it? Somehow, though, the assembly line mentality has come to define the totality of the workplace making it unbendingly consistent, within specification, controllable, predictable, and uninvitingly inhuman and mechanistic. Machines need not be creative and assembly lines building machines also need not be creative at least not after their initial design. That first assembly line was an immensely creative idea, based on the idea of interchangeability of parts, another immensely creative idea. And together those innovations changed the course of industrialization."

To expand on Phillip's opening comments, this reporter sees Collaborative Creativity, the first tenet of Mystic Management not as resistant to mechanization and robotics, but resistant to the mechanization of the human spirit and the treating of people as robots. Until such time as we totally remove the human element from the workplace, we might want to turn our attention toward dealing with people without breaking them, literally and figuratively. Collaborative Creativity respects the creative genius, the creative spirit and refuses to squash it in the name of consistency or profit or any other after-the-creative-fact notion. And this creativity is collaborative, team-built.

Again in Phillip's own words. "I'm not suggesting we haven't accomplished great things as a society. Wasn't putting three men on the moon and bringing them back a wonderfully creative idea, wasn't it magnificent? The idea officially took shape with the conception of the Apollo Program and informal discussions around a table in early 1959. The idea officially came to fruition ten years later with the moon landing. Today the stack of paperwork supporting a manned space mission stands taller than a Saturn V Rocket. This is the typical way of organizations. They begin and grow as scattered creative germs and ultimately evolve into carefully documented diseases. It's the natural order of things to move from simple to complex. One strain of the disease is bureaucracy. We've all been exposed and most of us don't like the symptoms. The vaccine must be formulated from the original germ. In this case bureaucracy must be infected with the germ of an idea, a creative germ. Collaborative Creativity is fueled by the energy flaring out from the human aura as individuals create. To create is to allow passage into the next dimension of doing business. To create is to breathe new life into the going concern."

Upon pressing Phillip and Christian for more detail they shared their view of Collaborative Creativity as a new business ethic. Like Plato on Ethics, the Hansens on Collaborative Creativity would prefer creativity for its own sake, because it is right action. They will, however, in the name of practicality settle for organizations embracing creativity because it will ultimately strengthen the bottom line. Regardless of the motive the pursuit of creativity should become a new dimension of corporate social responsibility.

To close the discussion of Collaborative Creativity, Christian cited the name of his company, Used Water Works, as an example of the collaboratively creative process. The company is in the water recycling business and the implication is that "used water WORKS for mankind." The company name was the outcome of a collaborative/team effort, a brainstorming session involving employees at all levels within the organization. The key is cooperation and the recognition and consideration of all ideas. Collaborative Creativity does not happen in a vacuum.

This reporter is not oblivious to the serious practical objections to the notion of Collaborative Creativity, and for that matter to all of the Mystic tenets. High ideals appear to have high price tags. However, striving for anything less than high ideals would be more expensive in the long run. There is no future and no profit in shortsightedness. The frightening part for some is that allowing creativity demands that one empower others. This brings us to the second principle of Mystic Management, Ego Empowerment.

Ego Empowerment is a bit of an oxymoron. It doesn't mean expanding one's own ego, but keeping it in check in order to empower others. Christian opened this section of the lecture with the following statement: "Ego Empowerment is the oxymoron in the new paradigm of collaborative management weltanschauung." It was wonderful. He looked intently at his audience and then at his father who simply shrugged and threw up his hands.

Phillip moved to the front of the stage and pretend-whispered to the audience: "I should have known better than to bring my son to the university. What he's trying to say is that even though Ego Empowerment is a bit of a contradiction in terms it fits the new model of quality/team management. And 'weltanschauung,' well, you'll have to ask him. Surely in a 'publish or parish' environment, poor Christian would perish."

"Now that's unfair," quipped Christian. "'Weltanschauung' gives us a global flavor and, besides, it fits right in. It does after all mean a comprehensive philosophy of the world and mystical contemplation."

"That certainly clears it up. We should have named our 'new paradigm' Weltanschauung Management. It seems to me we are having enough trouble with the word 'Mystic.' Nonetheless you can be credited with using the words 'empowerment,' 'oxymoron,' 'paradigm,' 'collaborative,' and, of course 'weltanschauung' all in a single sentence. Very impressive."

"You know, that's not very ego empowering."

By this time the audience was chuckling and getting the idea. How often are we simply put down because what we've come up with seems different, kind of silly? How often on the other hand does someone take the time to help reshape our silliness into something dynamic and powerful? Empowering others is tricky business. As Christian so aptly put it: "You have to be willing to accept, appreciate, reshape, and recreate, and all with no expectation of personal gain."

This reporter recognizes the apple pie sound in this and it is hard to argue against without being perceived as a troll. I think that's why many CEOs have gone along with empowerment as a part of a quality management strategy only to wake up in the middle of the night in a cold sweat at the thought of actually allowing others to make critical decisions. Often CEOs reassess what they have done and keep only those parts of quality management that deal with continuous improvement and customer service. They simply revoke empowerment, the employee enhancing part. It's that proverbial "throwing out the baby with the bath water." Without employee empowerment as the cornerstone there's nothing new in quality management. Well, that's not exactly true, there is statistical process control, benchmarking, reengineering, managing the white space, ISO 12000, and the Malcomb Baldridge Award. These are formal things that can be put in the strategic plan to benchmark progress. Empowerment remains the challenge that company executives simply can't handle. Empowerment demands something bigger than big business, and so the next Mystic Management Principle, Gentle Generosity, takes shape.

According to Phillip, "Empowerment is something we do; it's an action verb. Gentle Generosity is something we are; it's a quality. It's the quality that allows us to empower AND feel comfortable with that decision. It's freeing up our own insecurities while at the same time going the extra step to encourage others. It is, again, compassion"

Gentle Generosity looks like a very desirable trait. Christian asks the interesting question, "Who would more likely be associated with a Gentle Generosity, Attila the Hun or Winnie the Pooh and if you were President and CEO of a major global conglomerate with whom would you rather be compared? The Hun is a fighter, warrior, and conqueror. Pooh Bear is fat, yellow, and occasionally gets his head stuck in a honey jar. Which image would be most likely to enhance the bottom line and maintain the confidence of your Board of Directors and your stockholders? We've all heard and seen that nice people finish last; being liked is unimportant; good executives need to be self-strokers with no need for reinforcement or encouragement from outside themselves. And herein lies the problem: self-stroking causes hierarchical schizophrenia, a disease of organizational position. As one moves up the organization ladder he or she may seek council only from those at a higher organizational level. When one finally reaches the top one may seek advice only from oneself. Hence the adage 'it's lonely at the top.' Oh yes, and here is where the schizophrenia sets in; one is forced to interact with oneself while taking on and responding to all sides of an issue. This clearly demands more than one personality. Hierarchical schizophrenia is the number one killer of Collaborative Creativity and crippler of Ego Empowerment. A Gentle Generosity in spite of its Pooh image is the only known cure."

Listening to Christian convince an audience riddled with management professors and in-progress MBAs that they should give up the warrior image for a Winnie the Pooh one was quite something. It was truly a call to high ideals. Simply put, teamwork and collaboration are not warrior tools, they are the sum and substance of process orientation encompassing not only the ability, but the need, to interact with other individuals at all levels of the organization. Gentle Generosity is part of a win-win strategy and this does positively impact the bottom line and draw confidence from Boards and stockholders. The trait itself, to have Gentle Generosity, moves into the spiritual realm of Mystic Management and foretells of its next principle Karmic Kindness.

Karmic Kindness is the antithesis of the 'no pain no gain' philosophy. Phillip stated it very simply, "What goes around comes around and kindness is the better way. There is a wonderful bumper sticker out there that says MEAN PEOPLE SUCK. So do mean managers. Then, of course, there's the bumper sticker that takes it a step further COMMIT RANDOM ACTS OF KINDNESS. Sometimes I think we should stop reading books and simply check out bumper stickers. My contribution to the world of bumper stickers deals with paradigm shifts, SHIFT HAPPENS."

My reporter-self compelled me to look up the definitions of both karmic and kindness. 'Karmic' from the Hindu or Buddhist refers to the total effect of one's conduct during the successive phases of his or her existence. Karma has to do with destiny. Then there is kindness. 'Kind' takes up almost a whole page in my dictionary. To be kind is to be friendly, generous, warm-hearted in nature, sympathetic, understanding, charitable, humane, considerate, forbearing, tolerant, generous, giving, agreeable, beneficial, and natural, and, of course, compassionate. Now there is a powerful word, I had no idea.

Christian and Phillip stood close to each other and spoke in unison: "Karmic Kindness is the soul of the corporation. Each job you hold is a lifetime and each act of kindness in each of those jobs takes you closer to your destiny. And your destiny, whether you choose to attend to it or not, is community building and sustainability, it is equality and oneness with all those around you, it is love." The two men stood focused on their audience and silent for a full three minutes. They said nothing with their voices. The audience rejoiced in the silence and also said nothing with their voices.

It was one of the most intense periods I have ever experienced. I could not fathom how they did it without seeming totally ridiculous. The two men, father and son, standing together proposing love as a principle of management was mesmerizing. There was far more going on than met the eye. I had that same feeling I'd had earlier in the day as I left the restaurant. The lecture hall took on that same other-worldly aura. The sun-filtered light through the trees and through the tinted glass of the lecture hall windows turned the entire scene a subtle but definite pink. I have struggled for two weeks with how to write this segment without appearing ridiculous myself. The bottom line for me is that I've finally concluded that it is unimportant how ridiculous I might seem. What's important is the message, and I have communicated it the best way I know how. Each of us perceives our reality somewhat differently. And it is in these differences that we find the fifth tenet of Mystic Management, Inclusive Integrity.

Christian took the lead here: "Inclusive Integrity acknowledges differences, it is diversity personified, a celebration of diversity, and this celebration is not a natural tendency. In fact it's quite the opposite. The more like us another is the better we like him or her. It's the 'I'm okay, I'm okay' philosophy. The less difference between you and me the better. This behavior leads to the establishment of exclusive clubs. For example, there are Irish, Catholics, and, of course Irish-Catholics. There are Italians, Americans, and Italian-Americans. Once I even heard about a club of Irish-Catholic-Americans. Let's see, African-American, Hispanic, and I think it's Hispanic not from Spain or Puerto Rico or Mexico but only from South America. Then of course there's Jewish, but if they're from Israel or New York City, well, they're different. And there's Hansen not to be confused with Hanson, son of Hans. This has all the trappings of a market segmentation strategy. We might as well be discussing Chevrolet, Pontiac, Oldsmobile, Buick, and Cadillac, or Wrangler, Levis, and Calvin Klein, or maybe even Scott and whatever the quilted one is. We can't possibly be talking about human beings. Then again, if I'm a Buick and you're a Buick that's good. If I'm a Buick and you're either a Chevrolet or a Cadillac that's bad.

We're all GM but we look different and we handle differently. The fact that all three can get from San Diego to Seattle via the interstate is irrelevant."

Christian continued without falling through the thin ice as he skated upon and around his audience's values. He did manage to make his point and concluded by citing the all too common examples of employee performance being evaluated on how closely the job resembled the way the supervisor would do it rather than on whether or not the objectives were met. His closing comment on Inclusive Integrity was: "To accept diversity is not enough and to value it is a great beginning."

The final tenet of Mystic Management is Systems Sensitivity, "This is the synergy and synchronicity of it all. This tenet is the glue, the matrix, the connectedness of one thing to all things. It's the feedback loop, the reinforcer."

This reporter left the lecture hall at the university with a different impression of what might be possible for corporate America. This reporter left Phillip and Christian Hansen's talk with a different feeling about business, a distinctly non-statistical, untested, and spiritually motivated and hopeful future; a compassionate future. Shift happens.

CHAPTER 3

▼

THE ROCK SHOP PROSPECTOR (EARTH)

There were times when Phillip Hansen found himself quite amusing, not the serious professional. This was one of those times. It was early November 2022, about 6:30 P.M., and already dark. With the lights on and the drapes open Phillip could see his reflection in the study window of that old Waterford, Virginia, house. The specter-like figure in the window was about five-eight (five-eight and one-half to be exact), and more thin than fat (except around the fiftyish waist, fifty years that is). Phillip was not exactly handsome, but not too bad either, nor graying too much. All in all he was a pretty average looking fellow. Suddenly, it was as if he caught the giggles from his window-pane-divided reflection, and he just stood there laughing out loud along with the image in the window. He couldn't help himself as he thought about how horribly civilized he was and unaccustomed to such outbursts.

On this particular November evening he was hidden away in his beautifully appointed study over the garage doing one of his favorite things,
attending to his rock and mineral collection. He had been thinking about
labeling a newly acquired specimen when he was so rudely interrupted by
his window image. This particular specimen was a puffy-looking apophyllite from India, and a gift from his wife Jo.

Phillip and Jo had a very unusual relationship; it worked. Phillip took
time out from his apophyllite labeling to actively think about her for a
moment or two. Actually, as so often happened, she was probably thinking about him at that exact moment and the two joined thoughts. He
sensed her broad smile, blue eyes, and fiery red hair. He pictured her
reaching for the top shelf of the kitchen cabinet to fetch something he
himself was unable to reach without a chair. It's not that she was inordi-
nately tall at her five eight or he short, they were just screwed together differently. Jo was blessed with long arms, fingers, and legs all set neatly
around slender hips and long waist. Phillip, on the other hand, had a
lower center of gravity, perhaps more grounded, but less agile and stretch-
able. She was turbo charged and he had four-wheel drive. Together they
could go anywhere and do anything. Phillip often thought about writing a
scholarly treatise on "The Influence of Physical Size on Martial Bliss." He
was certain his colleagues would never get past the sexual connotations!

As his psyche returned to his Waterford study and the task at hand, he
placed the specimen gently on the big roll top desk so as not to damage
either the desk or the rock. It would be hard to say which would be the
greater travesty. The potential risk of damaging a prized possession was
somehow exciting (in lieu of rafting a river or bungee jumping off a
bridge). It added an adrenaline rush to the objectively mundane. Or
maybe it was Phillip's daydreaming into the nooks and crannies of the
Earth that added the element of excitement. Where was this apophyllite
found hiding? Was it in a small cavity in a mountainside? Did the discov-
erer have to dangle precariously from a rope on the side of some sheer
cliff? What act of superhuman courage and adventure did it take to

unearth this puffy looking thing so it might come under the scrutinous eye of Phillip Hansen?

Phillip began laughing aloud once again as he rolled a piece of paper into the old I.B.M. Selectric II typewriter and typed the number "462" within one-quarter of an inch from the top of the page. He then semi-yanked the paper out of the typewriter risking tearing the paper and probably destroying some inner working of the machine. He couldn't help himself, he liked the sound of the gears trying to resist his pull. Still holding the extracted paper with the number typed on it, he reached into one of the many desk cubbyholes and foraged out a hand-held paper punch. Grasping paper and punch he leaned toward the lamp and, sticking the paper in the bright light under the shade so he could see the pica-sized "462" at the top, he carefully placed the punch over the number and squeezed. With a crisp snap the tiny disengaged disk of paper with the number on it fluttered to the floor trying to hide from Phillip's determination to find it. Phillip's amusement at himself heightened as he imagined how he must look crawling about the study floor searching for a circle of paper about five-sixteenths of an inch in diameter.

Phillip cavalierly licked the pointer finger of his left hand and adeptly placed the finally-captured disk on the wet tip, number up. Balancing the circle on his finger, he searched his giant desk for the Duco Cement. Securing the twisted, half-empty tube in his free hand, he raised it to his mouth and, with his teeth, grasped the head of the small finishing nail stuck in the aluminum tube neck. In one quick motion he pulled out the nail like a grenade pin, pinched the bottom of the tube, and aimed the oozing glue at the exposed underbelly of his new rock. With pinpoint accuracy he dropped a minuscule glob of glue into one of the apophyllite's topographical anomalies big enough to inconspicuously absorb the circumference of the numbered disk. And then, like a plate juggler, Phillip flipped the tiny circle off his almost dry finger tip and splashed the blank side down into the Duco pool.

It was about here that his amusement with himself peaked. And no wonder. In his "other" life Phillip Hansen was one of the country's leading psychologists and respected as a pillar of sanity and stability in a decaying world society. In 2022, and before all the Mystic Management hullabaloo Phillip rested somewhere between social psychologist and industrial psychologist. His teaching, research, and writing fell primarily in the social realm; his income was generated more in the industrial area. Somehow his mental meanderings about social systems had caught the fancy of the private sector. The corporate giants were sure Phillip could come up with the perfect strategy for motivating and empowering the masses (lowly employees) to increase efficiency, job satisfaction, and profit margins all at the same time. At two thousand dollars per day Phillip saw no harm in trying. It seems his very presence had a positive impact worth far more than his seemingly exorbitant consulting fee. And Phillip knew why. It had to do with Eyespell.

To finish labeling his rock Phillip pushed at the numbered circle with the glue-crusted eraser-end of a #2 pencil, making sure to apply just the right amount of pressure with the "Ticonderoga." When he was satisfied that the label and rock were one, he smiled the smile of accomplishment, and escorted his new prize toward the lighted curio cabinet in the far corner of the room. He stopped short of his destination and spent a moment taking in the splendor of the various crystals, metallics, and colorfully crusted bits of the Earth reflecting the directed rays of the high intensity lamp recessed into the inside top of the cabinet. Phillip finally moved those last steps to the cabinet, and carefully opened the glass door, trying not to shake the more delicate specimens from their Lucite perches. He reached in and gently placed specimen #462 in a location of honor at the very front of the second-from-the-top glass shelf.

There was just one more thing to do before settling into the often practiced routine of touching, sensing the vibration, and reminiscing about pieces of the collection in the curio cabinet. Phillip needed to attend to the accountant-like task of entering the information about the apophyllite into his database. He had learned over the years that if such information was not recorded almost immediately, valuable tidbits were invariably lost, lost forever. He backed toward the computer table, still drinking in the images of his collection and, at the last possible moment, turned to begin his data entry task. The computer, humming in obedient readiness, displayed the database fields to be filled in. After attending to all the technical data Phillip finally came to the memo field of the database. This is where he would tell the story of the specimen. This final part of the meticulous and mundane recording task was fun and creative.

For Specimen #462, Phillip began writing, "It was no special occasion at all. I came in from the garage mumbling something about how I'm the only one who ever empties the trash around here, and Jo was standing in the kitchen with that smile she gets when she's up to something."

This smile always made Phillip uncomfortable because it invariably meant he would probably have to think about doing something fun, something not on his agenda for the day. Don't misunderstand, he always loved her ideas...afterwards. In fact, she is personally responsible for ninety percent of his fondest earthly memories. But in the moment, he almost always found her ideas unsettling to his routine. There are two kinds of people, those whose initial reaction is "yes" and those who need to think about it. As a thinker, Phillip automatically says "no" to most things in order to give himself some time to become grounded in whatever the new twist is going to be. Four-wheel drive.

He continued the entry writing, "I took one look at her and blurted out: 'No way, I'm not even slightly interested in what it is.' 'Okay,' she said, 'if you don't want it.' 'What do you mean, want it?' And so it was that she pulled a little sack from behind her back and said: 'You look like you need a rock.' And so it was that I came to possess this magnificent apophyllite. Number "462" will always hold a special place in my heart. You can feel Jo's vibration when you touch the stone. It's the only turbo charged apophyllite on the planet!"

Phillip had been a rock hound for years. However, he hated the designation "rock hound" in spite of his passion for amassing both a striking and valuable collection. He had a basic knowledge of geology and was an expert of sorts on the history of mines and mining around the world. Phillip would be the first to admit that he could get lost in some of the most objectively boring reading about old mines and prospecting. In his reverie he could sometimes almost feel the hairs on his mule's back as he imagined climbing menacing switchbacks in the high Sierra, or searching the parched desert for some sign of nature's planetary wealth. He could almost feel the freezing cold or the burning heat tearing at his aching muscles, and all endured in anticipation of that one big strike! Phillip would become almost confused when the phone rang or an airplane would jet overhead reminding him that it was not 1860, and he was not prospecting, except perhaps in some of the finest rock shops in the country. And it was that line of thinking that got him to laughing at himself again on that November evening. He was the civilized Phillip Hansen, "the rock shop prospector."

In all honesty Phillip didn't do all of his collecting in rock shops. He was actually in the field a few times. He loved being back off the main drag where it was often silent and beautiful. These times brought memories to Phillip that fused his very soul with the earth he was standing on. These experiences were nothing short of awesome, the kind of inner dimensional experience that makes one lose one's balance, almost.

Phillip refocused on the new specimen in his curio cabinet, apophyllite from India, number 462. His hand then almost unconsciously reached into the still open door of the curio cabinet and emerged with a flat polished sheet of purple lepidolite interspersed with pink tourmalines. He was often drawn to the pastel-colored specimens, especially the pinks. They spoke to his soul of another time and another place.

Phillip ran the palm of his hand along the smooth surface of the lepidolite. He smiled as he recalled that day at The Collector in Fallbrook, California. Fallbrook was just outside of San Diego. Phillip had read about it in one or another of his books. This was California tourmaline country.

There were mines everywhere, the Pala Chief, the Tourmaline Queen, and the Himalaya to name a few. Of course Phillip was looking not for a mine but for The Collector, a rock shop. The Collector turned out to be more than just a rock shop; it was owned by the Pala Mine and afforded him a special opportunity. This was Phillip's chance to collect tourmalines "in the field." The proprietress brought him huge drawers filled with rough tourmaline crystals to rummage through. With Phillip's imagination at work it was irrelevant that he was comfortably seated in a leather chair, leaning over a beautiful oak and glass table. Phillip was "in the field!" His journey through the boxes of tourmaline was no less perilous than Indiana Jones' in "The Temple of Doom." It proved to be the highlight of one of those marvelous vacations with Jo and their son, Christian.

Christian was in his teens at the time, and his fondest memory of The Collector was seeing his father as child-like, excited as he picked through those boxes of tourmaline. It was, perhaps, the first time he saw his father for who he really was. Or it might have been one of the few times his father made it possible for Christian to "see." The memory of sharing his true self with his son was important to Phillip. Moreover, Christian's insight from that memory was a catalyst that made all things possible for him later in life as he would champion a new paradigm from a new world. The exact words of their interaction rang through Phillip's consciousness.

"So, Dad, what are you doing? You've got a really silly look on your face."

"I am searching for tourmalines and it's hard to see in the dense forest."

"But, Dad, you're sitting at a table in a well-lit room looking through some drawers."

"Am I?"

"What do you mean?"

"I am doing exactly what I've created in my head. And if my mind is searching for tourmalines about a hundred and fifty years ago on this very spot, then that's my reality. You ought to see it. It feels like summer. The forest is dense and the sun is peaking through the trees. As I look down the ground is shimmering with colorful rays as the sunlight bounces off tourmaline crystals scattered virtually everywhere. It's absolutely magnificent. Would you like to join me?"

"Why not."

"Create it in your head and it will be. Sit beside me here in the forest and let's search together."

Christian Hansen was a lot like both his father and his mother, a blend of the best of each. He stood six-feet-two-inches tall and had a self-concept to match, not unbounded ego, just a healthy self perception. And he was not average looking, but downright handsome. There was an interesting aura about him. He was so special that he gave the appearance of the perfectly commonplace, ordinary, no different than discovering an end table next to the couch. There was no need to draw attention to himself, not yet.

Phillip started to laugh again as the psychologist in him caught the errors of his free associating with his curio cabinet "friends." Everything was just as he remembered it, except that the slab of lepidolite sparking the reverie about Christian was not from The Collector at all. This particular piece of lepidolite was purchased at The Comstock Rock Shop in Virginia City, Nevada, and some three years after the wonderful experience at The Collector. It always fascinated Phillip how the "feeling mind" has no regard for linear time.

He unconsciously reached into the confines of the curio cabinet once again, this time pulling out a substantial chunk of rose quartz. He just smiled at it as if it were an old friend. "This piece of quartz was not purchased in any rock shop," thought Phillip. "No sir, this piece of rose quartz comes directly from the local pet store." The "rock shop prospector" had stooped to a new low. While looking for some aquarium gravel, Phillip had happened upon two large chunks of rose quartz. The shopkeeper told him just to take them, he had no idea what they were or where they came from. How unusual.

Unusual in more ways than one. Not only did Phillip have no idea where they came from, whenever he held the smooth yet indented and striated pastel pink rock in his hands, a pink world floating in a star-bespeckeled galaxy far from the feeling of Earth entered his consciousness. This time was no exception. Phillip Hansen's hands clung to the rock as his mind soared beyond the confines of the study in that old Waterford house. He focused on that beautiful pink planet beneath two suns and four moons, the one he knew was "home."

CHAPTER 4

▼

THE MISSING EYESPELLIAN (EYESPELL)

Leo had spent the day and the better part of the evening intercepting Antonio, Melissa, Nancy, and Pete at their assigned re-entry points. "But," he thought, "there is still one adventurer out there, Phillip." Phillip had missed re-entry and there was no word from Kathryn confirming his whereabouts. With all the todo about Earth-plane vibrational leakage, no one had even considered what the consequences might be if one of the project participants failed to return at all. The exact time and place of each re-entry was established at the inception of the Eyespell Experiment in Earth year 1972. It was assumed all five would return twenty years later as planned.

An Eyespellian had never been lost, and the consequences of such a loss were mostly speculation. Eyespellians are inextricably connected to each other and to their planet. It's as if every cell or molecule on Eyespell reflects in every other cell or molecule; nothing on Eyespell exists in isolation. A Mystic Management anchor concept is connectedness or what the scholarly treatises on the subject call The Sixth Principle, Systems Sensitivity. This is the innate understanding that all things are interconnected and what happens in one cell affects all other cells. Systems sensitivity is the crux of Eyespell's planetary cell-matrix.

This cell-matrix so connects everything Eyespellian that the total consciousness of the planet could not help but be adversely impacted by the unexpected and premature loss of even one Eyespellian or, for that matter, one grain of sand on the planet's surface. The question is, to what extreme would Eyespell be disrupted? Natural changes in density, death for example, are anticipated and accounted for. The total consciousness of the planet embraces and absorbs the vibrations of such occurrences and restructures them into the total fabric of Eyespellian community. The cell-matrix keeps Eyespell virtually free of accident and sickness on an individual level. The matrix is in constant flux minimizing the impact of even the slightest vibrational shifts. What would be typically construed as an accident or illness is simply absorbed and re-manifested in some positive way. Even something as seemingly insignificant as a stray thought is captured in the Eyespellian consciousness and translated into a fragment of the planet's overall reality. Eyespell would appear extremely enlightened and advanced if Earth were observing Eyespell instead of vice versa. And so, in the face of a missing Eyespellian and concern about Earth-plane vibrational leakage Eyespell had much cause to be worried. The bottom line was whether or not Eyespell's cell-matrix could absorb and redistribute vibrational leakage and handle a missing Eyespellian without skewing the planet's reality in some heretofore unknown direction, almost certainly an undesirable and negative direction.

In the hope of reconnecting with Phillip, Kathryn remained on Earth until the last possible moment before catching the final panes of the re-entry window. When she finally arrived on Eyespell she was alone and somber; in disbelief that she had returned without Phillip Hansen. All attempts to re-establish the telepathy link with him had failed; nor did any of the more Earth-bound methods produce tangible results. Missing person bureaus and hospitals were checked; newspapers were scanned for accident victims. The search produced nothing. It was as if Phillip had simply vanished into thin air. During the entire twenty years of the Eyespell Experiment, he had been the easiest to track and seemed the least likely to experience any serious re-entry trauma. It was ironic that he was the focus of this last minute crisis.

In her head Kathryn reviewed the "link procedures" a thousand times and could come up with no explanation of how the telepathy link with Phillip could have been broken…except one: a near-death experience. If Phillip had entered the white space Earth people call the "tunnel" at the exact moment re-entry was to occur, a total telepathic amnesia was possible. In that one extraordinary case, one in tens of millions, Phillip could be cut off from Kathryn and could be earthbound forever; re-entry might be impossible. This was a frightening prospect. Eventually Phillip would intuit his Eyespellian heritage finding himself trapped on what would suddenly become an alien world, alien even though part of his memory would recall the event of his birth on Earth. For the first time on Eyespell someone cried tears of sadness…Kathryn wept for Phillip Hansen.

Thus manifested the first of many complex tangles resulting from the Eyespell Experiment and its presumption to directly fuse Earth and Eyespell. Each tangle would be unpredictable and each shrouded in its unique ambiguity, making interpretation and a course of action exceedingly complex. For example, in this instance, it was uncertain whether the sadness Kathryn experienced was an initial indicator of Earth-plane vibrational leakage or merely a residual energy flow confined to her own psyche, possibly even relief at her own successful re-entry? Although she had been on the Earth for twenty years she had never technically Earth-fused. Therefore, Kathryn dismissed the possibility of leakage, but who could be sure? In any case, unless she were to close her telepathy link and keep it closed, whatever her thoughts and feelings, they would ultimately become part of the cell-matrix and would become assimilated into the Eyespellian consciousness.

Her thoughts ran in several directions at once. "The up-coming debriefings of the four who have returned will hopefully answer the critical questions. Such a tangle! Perhaps all the worry has been for naught. Maybe there is no significant vibrational leakage. Just maybe my crying jag was not such an extraordinary event after twenty Earth years away from home. Just maybe Phillip is not separated from Eyespell. He's probably already home. Such optimism," she thought, allowing a brief smile.

By the time Leo met Kathryn at her re-entry point, she was no longer crying. He had arrived in time, however, to catch the telltale redness in her eyes. For now, he chose to keep the observation to himself giving Kathryn a twenty-year-overdue hug. It was a long embrace as Leo telepathically transmitted twenty years of Eyespell's "news" to Kathryn, filling in any details she may have missed through their long-range and often static-filled communications.

"It's wonderful to have you home, Kathryn. Four of the five are back and doing fine. The re-entry trauma is no worse than we predicted. However, at this point there is no way of telling if there has been any significant Earth-plane vibrational leakage. I am somewhat concerned about Nancy. It's nothing specific, just a feeling I can't quite put my finger on. She seems a little depressed, and she acted oddly when she first returned. And what about Phillip? Any thoughts?"

"Nothing we've not already discussed in our recent communications, Leo. I actually cried after re-entry when hit with the full realization that Phillip was left behind. I feel it is my fault. I can't believe the telepathy link was broken. My sole purpose for the past twenty years has been to keep track of the five of them. How could this have happened?" Tears began to well up again in Kathryn's eyes.

"Let's take things one step at a time." Leo grasped Kathryn's hands in a gesture of reassurance and continued. "Our four returned explorers are just chomping at the bit to meet with the Elders' Council. I told them we would do so as soon as you returned. Let's focus on the joy of their return. Together we will figure out what has happened to Phillip. Although he is not here I do not sense that he is gone from us forever. Your tears have not gone unnoticed in this connected place. Together we will make them tears of joy."

Kathryn smiled and felt comforted by Leo's words. She turned her attention back to the issues at hand. "Have you told them anything of their mission or their identities as Eyespellians?"

"No. They have been having momentary periods of recall, but nothing that yet makes complete sense to them, nothing specific enough. They have a lot of questions. Pete almost has it figured out. He knew immediately that this is home and he recognized Antonio and the others as old friends. He even remembered me. Even though he couldn't fill in the details he very much trusted his feelings. Pete's state of mind made me feel very encouraged. On the other hand there is Nancy. Like I said earlier, there is definitely something amiss there. She actually shrunk from my hug. Maybe I'm just being too sensitive, you know, hurt feelings. Of course, that in and of itself is symptomatic that something may be wrong. But, things seemed better after Pete's arrival. Nancy seemed more settled and the peculiar vibrations seemed to have dissipated."

Looking somewhat pensive, Kathryn finally said, "After twenty years of clandestine observation, it will be nice to deal with them face-to-face. Especially Nancy. Having to lie to her because of that thing with the tele-pathic bleed-through really bothered me. Such deception is so counter to what we believe in. Imagine Eyespellians lying to one another. For any rea-son. Without a doubt that was the most uncomfortable task in my twenty years as Project Overseer. At least until today when I was forced to return without Phillip. Oh, Leo, I missed you. It is so good to be with you again."

"Having you and the others back makes our planet almost whole again. It has been more difficult than any of us imagined letting six souls leave the planet at once. The whole planet can feel your presence, Kathryn Song."

Leo and Kathryn moved purposefully over the dune in silence to gather up the four returned adventurers, taking them to the Elders' Council as promised. Leo felt a mounting yet unidentifiable apprehension as they continued their silent journey. His apprehension would find its target when Nancy and Kathryn would soon meet.

Kathryn was very introspective as they continued walking their silent path. She thought to herself, "Why do Eyespellians have to be so curious? We have manifested an almost perfect world and yet we risk it all out of curiosity or the quest for a little more knowledge. There was no reason to get mixed up in this Earth business in the first place. And then to lose a loved one; to actually have Phillip not return!"

Leo looked her way and said: "Surely, Kathryn, if you wanted to keep your thoughts private, you would not leave your telepathy link wide open. Have you forgotten such basics after a mere twenty Earth years? And surely, you do not mistake our motives for mere curiosity, Kathryn. Curiosity is not our motive. Interest, love, empathy, compassion, caring, and the potential to help a struggling world, now these come closer to our motives. On Earth it is said of curiosity that it killed the cat."

"Leo, I am not myself yet. Of course I know what you say is true. I feel like a, like a…confused Earthling." For the third time since her return tears shone at the corners of Kathryn's eyes.

Leo let love flow from himself to Kathryn in an expression of unconditional acceptance. "Do not worry. There is nothing Eyespell can't handle."

They rounded a smooth bend in the path coming down from the moderately steep dune, and the four excited returnees stood waiting about one hundred yards ahead. After what seemed forever-in-an-instant, Antonio, Melissa, Nancy, and Pete were finally going to meet with the Elders' Council. They had been awaiting Kathryn's arrival on Eyespell almost three Earth weeks. During this time the foursome had expended most of their energy getting to know each other as if for the first time. The re-entry trauma was still moderate to severe and none of the four had completely regained their Eyespellian faculties yet. They were still mostly limited to the Earth concepts of linear time, three-dimensional space, and oral communication. This was not unexpected.

As Kathryn and Leo neared them, Nancy's eyes met Kathryn's, and Nancy instantly knew of the deception, knew that Kathryn had feigned to be her spirit guide. Nancy faced Kathryn and screamed: "You lying bitch! How dare you deceive me! How dare you!" The unmitigated hatred in Nancy's eyes and the contempt in her voice stunned the group into an awkward silence where a merry greeting had been expected. The smooth bend in the path began to tear and crack at the curved stress points. Thunderheads began to gather directly above them and the pastel serenity of the blue sun became engulfed in the thick pitch-blackness of the swirling clouds.

There was a sharp snap in the air, a psychic cracking of a whip. The planetary cell-matrix shifted and both the social and climatic environments began to refocus in a positive and more typically Eyespellian fashion. Nancy's anger dissipated and the path mended itself as the blue sun peeked through the rapidly-scattering thunderclouds.

"Earth-plane vibrational leakage," Leo muttered to himself as he motioned to gather the small group into a prayer circle. "Gather in a tight circle, and quickly," shouted Leo. "Nancy, I want you by my side."

"Why?"

"This is no time to argue, please do as I ask."

"What's the big deal? Why are you so upset over a little thunder and lightning? What is this place and, like I said, 'what's the big deal?' "

Melissa chimed in: "Yeah, what's the urgency here? I don't understand."

The group, except for Kathryn and Pete, began to question Leo's concern, and thunderclouds began to reform in a more menacing fashion than before. Leo ignored their questions and took a crystal from the purse at his waist. It was attached to a rope of light, and placing the rope around his neck, he held the crystal point down between his skyward-lifted palms. Within moments, all instinctively gathered into a prayer circle and were bathed in an umbrella of blue light as the blue rays of the planet's sun were focused through the crystal. Each instinctively knew to remain in the light until Leo lowered his crystal. They prayed as one until the yellow sun set in the western horizon and the blue sun barely hung in the south. They waited in stunned silence for nightfall and moved toward Elasia under the light of the first three rising moons of Eyespell.

Antonio was the first to speak. "Where are we going?"

Kathryn answered, "To Elasia, a beautiful and magnificent gathering place. It is this planet's only city. Elasia is one with its natural environment like two snuggling kittens one upon the other in an afternoon nap. The glassy spires of the city are hardly discernible from the intermittent mountain peaks. Bathed by the two suns by day and four moons by night, the pastel hues of the city blend with the landscape. Its ordinary city noises enhance the music of its birds and waterfalls rather than creating the harsh cacophony one might expect in a typical city."

"What is this place?" asked Nancy.

This time Leo answered. "This is the planet Eyespell. This is your home and this planet and its people are one, each mindful and respectful of the others' aliveness. And that, young lady, is what the big deal is. Those thunderclouds are as alive as we are."

Pete seemed particularly interested in this idea of aliveness. "Leo, I almost understand, or I should say, I feel what this aliveness is. I feel so connected to each of you and to this place. Tell me more."

Leo was delighted at Pete's awareness and was more than happy to provide more details. The group had been back long enough so that much of what Leo had to say should make sense at least at some intuitive level. "Elasia is central to the created reality of the Eyespellians. There is a synergy here. Eyespell's collective consciousness is manifested in every molecule, animal, plant and mineral. This is gloriously apparent in and around Elasia. Everything on Eyespell is alive and part of what we call the planetary cell-matrix. A less glorious example of the force of this cell-matrix was the recent cracking of the pathway on the dune and the ominous forming of thunderheads at the same instant as Nancy's negative outburst. The 'comings' and 'goings' in this place demand a wholesomeness of purpose and uncontaminated thought patterns in order to maintain its skewed lightness.

The concern about Earth-plane vibrational leakage cuts to the very core of Eyespell's existence as a planet of the light skew. A stray negative vibration, thought, or feeling if not immediately compensated for, could potentially come alive on Eyespell, creating itself over and over and over and with ever-increasing intensity. Eyespell is not a place of opposites. It is a place of light, a place of positive in the absence of negative. And the consciousness of this planet Eyespell is a fragile thing."

Antonio asked, "How many people are there on Eyespell?"

Kathryn took up the charge and said with a broad smile, "That's a practical question, Antonio. The entire consciousness of Eyespell and its light skew centers around community and unconditional love. Eyespellians number only about 250,000 in physical body. The total energy of the planet incorporates another million or so souls out-of-body within the planet's aura in transition between physical and non-physical reality, birth and death as Earthlings call it. We have no machines on Eyespell and no technology in the hardware sense. Eyespell is a manifestation of the thoughts and spirit of the total populace within its aura. We Eyespellians literally create our reality from thought translated into the cell-matrix. This beautiful desert, waterfalls, shelter, food, even existence itself are without exception, thoughts manifested. The formula is simple. We have manifested unconditional love and compassion as the basis for our planet's reality."

Leo interjected at this point, "A lesser vibration such as that produced by Earth-plane vibrational leakage, leakage such as the emotion displayed by Nancy, could manifest an Eyespell contaminated with the dark skew, producing a different and undesirable reality."

Taken by Leo's words Nancy embraced Kathryn. Nancy's anger was temporarily assuaged. Leo returned the crystal to its silk pouch and zipped his purse shut with a sigh of relief. The tensions had dissipated and Eyespell once again moved in love and light. With the gesture of a herdsman, Leo swung his hands in the air and exclaimed: "Off to see the Council we go!" There was a true sense of excitement in the air.

The Council Chamber was at the very center of Elasia. To enter it was akin to entering the very center of a huge crystal; it was like becoming one with the planetary cell-matrix, fusing with its very atomic structure. The feeling was out-of-body and utterly expansive. Leo, Kathryn, and their following entered the chamber.

It typically took several minutes to become grounded enough to focus on the finite dimensions of the room's physical reality. It was an enclosed amphitheater. There were twenty-seven descending and curved rows of stone-like seats as one might expect to have found in ancient Rome. However, like all of Eyespell, the amphitheater was alive. As Eyespellians met stone, perfectly contoured sensor-impact-chairs enveloped their physical bodies. A raised stage formed the twenty-seventh and center ring. With Eyespell's six Elders at the center and all perimeter seats occupied, the Council Chamber could hold three hundred thirty-seven Eyespellians in manifested physical presence. Such a configuration of Eyespellians was called a Full-Round Session. During a Full Round the three hundred thirty-seven maintained total telepathy link with all other Eyespellians, and their collective consciousness would seek enlightenment born of the very life force of the universe. The Eyespellians, in a very real sense, would "talk to God." All things imagined and all things real would fuse into the same cosmic stuff. The Full Round has always been the ultimate reality-creating experience on Eyespell, channeling the energy of the planet toward specific outcomes.

Due to tremendous vibrational sensitivity Eyespell was particularly vulnerable during Full Round. For this reason it was only rarely convened. The conditions needed to be particularly positive to guard against any unwanted outside influences. The slightest stray negative thought anywhere on Eyespell or within the planetary aura extending far into Eyespellian space could easily and instantly translate into an unwanted reality. With the positive light-skewed nature of the planet's current manifestation, it would take little for the universe to impose, matter-of-factly, its typical balance of light and dark on Eyespell.

Eyespell's defiance of the continuum of opposites suggests that reaching homeostasis on this planet would mean destroying its skewed lightness. Eyespell's light skew makes it open to a chaos unmatched in the normal scope of a more balanced, if less enlightened, planetary evolution. Eyespell's absolutely positive bent is also its most dangerous enemy. This seemingly perfect planet suffers from an innate, fragile, and self-destructive intolerance of anything unlike itself. Earth-plane vibrational leakage is a force unlike Eyespell and represents a diversity potentially cataclysmic in the face of Eyespell's absolute intolerance.

The small group began to descend toward the center of the chamber chatting excitedly among themselves. Leo moved ahead of his companions to take his place on the raised center stage at the twenty-seventh ring of the domed amphitheater. At the same time, the other five members of the Elders' Council were coming into-body at center stage. Each had a pouch containing a crystal at his or her side on a rope of light like Leo's. Each crystal's color vibration corresponded to the bearer's custodial charge for a portion of the light-skew.

Using the crystals, the Elders could bend light into the colors of the Eyespellian rainbow, a rainbow with an infinite range of hues, all in harmony with the primary colors of the planet's two suns and four moons. It was this type of light bending through his crystal that had enabled Leo to bathe the prayer circle in blue light. Leo's crystal corresponded to the blue sun and the blue-light corridor, the Corridor of Peace. Color fusion, the making of rainbows, and light bending are more than esoteric or aesthetic pastimes on Eyespell. Light is always the first manifestation of Eyespellian reality. Therefore, anything of the light skew on Eyespell is serious business.

The group continued making its way into the council chamber. The Full Round had been called in honor of their return. Each of the twenty-seven circles of rows in the council chamber had a specific vibrational level and each Eyespellian resonated to a specific row. The closer to the center, the more powerful the vibration, and the higher the row number. All of the vibrational levels were regarded with equal dignity and as essential to the total community of Eyespellians. Kathryn, like Leo, moved ahead of the group proceeding to the twenty-first ring of the amphitheater to take her designated place. The four Eyespell Experiment participants moved to the third ring only and stood waiting, intuitively knowing not to move closer to the center at this time. The rare meeting of the Full Round was about to begin. The amphitheater was rapidly filling to its capacity of three-hundred-thirty-seven, and Antonio, Melissa, Nancy, and Pete found themselves surrounded by a multitude of flowing and various pastel-hued robes. All were finally gathered in physical presence and the Full Round opened.

CHAPTER 5

▼

IN THE ATTIC (EARTH)

Christian Hansen was rummaging through a big trunk in the attic. He came across several notebooks of his father's writings that he had never seen before. His parents had lived in that old brick and wood house in Waterford, Virginia, for as long as he could remember. Christian had great fun exploring the attic during visits home. He felt like such a kid it was hard for him to believe that he was now thirty-two and his father was crowding fifty-eight. It was even harder to image that the new millennium was already thirty years old. He was too young to remember all the talk of its approach.

On this particular day, the rest of the family was on a trek to Harper's Ferry, West Virginia. Mom and dad, his wife, and the boys never seemed to tire of wandering through the old Civil War graveyards or standing on the famous rock outcropping that overlooks Virginia, West Virginia, and Pennsylvania. Sometimes they were sure they could hear the shouts of distant foot soldiers and see the lights of their campfires across the river. It was as if John Brown himself walked out of the past and gave personal tours inside people's heads. It was like that a lot when his father, Phillip, was around; he had a unique way of bringing things to life. There was a unique aliveness about him that seemed to connect everyone and everything around him.

Earlier that day in his attic exploring, Christian had come across a bunch of old photographs. His mind wandered into contemplation about his favorite one, a picture of his father in an idyllic setting. He was standing in a field of gorgeous wildflowers with a waterfall in the background and an absolutely magnificent double rainbow framing the whole scene. His dad must have been in his early twenties when the picture was taken. What intrigued Christian the most was the far-away look on his father's face. The look hinted at a sadness or disappointment with the beauty surrounding him. It was as if it paled in comparison to some incredible vision in his head.

The only time he had seen his father cry was years ago when the two of them were looking through these same old albums and they happened across this very photograph. His father had taken one look at himself as a young man in the picture, held the photo against his chest, and sobbed for several minutes. Christian vividly recalled that when his father had stopped crying, he had looked him deep in the eyes and said, "Thank you, Christian, for sharing this moment with me and allowing me to be human."

Christian was about twenty at the time. He had hugged his father and said, "You are the most human man I know. Somehow, your tears give me hope for my own future and my own humanness. They give me permission to just be." Christian never really understood that moment, nor did he question why the photograph brought his father to tears. But Christian had felt the penetrating and almost mystical impact of that interaction ever since.

His mind moved from reflecting on the old photograph to the pile of manuscript pages in his lap. Just as his awareness peaked, the pages seemed to intentionally slip onto the rough-planked attic floor. As he leaned over to collect the loose papers, a breeze sneaked through the attic and several sheets tried to escape behind an old bureau. He deftly stopped the getaway by maneuvering the entire stack of papers speedily upward and under his waiting chin.

He chuckled to himself as his eyes caught the words trying to fall off the page before he could read them. With his head still cocked from the capture, one eye shut, and the other eye almost parallel to the page, he managed to negotiate a couple of sentences.

> ...and still another book was started but never finished. There is no way to rationally describe what I think I have experienced. Every time I try, the spaces between the words are more provocative than the words themselves. Anti-synergy! The whole is smaller than the sum of its parts.

"Anti-synergy?" Now that got Christian's full attention; he loved it. He grabbed the pages firmly in both hands, settled back in the broken-down redwood lawn chair and, by the dusty light of the sun's rays spilling through the cobwebbed window, he began to read. Christian now focused his attic exploration on the neatly typed and somewhat yellowed pages.

> Somewhere in the flatness of the land, the relative sameness of the weather, and the contrast of excessive wealth along the ocean and excessive poverty less than fifteen miles inland, there was a terrible disconnectedness. Out of this sense of despair arose the theme of community and community building as a starting place. There needed to be a new paradigm if the Earth were to be saved.

Initially unnoticed, less than half a page into his reading the neat typing gave way to scrawled notes which unevenly marched down the page and onto the back of the first sheet. With some effort Christian was able to decipher his father's handwriting.

Community building is essential. A bridge somehow needs to be built between the microcosm of one person's experiences in the world, and the macrocosm or commonality among the experiences of all of us. Maintaining the dignity of every human being must be paramount while focusing on team building as a core strategy, eventually working toward a global team to solve global problems of economic and environmental incompatibility. In order to get enough attention I need to focus on something that is part of everyone's tangible experience. I need to highlight and restructure community from the fundamental building blocks of a collective unconscious bringing it slowly to a conscious and purposeful level. Through this process, Earth's healing journey might be initiated. But how can I presume to take on such a task? And where might I begin?

The handwritten text ended with these questions and picked up again in typed format in the middle of the next sheet. The pages weren't numbered and Christian couldn't be sure of the order of things, especially after chasing the pages around the attic. The perplexities of the puzzle, however, only increased his interest. He read on.

The Eyespell Experiment focused on the desperation of America's youth. The five planned suicides with four that actually happened within hours of each other were designed to get Earth's attention. However, they had little impact on anyone's consciousness. There was such a lack of community that the suicides went virtually unnoticed. They appeared as disconnected and isolated incidents fed into the national statistical mean for suicides, raising it ever so slightly. I am glad I was not the fifth. I am glad I did not die with the others as planned.

Christian thought the manuscript was becoming "curiouser and curiouser." The Eyespell Experiment? Although quite a scholar, Christian could not recall anything called the Eyespell Experiment. He could not even begin to process the reference to his father's suicide nor did he try. He continued reading with renewed fascination.

> Americans are searching to make sense out of their pasts. The altruism of the 1960s brought soul searching and revolution with no resolution. The narcissism of the 1970s made everyone 'do their own thing,' but too often at their own expense and the expense of others. The individualism of the 1980s made Americans self-centered, but certainly not self-actualized.

Christian twisted in his chair in an unconscious physical reflection of his psychological discomfort. He continued.

> Americans have gone from left to right, liberal to conservative, liberated to traditional and still haven't found what they've needed. They've become specialists, then generalists, then specialists again. In all of this maneuvering, while they have learned to access massive amounts of information, they have not gained much wisdom. A generation, once full of hope, has hit middle age. Their legacy is abject confusion feeding into a society fraught with hopelessness, and bent on violence, sex, drugs, crime, and suicide as means of escape.

Christian read on in spite of his escalating discomfort.

> All of this, and Americans have gained so little insight. For many, the inability to distinguish between what is physical and what is psychological is fashionably called a spiritual dilemma. And then there is more vacillation, a seemingly endless cycle. This is the American dilemma: Americans encircled, in the way of their own

growth and tripping over their own feet. The result is isolation, fragmentation, and an almost total lack of community.

The typeface again gave way to margin and back page notes done in Phillip's obviously excited handwriting. Christian struggled to piece the bouncing letters together.

> As an off-world observer, I feel that what is most profoundly wrong within the whole American culture is that Americans have lost a sense of community. They idealize the community that existed prior to World War II; know something made it sick during Vietnam; and feel alienated and truncated with the ever-increasingly mobile society and dominance of the distended family.

Christian's brain came to a screeching halt. "Off-world observer?" He had never seen that idiom before. Twice now, in less than three pages, his father had stumped him. He made a couple of mental notes and continued to the next typed page.

> America is a wealthy society. Her wealth is especially evident in her corporate structure. The output of General Motors alone is greater than the gross national product of some third world countries. How can this imbalance be in the interest of a world community? It isn't, and in the past twenty to thirty years the term "business community" has become as much an oxymoron as "business ethics." America's wealth is achieved at great cost, lack of community. America is a high anxiety society suffering from soaring blood pressure and at high risk of heart disease. Do people realize how broad this handicap is? This is symptomatic of lack of centeredness, lack of focus, lack of community, disconnection. Without a clear center, a healthy heart, where is the point of reference in America? What is the system and what is

the sub-system? How are things connected? What makes up the whole and how can one tell if something critical is missing?

In the margins Christian could barely make out the words.

Maybe that's what this new paradigm should be about, connection. It could pull together, for example, business, art, psychology, and spirituality. It could combine right and left brain and create a synthesis that generates synergy, a whole that is, indeed, greater than the sum of its parts—a synergy that shifts America's brokenness into integration focused on community building. This could be called…systems sensitivity." There was an arrow from the margin pointing to "systems sensitivity" with a note, "Systems sensitivity is the key, it's the exact concept and the correct terminology. From where is this information coming?

Christian looked up from the manuscript, now totally bewildered. The writings revealed a side of his father's psyche that he was unaware of, to say nothing of the nagging implications of references to "Eyespell Experiment" and "off-world observer." He had not known his father to criticize anyone or anything, much less lambaste the entire nation. It wasn't the absolute truth or falseness of what his father had written that seemed so uncharacteristic, it was the pounding harshness of some of the statements. There was an ill defined and nagging urgency behind the whole theme.

Christian was not sure what had given his father such a perspective. Was he not an American himself and just as much a part of the society as those he seemed to be criticizing so severely? Looking down again, Christian discovered a poem couched within the fiery prose.

Perhaps the greatest American travesty and the most dire symptom of lack of community is the prejudice which is openly displayed, one soul against another. Even to the point of murdering one another over the color of one's skin!

DAY OF RECKONING
To Martin Luther King, Jr.

Just as "they crucified the Lord" and others…
Hatred engendered in the hearts of man,
Hammers its nails of violence,
And fresh-flowing tears add weight to the human "cross."
Angry voices shriek "black" and "white" words,
And cancerous evil festering in the souls of brothers
Distorts all truth in spiritual mutilation.
"Assassination!" the headlines scream,
And rampant destruction is born of the senseless death.
What idiocy the premise! A cause cannot be slain!

Disquieting thoughts needle the national conscience,
And racism, by its negative quality,
Shackles the oppressed and his oppressor.
What right any man to blacken his brother by deed,
To raise the weapons of inequality against him!
No deity separates the children of the "family,"
Nor rains eternal love in unjust favoritism.
Were the roles to be reversed, what reactions?
Suppose the condemning became the condemned?

The "righteous" in their supplications
Denounce the violent element among them;
They, too, repudiate what is savage uprising.
All thinking men ask: "Is ruthless murder to be discounted?
Or injustice, a permanently prevailing condition?

Our land, a jungle of fear, triggering uncivil deeds?"
It is a day of reckoning…time to listen.
Unchaste hearts are but a cacophony
In life's great symphony of brother loving brother."

Poem by Bettie Rose

Unable to process what he had read thus far, Christian stretched his back and rubbed his eyes, and somewhere between the prose and the poetry, he dozed off. His unconscious ear heard the family car creating the unmistakable sound of fine gravel being pressed between rubber tires and Mother Earth. He bounded out of the old chair and took the steep stairs down three at a time to ask about the Eyespell Experiment and off-world observing. He felt like a little kid on the night before Christmas. And he was pretty sure that "Eyespell" and "off-world" were just well wrapped packages preventing him from seeing what was inside. Surely his dad, Phillip Hansen, would gladly help him open them up.

He rushed out of the house to greet them as the car slowed to a stop. Phillip instantly spotted the yellowed manuscript pages in his son's grasp. He stuck his head out of the car window and said, "I see you've been in the attic again, Christian."

CHAPTER 6

▼

A CRITICAL ENCOUNTER (EARTH)

It was no accident that Jo had come to be Phillip's wife and Christian's mother. She was a special individual. Although of Earth, Jo shared many Eyespellian characteristics; her vibration could easily resonate with a high row number in Elasia's Council Chamber. Aliveness, connectedness, and compassion were integral parts of her personality. She was said to have a healing solvent; just being around her was enough to put one at ease. Without Jo's presence in his life by the early nineties Phillip would never have survived the aftermath of having missed the re-entry window.

Back in September, 1994, a confused Phillip Hansen had arrived in Washington, D.C., where he would soon meet Jo. He had barely recovered from a near fatal accident in Boca Raton, Florida in 1992. The impossible had happened. At exactly the moment of his planned re-entry from Boca Raton to Eyespell, he was sent spinning toward the light of a near-death experience. Just as Kathryn had deduced, the statistically outrageous coincidence did indeed occur and sever his telepathy link with her and with Eyespell. Phillip's missed re-entry and near-death experience left him in a coma for several days. He awoke to find out about the suicide of his closest friend, Melissa Commings. Melissa and Phillip were the only two Eyespell Experiment participants who had had direct contact with each other while on Earth. Of course, they felt a natural attraction and remained very connected from the moment they met as pre-teens on a public Boca beach. As re-entry approached they had even planned a double suicide.

The combination of a missed re-entry, telepathic separation from Kathryn, coma, and the news of Melissa's death pushed Phillip into what he later dubbed the "time of madness." It was imperative that he "connect" with Jo before the onslaught of panic attacks and free floating-anxiety that would plague him for the better part of the next fifteen years. For both Earth and Eyespell it was critical that during the ensuing "time of madness," he not reach total despair and actually commit the suicide he had originally planned for his twentieth birthday. If he killed himself now, it would mean the end of his physical incarnations on Earth and Eyespell.

While the Eyespellians had no contingency plan to account for quirks in the Eyespell Experiment, the Universe, seeing the total cosmic picture, did have an alternate plan. In early 1994, through a series of prophetic dreams, Jo learned of Phillip and was made privy to Phillip's Eyespellian identity, his missed re-entry, and his anticipated move to Washington. The dreams clearly foretold the potential disaster to the two worlds should he commit suicide. Jo sensed it was her duty to meet Phillip and to become his protector. It was her cosmic responsibility to intervene. The gift of her solvent was needed to protect Phillip during his "time of madness." This period would eventually pass, and Phillip would rediscover his Eyespellian reality. Once that was accomplished Jo could go about her own worldly business.

The prophetic dreams, Phillip's identity as an Eyespellian, and her role in protecting him did not fall outside of Jo's experience. She was particularly sensitive to issues surrounding death and dying, and to put bread on the table worked as a counselor with a local hospice. However, her sensitivities went far beyond the worldly. She often connected with the energy of a dying person and literally helped the soul's transition to another plane. In this work she was constantly in touch with spirit and frequently took direction from her higher self and from all manner of Beings of the Light beyond her own consciousness. The dreams about Phillip were particularly lucid and specific about how, later in life, he would bring Earth toward something positive called the light-skew. However, in the early nineties he was a very fragile Earth-bound soul teetering between survival and suicide. Meeting Jo and being immersed in her special and unique personal qualities would be the essential ingredient to survival winning over suicide. The Universe elected and hailed Jo as Phillip's protector.

Early one evening, Jo slipped into her jeans and a peach-tone sweatshirt and headed for Georgetown. She decided to walk. Her mood was light and reflected in the rosy glow of her cheeks. Excited and filled with an inner joy she intuitively sensed an immanent encounter that would begin her mission to save an Eyespellian. Absorbed in these thoughts, she finally looked up to get her bearings. She was surprised to find herself so far along, already wandering the narrow path next to Georgetown's canal. She spotted a good-looking young man coming from the opposite direction. Everything inside of her told her this was the man she was to meet. As they neared one another, he moved aside to let her pass, a little late. Their eyes met, and Phillip's Earth-life was changed forever.

Transfixed, he was barely able to speak. Finally he said, "Excuse me. I didn't mean to crowd you, I guess I was daydreaming."

Looking into the murky canal Jo said, "It is a bit chilly for a swim. What were you daydreaming about?"

"Meeting a beautiful and intelligent woman along this canal and having a cup of coffee, buying a beautiful house in the country, and having one perfect child."

"Done! Where shall we go, for the coffee that is?"

"How about the first place we come to?"

"I always like a well thought out plan. In fact, I think you should feed me as well. Or, you could watch me eat and you don't even have to pay for it. I just think eating is great fun, as long as it's a vegetable that is."

"You're a vegetarian?"

"And an Aquarius."

"How impressive. Me too."

"Vegetarian or Aquarius?"

"Both and proud of it. You know we've only just met and I feel better than I've felt in some time. That must sound like a terrible line."

"Indeed, but I like it coming from you."

"That's it then, a veggie burger and coffee."

From the moment they met, in what appeared to be a chance encounter, Phillip perceived Jo as a "filter of light," a "solvent." She soothed his innermost thoughts still so terribly pained by the recent events from Florida. Her very presence was enough to "heal" his mind. The relationship between Phillip and Jo never stopped evolving. They balanced each other. While her "solvent" protected Phillip from the subtleties of the dark-skew from within his own mind, he protected Jo from direct attacks of the dark-skew coming from others.

Phillip's point of greatest weakness in protecting himself against "dark" vibrations rested within the workings of his own mind. He was his own worst enemy. He had frequent bouts of negative thinking, depression, worry, guilt, and discouragement. The possibility of suicide as an answer for Phillip was not an imagined concern. His vulnerability was life threatening and, indeed, very real. While in one of his funks there was the danger of his committing suicide out of sheer confusion between his Earth-born thoughts and his then unconscious Eyespellian-born thoughts. Somewhere in his brain was still implanted the Eyespell Experiment's directive to commit suicide even though his twentieth birthday had long since passed. Connection with this thought process, however veiled, was uncomfortable in even the best of moods. In times of despair and confusion, Phillip relied on Jo for comfort and the assurance that he was not totally mad.

Jo, on the other hand, relied on Phillip to protect her from negativity embodied at times in the physical life force of other beings. Sinister others, given the chance, would take pleasure in destroying Jo's purity, destroying her "solvent." Phillip had an intuitive gift for recognizing, and protecting Jo from, those who would either maliciously with intention, or accidentally in their own selfish need, deplete her of her "solvent." It was one thing to simply be around Jo and let her healing aura soothe you; it was totally another to try to psychically steal her gift destroying the healing solvent in the process. For Phillip, being bathed in her aura was enough to comfort him.

Each truly benefited from the relationship created through Jo's dreams and her belief in a higher purpose. For her, what may have begun as duty ended in love. She joyfully and freely married Phillip and it was etched in the cosmic plan that she give birth to their child, Christian Hansen. His heritage as Eyespellian from his father and of "special personal qualities" from his Earth-born mother would come to serve him and the planets of the light-skew during the approaching time of the Mystic Management.

CHAPTER 7

▼

MANAGING THE LIGHT CORRIDORS OF EYESPELL (EYESPELL)

Antonio, Melissa, and Nancy were highly animated; they chatted as they remained standing at the third row of the council chamber. Pete, a few feet away, stood silent completely mesmerized by the flurry of activity around him as the council chamber continued to fill. Falling deeper into his apparent daydreaming Pete slowly became aware that the flurry of activity was not coming from his surroundings at all, but from inside his own head. It was as if he were greeting and being greeted simultaneously by everyone present in the chamber, over three hundred people. Pete was experiencing complete telepathy link for the first time since his return to Eyespell. Unable to manage this newly rediscovered faculty, he simply sat down where he was and allowed his mind to receive and reach out.

The first image that came to him was Leo sitting cross-legged with a small group of young students in a semicircle, facing him. They were hanging on their teacher's every word. Pete instantly recognized that he was one of the youngsters, and he effortlessly knew what Leo was saying.

"Now my children pay close attention. This part is very important. The light-skew and its management on Eyespell are complex matters. Our legends tell of the creation of the light corridors and the inception of the Mystic Management to maintain them. This history is recorded in the *Book of Dreams*. Who can tell me about the *Book of Dreams*? How about you, Pete?"

Still watching his daydream Pete chuckled as his younger self all but fell face first in the sand in his enthusiasm to answer his teacher's question. The young Pete blurted out, "The *Book of Dreams* is a book of, a book of, ah, a book of dreams."

Leo laughed and said, "And a green and purple songbird is a green and purple songbird. Actually, Peter, you're not that far off, and your enthusiasm more than makes up for your imprecision. The *Book of Dreams* is composed of images rather than pages and a single image has been known to keep our historians and scholars in lively discussion and debate for hours, even days, at a time. It is, indeed, a book of dreams, complex ones laying out the fundamental Eyespellian truths. Our task today is to review and synthesize a number of the basic images relating to the light corridors and the Mystic Management. The *Book* provides much practical information about these matters. Look at the chart I have given you. In unison, tell me what the six essential elements of each light corridor are. Come on now, don't be shy."

Leo cupped his hands behind his ears and leaned toward his students. They sat at attention and pretended to be the instruments of a symphony responding to the conductor's undulations. Not exactly in unison they sang out, "The first essential element of each light corridor is it's crystal."

"Good," said Leo. "And what do you know about these crystals?"

This time Pete jumped in without hesitation. "Each Elder is in charge of a crystal that reflects the same color as one of the light corridors. There are six crystals and they've existed nearly forever. They have been passed down from Elder to Elder, and each is a perfect polished pyramid. They are identical in size and shape, and each one is made of a different gemstone. An Elder is never without the crystal of his or her light-charge carrying it either in a silk pouch at the waist or around the neck on a rope of light. The crystals focus energy on the spirit and emotion of our people."

Leo responded like a proud parent. "That's quite a dissertation, young Pete. You are quite sure of yourself after all. Does anybody here know the color of my crystal?"

The reverie continuing, Pete smiled again at the image of his much younger self. For the first time he realized that Antonio, Melissa, Nancy, and even Phillip were among the group attending to Leo's history lesson. Pete felt so connected. He found it hard to imagine that Phillip was not with the group in the council chamber on this day. He could feel him so clearly in his daydream.

As if on cue, Phillip popped up and tugged gently at Leo's robe and said, "Leo, show us your crystal. Yours is the blue one."

In unison the children said, "Please Leo, oh please, can we see it please?"

Leo reached into the pouch at his waist and produced a perfect pyramid of clear sapphire. It dangled from a rope of blue light as he held it in front of him almost touching the now misshapen semicircle of students. The sapphire pyramid flashed blue light that could be felt as it caressed the small group. An overwhelming peace came over them. Pete could feel it as if he were back there at that time.

"My crystal's not blue," said Leo.

Nancy looked at him and said, "You're just trying to trick us. Your crystal doesn't have to be blue, only its light has to be blue."

"Exactly right. You are all just too smart for this old man. So then, what's the next essential element of a light corridor?" Leo straightened his back and the semi-circle of pupils regained its shape.

This time Antonio spoke up. "The second essential element of a light corridor is its affiliation with one of the suns or moons. And I know the answer to your next question. Your crystal is of the blue sun."

"Wonderful, Antonio. And does anyone know what trait the blue sun represents?" asked Leo.

"You're getting at the third element. Peace is the trait for the blue light corridor. We could tell that just by the way we felt when you held out your crystal."

Pete recognized Melissa as the last one to speak and thought, "How odd sitting no more than three feet away from Melissa right here in the council chamber while at the same time being with her in childhood in a daydream that is so real." His thought shifted and he again heard Leo talking softly to his pupils.

"Okay, you've got the idea. The essential elements are a little out of order but no matter. An image from the *Book of Dreams* will clear it right up. I would hate to squelch your enthusiasm in my desire for perfection. I have given each of you a copy of an image that lists the six essential elements of each light corridor in the proper order, beginning with the color of the light corridor and ending with the Elder primarily responsible for that corridor. The order is color, crystal, celestial body, trait, mystic principle, and elder."

CORRIDOR COLOR	CRYSTAL	CELESTIAL BODY	TRAIT	MYSTIC PRINCIPLE	ELDER
YELLOW	CLEAR DIAMOND	YELLOW SUN	KNOWLEDGE	SYSTEMS SENSITIVITY	DANIEL
BLUE	CLEAR SAPPHIRE	BLUE SUN	PEACE	EGO EMPOWERMENT	LEO
WHITE	CLEAR QUARTZ	THIRD MOON	ONENESS	INCLUSIVE INTEGRITY	GRACINA
PINK	PINK TOURMALINE	FOURTH MOON	LOVE	GENTLE GENEROSITY	MYANA
RED	RUBY	FIRST MOON	ENERGY	COLLABORATIVE CREATIVITY	MATTHEW
GREEN	EMERALD	SECOND MOON	NATURE	KARMIC KINDNESS	REBECCA

The adult Pete watched and easily recalled the chart in its entirety. Leo, after giving his students several minutes to ponder the image, continued, "The combined infinite hues of the six light corridors make up Eyespell's light-skew. Even though an Elder is appointed to manage each light corridor, responsibility for the maintenance of the light-skew is shared to some degree by every citizen. Each of you is part of this sharing. Our being here together is an example of this. Our planet is a totally empowered society, to a person."

A young boy sitting beside Antonio spoke up. "I don't understand the word empowerment and I know it's important."

"Excellent point. To empower is to give power to equally, to share, to allow everybody to participate, to make everybody feel good about what we are doing. It's that kind of thing. This empowerment, although based on the highest of ideals, does demand structure. The day-to-day management of the planet's affairs rests primarily with the six Elders who make up the Elders' Council. The Eldersix, as we are often called, are looked to for leadership in both spiritual and corporal matters. Our leadership is that of consensus and respect among all Eyespellians, not of power held exclusively by the council. Does that help explain empowerment or have I raised more questions than I have answered?"

Everyone looked at Leo and sang out, "We think it's time for a break!" With that they jumped up and surrounded Leo, threatening mischief.

Pete watched the scenario continue to unfold. He thought, "I'm literally a part of my daydream." By the time he had finished this thought the daydream was quite a bit ahead of him. His mind had fast-forwarded through the break and picked up when the teachings resumed.

"Okay, settle down," Leo said. "The break is over. Now, back to the day-to-day management of the planet. Due to our telepathy links there is never a question of miscommunications or hidden agendas among Eyespellians. The net effect of this level of openness is that there are no politics necessary in our Mystic Management."

Pete was particularly interested in this part as he saw his younger self yell out, "Are we going to learn about the Mystic Management, Leo?"

"Relax Peter, I'm getting there," Leo said with approval in his eyes. "Mystic Management is our planet's management style. It is the antithesis of the typical power structures developed on other planets we have studied. Its six tenets are geared toward sustainability. Notice how everything seems to come in sixes on Eyespell. Six is our number of personality, magnetism, the community that is Eyespell. Anyway, the Elders have managed Eyespell in the Mystic tradition since the creation of the light corridors. This tradition, explained in the *Book of Dreams*, dictates how we manage our lives and our planet. The Mystic Management revolves around the six principles we are going to study. Okay, name one of the principles."

Pete saw himself enthusiastic and again yelling out, "My chart lists Collaborative Creativity as part of the red-light corridor."

"Yes, and Collaborative Creativity, is, in fact, the first principle. It promotes a management style that examines all ideas. Creativity for its own sake holds a position of respect, and is an integral part of decision-making in virtually every aspect of our lives. The decision making process is facilitated by one or more Elders, depending upon the light corridor or corridors. This is no simple task. Even with the aid of direct telepathy links, examining all available information and allowing for maximum creative input can be a lengthy process. Everybody's ideas are welcome all the time. Here on Eyespell creative is rarely synonymous with rapid.

Because we have no medium of exchange, much potential inherent conflict that would be caused by the correlation between time and money, for example, is eliminated. Since time is not money on Eyespell, and there is no economic gain or loss in terms of how long creative decisions may take, all things can be explored until consensus is achieved. Our lack of a typical economic system allows Collaborative Creativity to exist in the purest sense. Moreover, our ability to manifest necessary resources through manipulation of the light corridors eliminates the concept of scarcity. In the absence of scarce resources, Collaborative Creativity easily maintains its paramount position in our society."

The reverie split apart for a moment and Pete found himself connected to another set of thoughts. "This lack of scarcity is one significant result of the light-skew and good reason for Eyespellians to eschew balance. Balance would mean alternating cycles of plenty versus scarcity and a lesser ability to maintain a Collaborative Creativity. Earth-plane vibrational leakage, given its potential to cause scarcity and economic upheaval threatens, in its tendency toward balance, to destroy Collaborative Creativity." Pete recognized these thoughts as Leo's, but not from the daydream. He looked up, caught Leo's glance from across the council chamber and began to understand how telepathy link can take several directions at once. He again heard Leo's voice in his head, "It's time to get back to your reverie."

The daydream picked up without losing so much as a sentence. Leo was again talking to the semicircle of students before him, "The second principle, Ego Empowerment, also speaks of our rule by consensus. The focus is on shared management and group centered leadership. The orientation is other-directed rather than self-directed, with a mutual respect for the unique talents and abilities of every member of the Eyespellian community. We do not operate in a hierarchical fashion. For example, the six light corridors, our only organizational units, are different each from the other. However, no corridor is considered better or more powerful than the other. For example Daniel, head of the Eldersix and Keeper of the Yellow-Light Corridor, is no better or lesser than any other Eyespellian. His focus is on knowledge and he brings his personal qualities to bear on his light-charge."

Nancy waved her hands in the air with a question that just couldn't wait, "We shine with color. Does this have anything to do with what you're saying?"

"Now there's an interesting question, young lady, and pretty perceptive. I'm sure your parents have discussed this with you in a general way, but not in relation to the principle of Ego Empowerment. Each of us has a primary affiliation with a specific light corridor and we resonate with that light corridor. The color of our affinity corridor is reflected in the coloring of our skin, and the stronger the resonance with a particular corridor, the more obvious the skin tone. You used the words 'shine with color.' You're exactly right. These skin tones are not flat and consistent hues, but a shimmering fire of colors like those of an opal being slowly turned in the sunlight. If one were to look closely for example, Daniel flashes distinct yellow tones while I give off an obvious blue. These various flashes of color among the populace are a perfect blend with the hues of the planet and its two suns and four moons. Eyespell is literally a place of color and diversity that culminates in a feeling of oneness through acceptance and all-inclusive community. You have already learned total acceptance. What's new to you are the larger concepts of oneness and inclusive community.

Again Pete picked up Leo's present moment thoughts, "And the impact of Earth-plane vibrational leakage would be to fragment community. Even the physical color of Eyespell would change. Balance could cause a blending of colors across the planet resulting in a consistent and uninteresting off-white. The oxymoron is that the balancing vibrations from the Earth's dark-skew of negativity would produce a planet lighter in color. It would be like metaphorically mixing black pigment into a can of pastel blue paint in order to lighten it. The concept is disconcerting." Leo waved from across the council chamber and said into Pete's consciousness, "Sorry, I've interrupted again. Continue with your daydream; it is important that you fill in the details about Eyespell. You will have an important role to play in our future."

Pete did not have time to be puzzled by Leo's comment as his mind again reached out and captured the continuing daydream. The dream-Leo was back at his teaching. "Gentle Generosity is the third tenet of the Mystic Management. This refers to our always going the extra step to encourage others. It is the giving to someone else while simultaneously freeing one's own insecurities. Eyespell is a planet of positive self-concept and continuous positive identity formation. Our studies show that many peoples from far away planets are plagued with identity crisis. Unlike us, they do not know who they are or where they are going either individually or collectively. We experience identity-building through a collective conscious that each of us can relate to. Other places experience identity fragmentation through inconsistent interpretation of a collective unconscious fraught with confusing and stereotypical imagery. There is little ambiguity in Eyespellian identity. *The Book of Dreams* is filled with identity-building images that can be manifested through light combined with thought. A magnificent example is an image called the "Identity Garden." The "Identity Garden" is found in Dream V, Image 1. Mind link with me and let's image together."

Leo closed his eyes and brought the image of the "Identity Garden" into his head for his pupils to share.

The Identity Garden

The young monk had a dream about the most beautiful place he had never been. He was hiking up a sub-alpine meadow with the snow freshly melted to reveal carpets of wildflowers in honor of summer. And there, high above his path, hiding in the mountain's mist, he could make out a curlicue wrought iron gate hanging between the parting ends of a massive wall that hugged the steep slopes. As he approached the gateway, the dream stuff stretched and he found himself amidst a pleasant crowd of people making their way through the gate into what the cornerstone in the wall labeled, "The Garden of Identity." Immediately inside and stuck in the middle of the pathway, a little keep-off-the-grass-type sign instructed: "PICK WHAT YOU WANT."

The monk awoke with a host of new metaphors from the dream garden. There was the wall, constructed of the building blocks of short-term goals and sustained positive motivation. There were the tall and skirted firs of aspiration and inspiration in the alpine meadow. There was the fountain of unconditional love at the garden's hub. From the myriad flowers abounding one could fashion a bouquet of identity. There were curiosity, compassion, truthfulness, trust, self-assuredness, and a non-judging attitude, all in full bloom. There was limitless possibility for choosing psychological healthiness among the objects and flowers in the garden of identity. In a word, there was hope.

Leo opened his eyes to find his pupils still immersed in the garden each selecting a bouquet of identity. Finally Leo spoke, "The sharing of these images is a celebration and brings us to our greatest vibrational level. Constant sharing and giving produce a state of planetary self-actualization. Gentle Generosity is truly the heart of Eyespell."

Pete's consciousness returned momentarily to the council chamber. He was profoundly affected by the imaging in his daydream. He now knew exactly who he was. He recalled the details of the Eyespell Experiment, his role in it, and the concern about Earth-plane vibrational leakage. He also knew that he resonated with the yellow-light corridor and his natural place was in the twenty-sixth ring of the council chamber. For now, however, he chose to stay where he was and finish his daydream. Leo looked up and smiled in confirmation.

The students were reluctant to leave image and Leo had to coax them back to their lesson, "Bring your image with you into the next principle, Inclusive Integrity. Inclusive Integrity celebrates the light-skew as the coming together of six diverse light corridors. It allows for the complementarity of different qualities merging into a synergistic whole. While the guiding principles of the Mystic Management must remain intact, the specific management style within each light corridor is directly tied to its Elder and the Eyespellians affiliated most closely with that corridor. The manner in which I empower within the blue light corridor need not be identical to how Daniel empowers within the yellow light corridor.

Equifinality, the ability to do things in more than one way, is a respected concept. The bottom line is that we must maintain the light-skew through an empowered society. Exactly how that is done may vary from light corridor to light corridor and from individual to individual. Any questions?"

Leo paused for a few moments and then continued. "Of course I know there are never any questions in response to the question, 'any questions?' It's just a technique I use when I really want to move along. And so to Karmic Kindness, the simplest principle of all: what goes around comes around and kindness is the only way. Kindness is the nature of all things on Eyespell, whether one is speaking of the nature of relationships or literally the natural environment as reflected in the cell-matrix. Eyespell is compassion personified."

From across the council chamber Leo again added a footnote to Pete's dreaming, "Imagine the negative possibilities of Earth-plane vibrational leakage with regard to this principle. It would be difficult enough to lose creativity, to lose empowerment, to lose diversity of color, or to not be self-actualized. But, imagine the dark-skew balancing Eyespell's kindness with violence. This is a most frightening prospect. The recent experience with Nancy and Kathryn is a prime example. This minor confrontation was almost instantly translated into the cell-matrix and began to wreak havoc. You saw the thunderclouds and the path begin to crack. While temporarily averted, the overall effects of this leakage have yet to be felt, I'm afraid. I've done it again. Get on with your daydream lessons."

Leo's teaching voice drifted to the front of Pete's mind, "And finally there is Systems Sensitivity. This is the understanding that all things, whether of mind, physical reality, or spirit, are interconnected. What happens in one part affects all other parts. This is an essential element in manifesting all on Eyespell, and is the linking pin between the light-skew and the planetary cell-matrix. A single thought can be captured and manifested within the cell-matrix. This is why positive thinking is so important. The impact of negative vibrations could be very difficult for us to handle. The Elders always maintain their light-charges in the Mystic

Management tradition, holding the six principles paramount in the management of the light corridors of Eyespell. In a nutshell, that's the Mystic Management. Let's sit in silence for a few moments to capture the spirit of what I have said."

Pete watched as the children reflected upon their lesson. Phillip was the first to speak, "Leo, if the light-skew is the manifestation of all six light corridors into the planetary cell-matrix, is it the cell-matrix that gives Eyespell its physical reality of total connectedness?"

"Yes, yes, now you're getting it. The body of Eyespell, its physical being, is manifested through the reality-creating process itself, and this process is a most fascinating aspect of our planet's culture. Observing an Elder manage a light corridor for the purpose of creating, within the light-skew, a new vibration that is ultimately manifested within the physical cell-matrix is truly a magic show. It is the Mystic Management in action."

"Can you give us an example, Leo?" asked Antonio.

"Ah, let me think of a good one. Yes, yes a wonderful example of this reality creating activity was solving the problem of transportation. We had a need to get from one place to another on the planet's surface as well as travel among the four moons.

The Elders' Council met and using the principle of Collaborative Creativity, opened the transportation issue to all ideas. There was much discussion. The gathering of information and consensus reaching among all Eyespellians took a very long time. Nonetheless this was a joyous process and is an integral part of our culture. There was no hurry to complete the task. That's not to say we worked only on the transportation problem. It is not uncommon for us to have hundreds, even thousands of reality-creating tasks occurring simultaneously, depending upon the complexity of each.

Ultimately, a fascinating decision was reached; it was decided to keep the planet machine-free. Any transportation system would, therefore, have to be energy based and capable of instantly transporting Eyespellians from place to place. The energy focus of this task placed it squarely in the red-light corridor, and under the auspices of the Elder Matthew.

Matthew, keeper of the red-light corridor, gathered all Eyespellians within his light-charge and together they walked in prayer to the Red Sand Desert in time for the rising of the first moon. The red-light corridor has the greatest number of people affiliated with it; a full thirty percent of the population is needed to manage its skew. What a sight! A team of approximately seventy-five thousand gathered into a great spiral moving slowly in a clockwise direction. Already in deep meditation they began to focus on Matthew's ruby crystal now extended at his fingertips toward the heavens. Suddenly the red light corridor opened. Its energy exploded like a volcano through the crown chakras of seventy-five thousand Eyespellians set on the identical conscious image of the agreed-upon trasporter system."

Leo had become effusive in his description and his pupils sat transfixed and wide-eyed, fully imagining that they were there, themselves creating the transporter system. Pete stood up waving his arms and making explosion noises, "Was it like this, Leo?"

"Even greater. After the thought or the word or the logos, an explosion of light is always the first kernel of reality creating. As the light passed through the consciousness of those seventy-five thousand set in prayer, the image was projected like a laser onto the red sands. This was the connection with the cell-matrix and, poof, the thought was converted to physical reality. Deeply resonating, single-syllable chanting, and tremendous fireworks of red light accompanied the whole process. Then it ended as abruptly as it began. The red-light corridor closed. What was left behind was the comprehensive system of energy vortices that allow us to freely and almost instantly travel in physical body around the planet surface and to its four moons. And we're all familiar with that."

"Wow, what a story," said Melissa. "Is any of this dangerous?"

Leo thought for a moment, then said, "I'm not sure dangerous is the right word. The most important conditions for accomplishing this are the purity of the color in the light corridor and the exact sameness of the image in each person's consciousness at the time of the corridor opening. Any stray color or thought would produce a result different from that intended. The only thing that might be construed as dangerous is the possibility of negativity entering the system during reality-creating. This has never happened."

Leo practically yelled into Pete's head, "Until now anyway! I never really thought about it much back then because the possibility seemed so remote. Sorry, finish up your daydream, Pete."

"Just one more thing, then we'll quit for today. The most dramatic, exciting, and beautiful outcomes of our ability to reality-create through manipulation of the light corridors are exhibited in our natural surroundings. Just look around you. In the scope of things Eyespell is a comparatively small planet, about the size of Mercury in Earth's solar system, for example. We are located at the fringe of the Pinar Galaxy in a small solar system with only two sister planets, both uninhabited. But you already know this. Our planet's most unusual characteristic is its configuration of two suns and four moons. In all the universe known to us there is nothing quite like it. We have spent much time and energy designing the natural environment of both the planet surface and the four moons. Although Eyespell appears pink from outer space, it's actually made up of an infinite-color array. Each of our six deserts, for example, displays the full color range of a particular light corridor in its shifting sands. The Green Desert shows off streaks of every imaginable shade of green in constant and shifting blend. How many of you have been to the Green Desert?"

Everyone in the group raised a hand and the girl next to Nancy said, "I've been to all six deserts and I think the green one is the most beautiful." As she turned her head in the soft light, barely perceptible flashes of green reflected back from her cheeks. She continued, "From my other studies it seems that the term desert is a misnomer. Other than the sand itself, our deserts display none of the parched characteristics commonly associated with them. For example, they are neither overly hot nor dry like the deserts on the planet closest to our yellow sun. Our deserts are wonderful places to walk."

"And to meditate," added Leo. "Meditation is something you will spend a great deal of time doing. Walking meditation is indeed the great Eyespellian pastime. Our deserts are also places of beautiful mountains, streams, waterfalls, meadows, small forests and all manner of other undesert-like topography. I am pretty sure we just love the word 'desert' and we are truly fond of creating colored sands."

"Except on the moons," blurted out Antonio. "I've been to the first moon with Matthew, keeper of the red-light corridor and I didn't see one grain of sand."

"And what are the moons like?" quizzed Leo.

Melissa volunteered, "They are like magnificent gardens. Each moon favors a light corridor in its color array, but there's no sand. I have only been to the fourth moon. It's a wonderful predominately pink garden; there is every imaginable flower in every shade of pink the mind can comprehend. The birds and cats are shades of pink, and even the water has a pinkish glow. However, I've seen pictures of all four moons. Well, we all have, and I think the most spectacular picture in the gallery in Elasia is of the third moon. It is a garden of white light taking in and reflecting back the entire light-skew in an explosion of color that is beyond all imagination."

"Indeed," added Leo, "the third moon is within Gracina's light-charge and is truly a place of unparalleled beauty and oneness. On that wonderful image let's stop for today."

Pete awoke from his daydream and again caught Leo's glance from across the council chamber. Leo sent still another message to Pete, "A looming concern with Earth-plane vibrational leakage is the manner in which the dark-skew might change the colors of Eyespell. The current threat is like the black pigment in the pastel-colored paint. I think I need to close my telepathy link before I contaminate the council chamber with my worrisome thoughts, if I haven't done so already. I am glad you have finished your lesson, for the second time." Leo smiled and prepared for the council opening.

Pete got up from where he was sitting and made his way down the council chamber, greeting Antonio, Melissa, and Nancy with a broad smile as he moved past them on his way to take up his proper place in the twenty-sixth ring.

CHAPTER 8

▼

THE VALLEY OF THE BLUENOON (EYESPELL)

Daniel, keeper of the yellow-light corridor, custodian of knowledge, and head of the Elders' Council, stood at the center of the Council Chamber. His crystal, on its rope of light, lay beautifully displayed against his flowing yellow robes. When Daniel moved, the crystal appeared to throw sparks of light as it swayed almost imperceptibly across his chest. With eyes lifted, palms open, and arms stretched toward the heavens, Daniel "spoke" the opening meditation into the minds of all Eyespellians. "In the light-skew of two suns and four moons manifesting six primary planetary light corridors, may the crystal charge of each Elder be preserved. The Full Round is open."

With the final word of the meditation, a color ray emanating from each of the six Elders' crystals burst into "flame," merged in the high reaches of the amphitheater, and created a laser-like light show inside the dome. The fabric of the dome and surrounding structures amplified the intensity of the colors until finally, the surface of the planet surrounding Elasia was ablaze with Eyespellian rainbows. The sight as seen from the dunes outside the Council Chamber was cosmically impressive. The view of Elasia from an outer-space perspective during a Council opening would be considered a spectacle in the category of miracles. And, in fact. the best spectator "seats" for this show, were at the fringe of Eyespell's furthermost aura. Most Eyespellians reserved these incredible seats through purposeful meditation that would put them out-of-body above the planet several hours before a scheduled Council opening. The whole ceremony was nothing less than expansive, grand, and literally out of the world.

As Daniel spoke, the planetary cell-matrix resonated with his light-charge. Daniel could not only be seen and heard, but felt. All beings were connected with every fiber of Daniel's being. He was one with the planetary cell-matrix. The closer one sat to the twenty-seventh Council Chamber ring the more intense the experience of total oneness with Daniel and with the planet. There are no words to adequately describe the depth of this experience, and there is no image that captures the spectrum of color flowing from the Council Chamber. This is truly of another dimension.

As Daniel's presence combined with the power of the laser-like lights opening all of Eyespell's light corridors simultaneously, Antonio, Melissa, and Nancy instantly and fully regained their Eyespellian identities and faculties. This allowed them to move from the third row where they had been standing to rings fifteen, sixteen, and twenty-two respectively. Their sensor-chairs enveloped them and they finally became one again with each other and their home, after twenty long and difficult Earth-years on that plane. Pete was already comfortably seated in the twenty-sixth ring and at some level still in touch with his reverie about the Mystic Management.

Leo watched pensively as Nancy settled into her place in the twenty-second ring. It made him extremely uneasy. She was, afterall, the one who just weeks before had triggered upon her re-entry Eyespell's first, although minor, episode of Earth-plane vibrational leakage when she avoided his hug. And only days before she had caused the first serious episode upon encountering Kathryn. Now this same individual was in the Council Chamber during an opening of the Full Round! By this time Leo had closed his telepathy link so as not to contaminate the Council Chamber with these worrisome thoughts. At this point, only Pete knew what was going on with Leo. It was, however, unprecedented for one of the Elders to go into open council with a non-activated telepathy link. Leo felt he had no choice. He could handle his charge of preserving the "peace" only if he could preserve the purity of his blue-light corridor. He was uncertain whether or not his crystal may still contain even the slightest manifestation of Nancy's anger and hostility. To expose open council to such a potential risk would be unconscionable.

Leo's closed telepathy link did not go unnoticed for long. Daniel said, "This is the first time that one of our Eldersix has come to open council mind-shrouded. This is a dangerous sign. Leo, peace-keeper, what so threatens your spirit?"

"With all respect to you and the Council, I am gravely concerned about Earth-plane vibrational leakage. I have experienced it first-hand, and if it seeps into our planetary cell-matrix the light-skew will be disrupted. A strong vibration could cause a permanent rupture in the cell-matrix. No matter how infinitesimal, such a rupture would begin to move the planet toward homeostasis, a mixing of light and dark. And what impacts the planet impacts the people. That which is Eyespell, is simultaneously Eyespellian. The Mystic Management principle of systems sensitivity, above all others cannot be compromised. All things are interconnected, are one. If Earth-plane vibrational leakage contaminates one part, it contaminates all parts of the cell-matrix.

Gracina, keeper of the white-light corridor, custodian of oneness, supported Leo's position. Herself the essence of white light, she literally captured those around her in an aura as bright as the third moon of Eyespell. "What Leo says is true. If oneness is broken there is no assurance that we will be able to heal ourselves. Perhaps it is time to hear from our returned children about all that has transpired in the last twenty years on the Earth plane. Only then might we be able to determine the real dangers to our planet. With the non-return of Phillip, my charge to maintain oneness has already been compromised. The loss of one of our children leaves a great void within the crystal energy of the third moon. I think our collective and unconditional love for Phillip is compensating for, at least temporarily, the altered white-light corridor his absence has created. And this is to say nothing of the added energy Myana has had to expend of necessity in maintaining the pink-light corridor from which unconditional love resonates. The skew within the white-light corridor is shifting even as we speak."

The pressing reality of Phillip's non-return, Leo's closed telepathy link, and the potential ominous consequences of substantial Earth-plane vibrational leakage, forced the Elders' Council into unprecedented action. The Eldersix prematurely ended the Full Round and moved into closed session. There could be no further contact with the returning Eyespellians nor with their overseer, Kathryn, until things were sorted out. The Elders shielded the center ring from all outside vibrations and went into a state of oneness in mind-link-orbit around the third moon of Eyespell.

This action by the Elders immediately kindled feelings of rejection within the small group returning from Earth. Dismayed they left the Council Chamber. With Leo unavailable, Pete and Melissa looked to Kathryn for leadership and perhaps consolation. But there was immediate friction in the group.

Nancy was quick to point out, "I sit at ring twenty-two. Kathryn sits at the vibrational level of only the twenty-first ring. Why would you follow her advice? Besides, I don't trust her."

She had no sooner spoken the words when Antonio pressed between them and stated matter-of-factly, "Pete is of the twenty-sixth ring and almost an Elder. He's the one we should be following."

Pete seemed embarrassed, and Kathryn, for the fourth time since her return, became teary-eyed. It began to rain. It was uncertain whether the clouds were natural phenomena or clouds of dissent, perhaps intent upon whetting some new and unfamiliar appetite for conflict on Eyespell. For the second time since their return they were reduced to an awkwardly silenced and fragmented group of individuals, quite un-Eyespellian-like.

As the Council remained in Oneness around the third moon, events on the planet's surface were worsening. The light-skew was definitely being pulled toward homeostasis. Eyespell was suffering from Earth-plane vibrational leakage of a serious and global nature. Signs were everywhere.

The first serious catastrophe was that the Eyespellians who had been out-of-body above the planet watching the spectacle of the Full Round, were harshly and instantaneously jerked back into their bodies. As a result they suffered something akin to re-entry trauma. There was widespread loss of Eyespellian perception, telepathy, and connectedness. Even though the negative impact on these powers was temporary, the cell-matrix had already been damaged. Leo's greatest fear had manifested. The cell-matrix ruptured slightly and was wreaking untold havoc with the light-skew. The literal fabric of Eyespell was being compromised.

The Elders, even in their state of oneness, were unable to immediately mitigate the situation on the planet surface. Eyespell was beginning to experience opposites. An example painfully obvious to the Elders was the contrast between their state of oneness and the temporary fragmentation and total loss of connectedness among the general population. It was as if the planet had been thrown back several hundred thousand evolutionary years in an instant, in the reflex of an eye.

The psychological disruption caused concurrent fractures in the cell-matrix itself. There were thunderstorms, mild earthquakes, and millions of tiny stress cracks beginning to form on the planet's surface. The healing blue sun remained hidden behind a darkened atmosphere for long periods of time. Growing things began to die. The various species of cats and birds making up Eyespell's animal population began to revert to an untamed and ferocious state. There were disharmony, danger, and fear among the living things of Eyespell.

Suddenly everything went still; there was an incredible electrical snap in the air and the climate of Eyespell once again quieted itself. The cell-matrix, responding to the powerful positive vibration of the Eldersix in oneness, was able to compensate for the devastating vibrational leakage…this time. But what of the future? The Elders broke the mind-link orbit around the third moon, each of them moving swiftly to manage their respective light corridors in an attempt to protect the light-skew from further disruption.

* * * * * * * *

The blue sun of Eyespell reached its zenith each day above a very holy place. Leo, guardian and manager of the blue-light corridor, urgently made plans to go there. The Valley of the Bluenoon, as it was called, was the most sacred place on all of Eyespell. Bluenoon was twenty-seven miles due south of Elasia and, for Leo, a two-day prayer-walk with a company of fifty-four pilgrims.

In good times, the pilgrimage was a festive occasion for young Eyespellians. They typically donned their colorful rainbow-hued robes and set forth from Elasia in good cheer. They would savor the opportunity to go off into the desert with an Elder, learning more of the light-skew and the cell-matrix. This day, however, the company was a select group of Eyespellians with special affinity to the vibrations of Leo's crystal and the blue-light corridor. The pilgrimage was not one of excitement and learning, but rather one prompted by the critical and urgent business of survival.

Leo emerged from the Council Chamber and found that the fifty-four pilgrims were already preparing for the journey. The robes chosen for this day were not of the hues of festivity, but of the solemn and serious monk's brown. The left sleeve of Leo's robe carried the symbol of the blue light corridor. The rays of an embroidered blue sun stretched from near the top of the shoulder to the bottom of the loose sleeve. He wore nothing on his head or feet, his crystal resting over his heart on its rope of light. The fifty-four pilgrims in their plain brown monk's robes also wore nothing on their heads or feet. Around the waist of each was a silver fabric rope laced at the front in a complex series of ties forming a knotted frame around a polished talisman of blue lapis lazuli with shimmering golden pyrite inclusions.

Leo led the group away from Elasia's center toward the dunes to Bluenoon. It was evening as they walked under the light of the first three rising moons. The fifty-four Eyespellian pilgrims walked behind Leo, two-by-two, in a perfect line of twenty-seven rows. Leo would raise a chant and each row would follow in succession in the same tone. It was an eerie-looking brown line of chanting monks with moon-glistening talismans that moved mindfully over the dunes on that uncertain evening. Arrival at the Valley of Bluenoon would be precisely at the light of three full moons the following night. It was not unusual for an Eyespellian pilgrimage to walk and chant for many days without stopping to rest, eat or drink.

Leo's and the pilgrims' states of consciousness moved gradually to higher and higher vibrational levels. The slowly marching column became one with each grain of sand turning and rolling under the forward motion of each monk's soles. The lapis talismans swayed gently back and forth in sync with the crystal of the blue sun pressing against Leo's heart chakra. The chanting tones gathered and rose like invisible force fields against the waves of Earth-plane vibrations still threatening to fragment the planetary cell-matrix. The ground upon which the pilgrims passed was instantly healed. With each footfall the cell-matrix responded as if it were alive and itself the fifty-fifth pilgrim. The planet healers reached the fringe of mountains overlooking the Valley of the Bluenoon on the second evening of their journey. The third moon of oneness was beginning to rise in the already lit two-moon night sky. Later in the evening when the monks were in place over the valley the fourth moon would rise, the moon of uncon-ditional love and compassion.

The valley itself was crater-like, totally surrounded by jagged peaks ris-ing sharply out of the beautiful Eyespellian desert. It was exactly one and one-half miles across with a tower-like formation jutting out of its center and standing one-hundred-fifty feet above the highest of the encircling peaks. The formations around the valley had sheer sides. They dropped like vertical glass sheets to the valley floor several hundred feet lower than the enveloping desert. From the path worn around the top perimeter of the crater there were four sets of carved steps leading downward in steep descent, one stairway at each point of the compass.

The pilgrims began to slowly walk the perimeter path above the valley. They ever so gradually spaced themselves at long and equal distances until the entire circumference of the Valley of the Bluenoon was encircled by chanting monks revolving counterclockwise at an almost imperceptible pace around the valley. This living circle continued its ceremony under the light of the four full moons of Eyespell.

Just as the blue sun lifted from the northern horizon and the four moons set, Leo began to descend the staircase at the north point of the compass. The encircling monks immediately realigned the space between them, and stopped their movement at fifty-four equal intervals atop the crater. Arms at their sides with palms open, and facing the valley center, they chanted in a tone that focused the very molecules of air toward the tower at the valley's center. As the sound sent its energy toward the tower, the talismans at their belts began to send points of light following upon the sound waves.

Leo continued to move down the stairs, eyes focused on his destination at the center of the valley. As the blue sun moved higher in the sky, he made his way to the base of the tower. The monks above continued their energy focus and chanting. Leo removed the crystal from around his neck and held it point upward. With this gesture, he appeared to float to the uppermost plateau of the tower. Waiting for the bluenoon, when the blue sun would reach its zenith directly overhead, Leo sat cross-legged squarely facing north with upward pointed crystal at his chest. The fifty-four pilgrims ringed the tower in prayer.

At exactly bluenoon, Leo lifted the crystal directly above his head with the fingertips of both hands. The clear crystal caught the full intensity of the blue sun. The rays of lapis blue and pyrite gold from the talismans inched up the tower with the monks' concentrated meditation. The sound of their chant reverberated against the glassy walls and the entire Valley of the Bluenoon turned an all-encompassing iridescent blue as the rays of the sun flowed into and back out of the crystal. There was Peace in the Valley of the Bluenoon as heretofore only described in accounts of the dawn of Eyespell's light-skew. It was as if the planet were re-born.

Leo and the fifty-four stood their vigil for three consecutive bluenoons. Leo then replaced the rope of light and crystal around his neck, floated down from the tower, and purposefully ascended from the valley floor by the stairway to the south. The pilgrims journeyed the two days back to Elasia, still in prayer and chant.

Seven evenings after the beginning of the pilgrimage and with only the fourth moon lighting the landscape, Leo re-entered the twenty-seventh row of the Council Chamber. The peace had been preserved; Eyespell again moved in the uncontaminated light-skew. The Council of the Elders was to meet the following day.

By the rising of the yellow sun, the Elders, the four returned Earth travelers, and Kathryn were at their places in the Council Chamber. Matters of the Eyespellians' adventures on Earth were to be taken up directly. Leo and the other Elders were still in monk's garb, having barely finished their tasks of repairing the cell-matrix. While there would still be no meeting of the Full-Round, the four returnees and their overseer were comfortable to finally be meeting with the Elders' Council. They were anxious to share their Earth experiences.

Daniel stood and faced the five Eyespellians in the Council Chamber. "Please forgive our delay in hearing your stories. Our sincere interest in each of you who spent twenty years on Earth for the Eyespell Experiment is shared by all of the light-skew. Antonio, you were the first to re-enter, and you shall be the first to share your Earth experience with the Council. Give us just a few minutes to complete our check of each light corridor. We need to be sure we are clear of Earth-plane vibrational leakage."

CHAPTER 9

▼

A HOLE IN REALITY (EYESPELL)

Kathryn looked at Leo with an almost devilish smile. Sensing there was still time before Antonio was to begin, Leo stepped down from the twenty-seventh ring and approached Kathryn in anticipation of a good story. He stood face-to-face with her, gently grasped her hands in his and said, "Come on, what secret are you hiding behind that smile?"

"Your monk's garb and the success of the healing pilgrimage reminded me of a story I read on Earth not too long before returning to Eyespell. It was a satire about the role of monks on Earth. I sometimes wonder if the author knew how close to a universal truth he came in his musings? It's sort of a cosmic joke; the irony of one planet being the reality of another. Access my telepathy link and let me share the story with you."

In telepathy link, the essay was instantly transmitted to Leo.

A HOLE IN REALITY
by
John P. Cicero, Ph.D.

There are three significant types of holes in the universe: black holes that absorb everything, white holes that absorb nothing, and holes in reality which I will explain. On Friday, March 29, 1985, I first suspected that holes in reality existed. Some days are just strange in their happenings and I remember this one clearly.

First thing in the morning, my wife dropped the glass coffeepot on the ceramic tile kitchen floor where it shattered into countless pieces. Upon arriving at work later that morning, the first fellow I spoke with related that he had barely bumped the glass shower doors enclosing his tub and they fell out of their tracks cracking upon the bathroom floor. When I arrived at the secretary's desk, I overheard her explaining how a stone had hit her car's windshield on the way to work, leaving glass literally hanging from the rubber moldings. The sliding glass door in another gentleman's study apparently exploded for no reason at all. He said it was as if the door were hit by an invisible bullet; there was simply a loud "bang!" The door splintered from the center out, leaving the safety glass in the frame like a million-pieced puzzle. All day it seemed as though people everywhere were breaking drinking glasses, dropping dishes, knocking over knickknacks and, in every imaginable way, unintentionally ridding the Earth of all objects made of glass. Why?

I think this phenomenon has to do with physical reality being an illusion. This is not an idea original with me. For example, statements from renowned physicists suggest that the next level of physics will be achieved through meditation. Some preliminary proof rests in the fact that no atomic particle, the very building block of physical reality, had ever been discovered until after someone suggested that it was there.

And so we come to the hole in reality concept. On a given Friday, an inordinate amount of glass is breaking for no apparent reason. There is more glass broken than sheer probability can account for! If physical reality is nothing more than illusion and if physics might advance through meditation, might not meditation be the key to all that broken glass? After all, meditation is doing for the cosmos in the late 1980s what the CB radio did for the freeways of America in the late 1970s. "Om" is the "Breaker 19" of the eighties.

Anyway, back to the hole in reality. Assume that the cosmic mind is always awake, always pulsating. The vibration is always there. Have you ever wondered why? I think the force behind this constant vibration has to do with monks and I think monks have to do with the hole in reality.

Have you ever stopped to think about how anachronistic monks who meditate behind cloistered walls are? In a high technology world, what is their purpose? For that matter, what has their purpose ever been? I think I know. I think that chanting, meditating monks keep us connected to the Cosmic Consciousness. I think chanting, meditating monks generate the minimum acceptable levels of vibration necessary to create and maintain the illusion of physical reality.

On Friday, March 29, 1985, one of the monks must have fallen asleep while meditating. Perhaps, just perhaps, that particular monk was in charge of glass-reality. And then just like that, poof! All that broken glass. A hole in reality.

"I should like to take a trip to Earth to meet this gentleman in his dreams," Leo said with a twinkle in his eye. "His musings have hit upon universal truth. I wonder how many others on Earth are of like mind? We on Eyespell may not be prepared for Earth-plane vibrational leakage, but just maybe the Earth is more prepared for Mystic Management that we think. I am glad you have not lost your sense of humor, Kathryn Song. Thank you for sharing 'A Hole in Reality.'" The Council was finishing up its previous business and was ready to listen to Antonio's Earth tale. Leo again took his place in the twenty-seventh ring.

CHAPTER 10

▼

THE REAL WORLD (EYESPELL)

Kathryn moved quickly forward and addressed the Council before Antonio had a chance to begin his tale. "With all due courtesy and respect to the Council and Antonio, I would like to share my perceptions of the Eyespell Experiment with you before we address the specific Earth-life-times of Antonio, Melissa, Nancy, and Pete. I feel that my insight as over-seer of the Eyespell Experiment will help put our findings in perspective. Is that agreeable to everyone?"

Daniel thought for a moment and said, "With the complications from Earth-plane vibrational leakage we are, indeed, having difficulties keeping the recent events in context. Your request is not only appropriate, but the logical starting place. It is unlike the Elders' Council to miss such an obvious point. Antonio, we apologize, but again we must delay the telling of your tale."

Kathryn began by detailing several observations about the incidents on Earth and her perceptions of the Eyespell Experiment overall. However, her manner was out-of-character, somewhat officious. "The catalyst for the Eyespell Experiment was the observed hopelessness of Earth's American youth. We thought that five premature self-induced deaths, occurring essentially simultaneously would communicate a message to Earth that something was drastically amiss. The deaths of our five Eyespell Experiment participants on their twentieth Earth birthdays should have carried a dire message to the American people. The suicides, we hoped, would be a warning that the society needed to take on the serious business of recognizing its emotional sickness and begin the healing process."

Kathryn continued, but in a more agitated tone. "None of us antici-pated the dramatic increase in teenage and young adult suicide on planet Earth, the United States in particular. By the time our re-entry window was reached, twenty years into the experiment, a mere four deaths, one in New York, one in New Mexico, one in California, and one in Florida, went almost unnoticed and, certainly were not perceived as related in any way. And, of course, the fifth suicide never happened, but that's another story. Here on Eyespell even a little depression would prompt a meeting of the Full Council. A self-inflicted death is simply not in the realm of our Eyespellian reality. Five such deaths within a short period, from our per-spective, seemed outrageous and cataclysmic and would surely be noticed. We were wrong in this central assumption; on Earth they weren't noticed except for a brief notation in the respective local newspapers. The suicides did not produce much interest at all much less some wake up call to impending social disaster. Antonio and Pete made the obituaries and Melissa's story was only a couple of columns in the local section of the *Boca Raton News*. And Nancy is still officially listed as missing. Apparently the mesa she jumped off was in a remote location and the authorities never did find a body.

As you can see, a major flaw in the experiment was its inability to gen-erate any significant interest. The separate lives of our four returnees ren-dered their concurrent suicides unnoticed as such. It is highly unlikely that any single individual would have seen more than one of the obituar-ies, much less made any cognitive connection between the suicides. We failed to account for the lack of community among people on Earth, especially given the condition of substantial geographical separation among our participants. The planet Earth has not evolved abilities that even approach the sharing aspect of total planet telepathy link. Perhaps this mission's failure was due in part to Eyespell's blindness to the lack of community on Earth."

Kathryn paused and cooly stated, "CNN twenty-four hour news is the closest they come."

Pete chuckled at Kathryn's cleverness but found the hint of sarcasm in her voice particularly reminiscent of Earth. He also found his reaction a bit disquieting and reminiscent of Earth. He wiggled uncomfortably in his chair and caught Leo's worrisome glance out of the corner of his eye.

Oblivious to her subtle and uncharacteristic Earth-mimicking behavior, Kathryn continued on, "Only something spectacularly horrifying would have gotten the kind of attention we had hoped for, the kind of attention necessary for the success of our efforts. For example, had the five been close friends committing joint suicides, maybe they would have received brief national attention…maybe. And then only if the method was truly savage or bizarre enough to make it newsworthy. Mere suicide was simply uninteresting news."

Kathryn stood for a moment smug and almost indignant, staring at the Elders. Before anyone could react she blurted out, "Then, of course, there is Phillip, who is missing altogether! As sophisticated as we Eyespellians think we are, the Eyespell Experiment is probably worse in its research design than much of what comes out of the colleges and universities of Earth. As you well know, I was uncomfortable from the beginning and to appease me you sent me to Earth for a first-hand look. I wish I had been more assertive at the onset of this foolishness. There was never consensus on this issue, and as far as I am concerned that is a violation of our Mystic Management we supposedly hold so sacred."

The Council was not accustomed to the controlled vehemence that Kathryn expressed. The Elders found the situation uncomfortable not because of Kathryn's disagreement with aspects of the Eyespell Experiment, but because of her tone and body language. The Eldersix attributed Kathryn's behavior to another manifestation of Earth-plane vibrational leakage. They could sense a slightly negative vibration in several of the light corridors. But the fluctuation lasted only a fraction of a fraction of a second and did not translate into the cell-matrix as the physical reality of the council chamber remained unchanged. Relying on their recent activities for reinforcing the light corridors, and the power of the pilgrimage to the Valley of the Bluenoon, they decided to stand fast against this new attack of Earth-plane vibrational leakage. But, something needed to be done and done immediately to change Kathryn's psychological temperament and to balance her. The Elders chose unconditional love, total acceptance of Kathryn as the best defense against Earth-plane vibrational leakage. She was to be embraced rather than feared.

Daniel moved closer to Kathryn and, looking into her eyes, spoke in a caring and positive tone, "In spite of your concerns about the project, Kathryn, as appointed overseer you gave unselfishly to the accomplishment of your task. While tracking our participants in Earth-fusion, you collected precise and first-hand information. You recorded the life circumstances you observed which might have logically led to their suicides as Earth beings. In addition to the data specific to Antonio and the others, you also amassed a great deal of information about what was happening generally in the experiment zone. You were able to tap the mood of America in a generic sense. We would be very interested in your perceptions."

Kathryn, unaware of her recent inappropriate demeanor, seemed genuinely pleased with Daniel's query. She responded very positively to Daniel, and, in an almost bubbly voice said, "I documented two recurring themes in American society: (1) the individual's search for inner identity, positive self-esteem, and community and (2) the search for what was idiomatically called the 'real world.' These two concepts seem inextricably intertwined, and represent the nucleus of much Earth literature and debate.

My hypothesis is that the previous Earth generation, the one just before the arrival of our participants, had expended so much of its time and energy concentrating on their own identity and reality issues that they directly, albeit inadvertently, produced hopelessness in their offspring. Of course Antonio, Melissa, Nancy, Pete, and Phillip Earth-fused as part of that generation of offspring. The stage was set for the Eyespell Experiment."

Gracina and Myana chimed in simultaneously, "What an incredible lack of connectedness and compassion to have instilled this hopelessness into an entire generation." Myana continued, smiling warmly at the contrast of her own connectedness with Gracina, "You must have found it impossible at times to be so close to such intense feelings of isolation and hopelessness. We all owe you a great debt of gratitude for being our Earth eyes, ears, and heart." The Elders leaned forward and swept Kathryn Song into their collective aura in expression of the ultimate Eyespellian complement.

So far, the strategy of embracing her to dispel the Earth-plane vibrational leakage was working well. With overflowing exuberance Kathryn used her mind link to directly share several writings from a wide variety of subjects that she had collected over the past twenty years. She thought to herself, "What a wonderful interaction, although it's odd; something feels unbalanced. It's almost as if I'm being manipulated, but that's ridiculous, Eyespellians would have no reason to manipulate. I wonder if Earth affected me more than I think? Anyway, back to the matter at hand, the writings from Earth."

The Council mind-scanned the writings with great interest. A piece of particular interest was an article from a magazine targeted to college-age students who would be entering the job market in the not-too-distant future. It was titled, "Work And The Real World." The author was a Professor of Business at a small southeastern school; neither the name of the article nor the professor was recorded.

Work And The Real World

No matter where I have been or what work I have been doing, someone has always been quick to point out that the "real world" was someplace else. No doubt, you have had a similar experience. If not, you will. Consider this, I have over thirty years of varied work experience. However, according to many other people, none of those experiences qualify as real world encounters. I have been a college professor and administrator; a middle manager for a fortune 500 company; a consultant to business, education, and government; a sole proprietor; an artist; and a psychotherapist. If none of my experiences qualify as real world, I can't even imagine how challenging the real world must be and how brave the souls must be who claim to have traversed its hard-knocks topography.

As a younger man, when the opinion of others influenced me more, I left a very comfortable management faculty position specifically to gain some expertise in that real world that everybody was talking about. Thirsting for reality and significance, I entered the corporate milieu. I even projected that I might better serve my students at a later time with some real world experience behind me. I could justify temporarily giving up what I loved, teaching, in order to someday be a better teacher, a teacher minus the stigma of never having worked in the real world.

I wasn't on that new corporate job a week before a fellow employee made it very clear that the real world was in a different part of the corporation! It definitely was not where I was working. It was in some other department, some other function.

It's fascinating how people are always pointing out where the real world is. And, of course, it's never where you are. It's always someplace they are or have purportedly been. At the very least, they intimately know someone who's in the real world.

If you're in training, the real action is in sales. If you're in sales, the real action is in some other company. And if you're in sales in that other company, then the action is someplace else altogether…"and I know a guy who…"

The implication is always that the real world, a place where you never are, is somehow harder, tougher, more demanding, dangerous, elite, faster, showier, more exciting, more dramatic, and clearly out of your reach. And, of course, the younger you are, the more elusive and further away from the real world you are, just ask anyone older than you.

The result is uncomfortable at best. Our identity and self-esteem suffer in this quest for the elusive real world. The desire to belong, to be a part of some defined community, the desire to be relevant, distorts our view of our present individual reality. Our world collapses into cloudy confusion. In this confusion much time and energy are spent trying to rid ourselves of the inner "shoulds" and "I'm not good enoughs." In this quest for inner growth we often become detached from our own reality, whatever that reality is (i.e. college student, teacher, administrator, manager, artist, psychotherapist, or whatever).

Indeed, our individual present moments, the only "real world" we have, slip right past us and we watch; we watch as if spectators at our own lives.

This is a game for which the price of admission is too high. Wherever you are is real enough. After over thirty years of working in jobs deemed "non-real-world" by others, I still can't tell the difference in value or "realness" between the stresses of tomorrow's mid-term examination, tomorrow's neurotic patient, tomorrow's art show, tomorrow's planning report, tomorrow's cash flow, and tomorrow's anything .

Be assured that you are in the real world by virtue of your existence and survival, no matter what the task at hand. As it has been so aptly pointed out, "Wherever you go, there you are."

Kathryn commented, "It's astounding to think that something so obvious to us needed to be produced in writing and published as good advice to the up-coming generation. Imagine the pain in the uncertainty of not knowing if what you do is meaningful and valued by others. It would be like saying that one positive trait, like knowledge, is somehow better than another, like peace. And imagine, all this according to a source outside ourselves. What a foreign concept, and for what purpose? It gets even more complicated and convoluted. Here's something I scanned off a fellow's desk. I have no idea if it was ever formally published, and it did not have a title."

This book is about my reality. It's about identity and there's nothing more real for each of us than our identity, the essence of who we are. Achieving identity is a unique experience for each of us and, certainly, each outcome is unique. However, I believe we are all part of a collective unconscious. All of our worlds are real as we define them, as we choose the approach, as we choose and interact with the exact experiences of a lifetime. The only reason to read about my reality, my identity search, is that there may be points of connection along the continuum of that Collective Being. We might, therefore, be able to share something and feel less alone for a moment. Ultimately, our choices are our own and our reality is what we create for ourselves. The real world is wherever we say it is. Part of being in my world is to understand my depression.

In my case, a fumbling for identity and my depression are very much cause and effect related. How can we fit into our chosen life without becoming a mere reflection of someone else's values and beliefs? We learn conflicting truths that play havoc with our identities.

We are taught that it is important to be an individual and to stand up for what one believes in. We quickly learn, however, that to get ahead, it is seldom who we are that matters, but who we are perceived to be and who we know that counts.

Then, armed with this level of inconsistency, we often insist upon telling our children that "He who has the most wins." Wins at what, life? What cognitive dissonance this creates as we continue to give mixed messages. For example, we tell our toddlers things like, "Now share your things with Jimmy at day care." Would we as adults share with anyone, any of our toys, our grander and equally important toys? Think about this type of clash between ideal and real culture.

We also tell our children that "Honesty is the best policy." Yet, they routinely see us lying. For example, when we don't want to talk on the phone: "Tell them I'm not home or I'm in the shower and I'll call back." They know we cheat on income taxes or exceed the speed limit when we're pretty sure there's no cop around. And we do these things because that's how the game is played.

It's not really about honesty. We tell the children that "It's what's inside that really counts," and yet it's obvious that the ugly, perhaps overweight, kid with braces, orthopedic shoes, thick glasses, and acne doesn't really have much of a chance even in the kids' world. Indeed, children can be cruel as part of the socialization process.

But think about where the most noxious racism, classism, and sexism thrives. Think about where the most cruelty is. It exists in all institutions where adults live, work and play, setting the examples for the next generation. Observe the worlds of business, government, entertainment, education and sports. Where exactly are the desirable role models? What part of human unkindness is just part of growing up and what part is set up as the model to emulate when achieving adulthood?

No wonder we become emotionally insulated as adults and can barely identify what we really think and feel. We don't know what we think and feel because we've grown up with so many cultural contradictions. We have all we can do to make any sense out of it and stay sane. Perhaps the insane are the only ones who have insight into the craziness of this place and time? The rifts are continuous. We are told one thing while constantly experiencing another. Identity crisis is squared and then squared again with each cognitively dissonant experience. Some of those experiences are stored into memory and, with later conscious recall, become the stimuli for negative acting-out behaviors such as aggression, scapegoating, and gossip. Other experiences are placed into the unconscious for later expression through defense mechanisms such as substance and alcohol abuse, and even suicide.

To achieve self-preservation and to enhance the illusion of growing up, we bury the inner child. We bury the child under our perceptions, reactions, and pseudo-solutions to the anxieties of growing up. We keep this child hidden under the surface. The result is that, as physical adults, we feel impotent, hostile and anxious. There is often a free-floating anxiety whose source and solution are also buried within the psyche of that inner child. Maybe this is just another type of child abuse our culture fosters, cultural catatonia and societal schizophrenia.

"The poor man," said Kathryn.

In response to this sharing, Rebecca, keeper of the green-light corridor of nature, removed the emerald crystal from its pouch, placed it around her neck on its rope of light and almost tearfully addressed the Council. "Earth's pain is overwhelming. The magnitude of inner conflict is debilitating. The distance between the psychology of individualism and the possibility of inclusive community rips at the spiritual stamina of the planet. It is no wonder we chose not to look on in passive observation. The Eyespell Experiment was necessary and I, for one, am not certain it was a failure. We sometimes forget we are an intuitive people; it is not so much what we know, but what we feel that makes the difference. I sense the beginning of a healing on the Earth and I feel strongly that our efforts will play a central role in that new age."

Myana came forth removing the pink tourmaline of unconditional love from its pouch, placing it around her neck in a gesture of love. She added, "I am reminded of an image in the *Book of Dreams*, "The Identity Garden." It is one of my favorite image-writings. Perhaps we could focus together on that image and in unconditional love send some positive identity energy to the Earth."

Leo stepped forward and asked that Pete, with his refreshed memory of Eyespell be allowed to lead the group in image. Pete smiled and effortlessly retrieved the image of "The Garden of Identity" from his recent daydream at the council opening just days before. The vibration of "The Garden of Identity" was sent toward the Earth in a loving and healing gesture. The purpose of the Eyespell Experiment and the unselfish motivations of the Eyespellians continued to unfold.

Allowing an appropriate interval of time to pass, Kathryn shared another bit of prose from Earth, prose that again smarted of identity crisis and lack of self-esteem. She sat back in her sensor-chair and offered several pages, beginning with a section titled, "A Matter of Misperception."

A Matter of Misperception

Right around my thirtieth birthday, I mustered up enough courage to ask my mother why she used to spit at me when I was a child. I had finally developed enough self-esteem to ask this delicate question. And, I wanted to know if she realized what an awful thing spitting at me was. She was horrified, denying the whole thing.

I remember that when I was a child and my mother became angry with me, she would rapidly wave her hands back and forth in the air and follow me with quick, short steps from room to room. She would swear at me in Italian and, then she would shake her finger at me with teeth clenched and her lips tightly pursed. This struck terror in my heart. And then came the really scary part. Positioned within inches of my now trembling body, she would utter several guttural sounds, move her head jerkily forward, and just as her head snapped to a stop, a faint bit of saliva would shoot in my direction. What kind of an animal was I to cause my own mother to behave in such a barbaric way? To cause your very own mother to spit at you must mean you're despicable!

After a few sessions with my therapist, I confronted her again. She still denied it, emphatically saying she would never do such a thing. But this time, I really cornered her; I gave her specific examples and ran around the kitchen acting out the whole horrific scene. I screamed those awful utterances and, with all the nastiness I could muster, I spit at the imaginary child huddled in the corner. I did it twice, just for effect.

By this time, my mother was laughing uncontrollably. Frankly, I was appalled at her behavior. When she finally collected herself, she told me that I had just solved one of the greatest mysteries she'd had as a parent. She proceeded to explain that she never did understand why I would instantly shape up whenever she would hover over me and yell in Italian, "And you, and you, and you!!!"

"And you," in my mother's Italian, came out, "Et tu; et tu; et tu." Now, say "et tu" with any speed and gusto and a little tracer of saliva can't help but shoot straight out from between your pursed lips. What a misperception and what a relief; my mother was not a beast and I was not a worthless being.

Many puzzling and upsetting things happen to us on our journey toward self-fulfillment. Identity and positive self-esteem become more and more elusive. It is literally as if we keep falling through the real world, never quite landing in it. It's as if our reality is full of holes; we can't find solid ground. I wonder how many misconceptions and miscommunications are never explained and resolved? And I wonder what these do to our identity and self-esteem? Perhaps we learn to fear and avoid others' expectations of us altogether in order to defray the cost of misperception. By adulthood we learn to be totally alone.

The Council was attentive to and compassionate toward the recurring themes of identity and reality, and much saddened at Earth's seeming inability to deal effectively with such issues. "Telepathy link offers such an easy solution to the complex problem of aloneness," said Matthew. "The energy from the red-light corridor could go far in stimulating the nine-tenths of the brain that Earthlings simply can't or don't use." The Council members simultaneously shook their heads in agreement.

Everyone seemed pleased that Kathryn thought to bring some unknown right-brained stuff for the council to scan. It showed Earth's potential in spite of its propensity toward the dark-skew. The Council had by now forgotten how Kathryn initially made them feel chastised, and again the light corridors maintained their positive skew. Leo thought for a moment and then, to even further accentuate the positive, said in his most accepting and warmest voice, "Kathryn, you have, indeed, picked up some wisdom during your Earth travels."

Kathryn was pleased at Leo's perception. Still unaware that her earlier behavior toward the council was out of the ordinary, she accepted the complement, but with that nagging thought, "They are patronizing me again, the bastards." Then she said aloud, "I think I have shared all I need to for now. We can scan more from these crazy Earthlings later. Let's hear about Antonio's life on earth." Her tone clearly and purposefully usurped the more typical approach of turning the meeting back to Daniel and asking what he would like to do next.

Daniel, caught off guard by Kathryn's command-giving, simply nodded approval. All could sense Kathryn's pride at taking charge, and all had heard Kathryn's inner comment, "…the bastards." It was Earth-plane vibrational leakage in still another guise. However, disruption of the cell-matrix was somehow again averted. Antonio seemed reluctant to begin his tale and all remained quiet in the calm before the storm.

CHAPTER 11

▼

DIVINE INTERVENTION (EYESPELL AND EARTH)

Antonio, although bewildered and taken aback by Kathryn's behavior, was anxious to finally share his Earth experience with the Council. Mind-link would have been the quickest way to glean his thoughts, but despite their telepathic powers, Eyespellians loved a good spoken story. They enjoyed talking and listening.

At the urging of the Eldersix, Antonio began, "It is strange to look back upon my Earth life. It's like looking at someone else or imaging with the *Book of Dreams*. The fact that I have Earth memories from birth to twenty years of age is absolutely incredible. What's really peculiar is that my Earth memories include absolutely no inklings of Kathryn, or anything Eyespellian. It's as if the Earth experience is a totally separate consciousness and, yet, somehow fused with my total being. I am Eyespellian, but have the experience of a simultaneous life on another plane. The concept of life on more than one plane is not unusual; it's the present moment duality of memory that boggles my senses. What I cannot determine is how my Earth life affects who I am now. I only know that it does."

The Eldersix, and especially Matthew, were very attentive to Antonio's description. "Antonio, try to explain exactly what you mean by 'duality of memory,'" asked Matthew.

"It's really a hard concept to get a handle on. I don't know what else to say, but I'll try again. There are several things to consider. Let's start with my Earth-time. During those twenty years I had no recollections of Eyespell. Then there's right now. I recall the twenty years and sense nothing Eyespellian in that part of my memory while at the same time its all part of who I am now."

Daniel got to laughing, "My boy, this is truly a puzzle and I seem to be missing a piece or two. Try again for this old man."

"This is embarrassing. I haven't had this much trouble communicating since our lessons in the desert with Leo."

Melissa, Nancy, and Pete chimed in, "Go Antonio!"

Pete continued, "Seriously, I think you're on to something here. I have many of the same feelings, but I can't get a grip on it, exactly, either. Keep at it and we'll see if we can help out."

"Okay," agreed Antonio. "I wish Phillip were here; he was always the articulate one. Here goes. It's like being two distinct people, Antonio the Eyespellian and Antonio the Earthling. It is not Antonio the Eyespellian simply remembering being on Earth for twenty years. It's as if my Earth time has it's own soul, a soul somehow now mixed with my Eyespellian essence."

This was an unanticipated surprise. It simply had been assumed the time on Earth would be nothing more than a memory, a collection of data. It had not occurred to anyone that those twenty years on Earth might represent a life separate from anything Eyespellian, in a sense, a life within a life. The impact in terms of Earth-plane vibrational leakage was becoming more uncomfortably clear. The Earth experience was not a mere memory, but an integral part of Antonio's present reality. The question was no longer if there would be continued Earth-plane vibrational leak-age, but with what consequences and to what extent. It was one thing to dissipate external leakage at some physical level; it would be like cleaning one's aura of negative vibrations. That risk had been assessed twenty years ago at the onset of the project. This was quite another matter, internal leakage, involving not just memories, but soul fusion. The returnees had brought permanently to Eyespell, as part of their very essence, a soul dis-tinctly of Earth. There was no way to anticipate the implications.

Once again Antonio's story was delayed as Daniel immediately queried the other returning Eyespellians about their memory patterns and the sense of an Earth soul. Melissa, Nancy, and Pete confirmed that they were having the same sensations Antonio described. Kathryn was not. Her experience was that of an Eyespellian who simply spent twenty years in another place, on another planet. The distinguishing factor was that Kathryn did not Earth-fuse; she did not experience being born an Earthling. Even without Earth-fusion her propensity toward severe Earth-plane vibrational leakage was quite surprising. The assumption was that Katherine would be unaffected.

Matthew spoke to the Council. "I think I understand what has hap-pened here. As you know, through the red-light energy corridor, the five Eyespellians were transformed into light energy and sent to Earth to be born. Our travelers arrived on the Earth as points of red light. In this form they each searched for and entered an unborn fetus just as it was dying of natural causes. Each fetus entered already had a chosen life path that could easily end now or later in suicide and, therefore matched the needs of our experiment. If the choice was to end life now, the Eyespellian point of light was to enter the fetus immediately upon the God-soul leaving the body. The Eyespellian light energies, already containing the souls of our beloved children, were designed to sustain life on Earth for only the pre-determined twenty years. Our plan was that the body would be of Earth and the essence or soul would be that of Eyespell. At the end of twenty years, the soul would return to Eyespell through planned re-entry taking up residence in the bodies of our travelers as we see them before us today."

Matthew paused and thought for a moment, "I knew the moment our light energy fused with the first unborn child that we had somehow connected, forever, our destiny with that of planet Earth. When our point of light entered the first womb, the God-soul returned lest we overstep our cosmic bounds. I never mentioned this because I was not absolutely sure about the return of the God-soul until today. As Antonio began to describe his feelings and the dual memory within his psyche, my suspicions were confirmed. Antonio's and the others' Earth lives are integrated with their Eyespellian essence, not just in memory, but in soul. The God-soul returned and, in a sense, was superimposed on the Eyespellian essence; two souls coexisting. This commingling of the two souls is a truly extraordinary and unexpected outcome. In light of this revelation, while Phillip has missed re-entry there is nothing to suggest that he is not still alive and well on the Earth-plane. Much of the Eyespell Experiment that has taken us by surprise is the doing of God and His Universal Law rather than the inadequacy of our experimental design. The question is, what are the lessons for Eyespell?"

The Council Chamber remained still for some time as each Elder merged with his or her crystal charge to get a better sense of what Matthew was saying. Rebecca was the first to break the silence, "I keep the green light corridor. I maintain the physical balance of the planet and the harmony between the cell-matrix of the planet and the feeling-matrix of our people. The vibration within the emerald crystal is shifting. There will be natural disturbances on Eyespell. We need to go to the old books and relearn how to prepare ourselves for disharmony with nature."

Each Elder spoke of the potential dangers to his or her light-charge. There was talk of sickness, conflict, chaos, ignorance, and isolation. There was allusion to lethargy, hatred, and abject poverty. Such thoughts and such words had not been a part of Eyespell's reality for millennia. As their mind links were open the impact of what had just occurred in the Council

Chamber quickly spread throughout the planet. The people of Eyespell were stunned at the grim prospects. Daniel adjourned Council and called a meeting of the Full Round, the council of the three hundred thirty-seven. The planet was to prepare for total mind-link. The Full-Round would commence in three days and would open under the light of the third moon of oneness to discuss what would become of the planet of the light-skew.

Antonio still had not told his story. He and the other recently returned Eyespellians were again put on hold. The importance of the details of their Earth lives had been overshadowed by the uncertainty of Eyespell's future in the face of Earth-plane vibrational leakage and a quickened movement toward the dreaded homeostasis. The cycle of Earth-fusion and re-entry to Eyespell for four of the five participants in the Eyespell Experiment was complete. The cycle of lightness into darkness for all Eyespellians was just beginning.

Phillip, the missing Eyespellian, was the only part of the circle not closed. The Council recognized he might still be alive on Earth and could be the single strand of hope in the broken light-skew. If Eyespell was to move toward the dark-skew, perhaps Earth could move toward the light-skew. Perhaps some balance could be achieved on a Cosmic plane allowing both planets to ultimately rest in the light. Perhaps Eyespell would not be permanently contaminated by Earth-plane vibrational leakage, and perhaps Earth could become more like the planet of the light-skew.

The Eyespellians felt humbled by the Cosmos. While the Eyespell Experiment meant one thing to Eyespell it meant quite another to God. Phillip's non-return shifted from being a devastating loss to being the crux of the Divine plan for Eyespell and Earth.

CHAPTER 12

▼

THE TIME OF MADNESS (EARTH)

Phillip felt something between severe anxiety and intense relief when his son Christian met him in the driveway holding what he recognized as those old manuscript pages he had stored in the attic. The rest of the family, oblivious to the yellowed papers clutched to Christian's breast, couldn't wait to share their Harper's Ferry adventure with him. Christian however, was so intent upon finding out about The Eyespell Experiment and what his father meant by "off-world observer," that he barely acknowledged the arrival of the rest of the family. He absentmindedly patted the kids on the head and gave his wife and mother token pecks on the cheek. He held up the manuscript and said "Dad, I have a couple of questions about some of your writings."

Phillip strode purposefully toward his son and, putting out his hand, said, "Let me see exactly what you have there." Of course, he knew without looking; he could feel his son's questions and could sense his overwhelming curiosity.

"Oh, yes. Some of my more flamboyant stuff. I sure do remember the feelings behind those words. I was a much younger man then and had some rash opinions. I thought I had thrown all of this in the trash years ago." Phillip was well aware he had not thrown those pages away. In fact, the rest of that fiery old manuscript was tucked neatly away in a leather case in his study.

"Now, Dad, do you expect me to believe that? You've never lost track of anything you've ever written, or said for that matter. And especially something as peculiar as this. No way!" Christian stood very still and looked his father straight in the eyes.

Phillip smiled and said, "Just checking. So, what has you so overwhelmingly curious?"

"Two things, 'Eyespell Experiment' and 'off-world observer.' I've racked my brains and can't come up with anything even approximating 'Eyespell Experiment.' The name is unusual enough that I would remember it; after all, I don't have such a bad memory myself. And the use of the phrase 'off-world observer' is most curious, indeed. It sounds like you're from another planet or something!" Christian cleared his throat and laughed a very uncomfortable laugh.

Phillip slapped his son on the shoulder and while gently pushing him by the elbow said, "I think it's time you come with me and have a look at another part of that manuscript." Phillip led his son to the study and produced the leather case. "Sit down here and read. When you have a few more pages under your belt, call me and I'll share the rest of the story with you. And, just for the record, I mixed those pages in with the other stuff in that old attic trunk knowing that when the time was right, you would find them. One other thing, I love you." Phillip hugged his son and, for the second time in Christian's awareness, cried.

He sat in his father's sand-colored, corduroy-upholstered recliner. He was barely able to gather his wits about him. The roll top desk stretched directly in front of him and across the room. His father's curio cabinet, glistening with its wondrous rock and mineral treasures, stood to his immediate right. While Christian was not scientifically interested in, nor particularly knowledgeable about his father's collection, the cabinet always caught his attention. He was especially attracted to the pastel-colored specimens. His favorite was the large chunk of rose quartz on the next-to-bottom shelf. When he was alone in his father's study he would often open the cabinet and just stand there holding the chunk of rock close to him, like an old friend. The vibrations were incredible.

What started out to be a typical day of attic exploring was turning into something quite extraordinary. He opened the leather case his father had given him and removed the manuscript. He picked a place at random to begin reading.

You are all frantically fragmented, running around making money, exercising, eating right, dying anyway, breaking up relationships, and, ultimately, feeling isolated. There is always the nagging realization that even though things aren't terribly wrong, something is just not right. Everything looks so pretty and in place, but it can be artificial, automatic, contrived.

The environment is dead; there is no heartbeat, no heart, no center, no downtown, no community. There are just shopping malls decorated with artificial plants and chlorinated fountains.

Under the pressure of having no sense of community you tend to cocoon. You go home after work and hole up alone with your families. Well, you may be in physical proximity to your families, but there is no mutually satisfying interaction. There is just a sharing of some defined space.

Someone is watching T.V. while someone else is Nintendo-ing, while someone is reading, and someone else is meditating. You are all back home exhausted from being 'out there.' Home, yet not at peace. You're desperately trying to heal yourselves of all sorts of physical, emotional and mental pain.

You are missing community. You don't know how it looks, or what it feels like, or where to find it. You know that a key determinant to longevity is the degree to which you become involved in meaningful, ongoing support systems, and other-directed activity. And still you are alone.

Inner work, outer work; action-reflection-action, in an ongoing cycle. You collect lots of information about what your reality ought to be. You obsess about the right personality type, friends, job, family, children (how many and when), where to live, what to drive, and how to help yourselves if you fall short in any of the categories.

One thing is certain. As you are now, greed will bring you to a point of social disaster. Even cocooning will become impossible. If Americans do not begin to voluntarily change toward a community-based way of life, necessary change will be initiated and managed by outside forces. America needs a new paradigm of sustainability. If you don't do it yourselves it will be done by other peoples and other nations. This has always been the way of history.

It seemed like more of the same, and Christian did not feel any closer to solving the mystery. He was becoming restless in his need to confront his father directly. However, he was well disciplined and learned long ago that his father's way, while sometimes mysterious, almost always proved to be the better alternative. In fact, he honestly couldn't think of a time when his father had misjudged a situation. And perhaps for the first time on any conscious level, Christian was beginning to realize that his father was not who he appeared to be. His father was, indeed, an unusual man. He continued to read from a different part of the manuscript.

At the turn of the century the new management practitioners began to stir the Industrial Revolution into something more concrete. By the 1920's, schools of business actually became legitimate places for study and even a kind of worship.

Many people in previous generations died unhappy because they did not make a million. Should you, too, die unhappy for lack of ten million? And will your children die unhappy? And for lack of how much?

The old paradigm with its bent for success is destructive; it kills people. World resources are being depleted, the world population is soaring, there are food riots in South America, and revolutions of rising expectations in the Eastern bloc are happening. And all of that is going to affect you. Newspapers juxtapose 1000% inflation and food riots opposite advertisements for things like Rolex watches and Mercedes.

Look past the front pages of most newspapers and the predominant use of space is advertising—advertising of sales, specials, and superlative labels with which you can adorn yourselves. Each week boasts its unique combination of sales. Holidays have become secularized as you see Halloween set up the week after Labor Day, to be followed by Thanksgiving, and then Xmas, taking the 'Christ' out. The pre-Christmas sales cover November and most of December. January hosts the post-Christmas rush. Thank goodness for Valentine's Day and St. Patrick's Day to close the gap before Easter! In all of this hubbub malls have become an important socializing venue. For many families the primary outing they take together, once a week, is to the mall to take advantage of the week's specials and to shop for the upcoming holiday. How much about culture and community can we learn at the mall?

One can certainly assimilate all the latest trends: what tennis shoes are for executives versus those for nerds; how many earrings need to be hung in one or both ears; how tight and how short the skirts will be for half a season. And then there are the latest gadgets, gizmos, and toys offered at the high-tech stores.

In all of this there is no humanity. There is no heart. What will the turn of this century produce to offset the knowledge produced at the turn of the last? Or, will this be your society's last? How can you continue to be so blind to corporate global reality—international suffocation, asphyxiation by undigested knowledge?

It was still that same condemning tone, that same pounding. Christian thought, "A couple more pages and then I want some answers from Dad." He picked out another section of the manuscript at random.

How can it be that in some places the man-made landscape rivals God's? The only hills here are the interstate bridges over the secondary roads. Here in Southeast Florida, rivers and lakes are diesel-dug deep ditches, and the closest thing to seasons is outside versus inside. The leaves fall off the trees at random, flowers blossom in what's called hard winter, and even the tiny ants bite and sting!

The neighborhoods are clothed in oscillating sprinklers and malibu lights at dark. The man-made lakes and palm trees encircle the perfectly kept stuccoed houses. The illusion of serenity is frequently shattered, however, by screaming alarm systems in those same neighborhoods, neighborhoods that have become unsafe.

In the 18th and 19th centuries a town typically had a town square, with the city hall on one corner and the church predominantly positioned on the other major corner. In the 20th century, you switched to a different model. The bank, your new worship center, sat in the middle of town. Over the years, it became increasingly ornate and expensive as it replaced the church as the new symbol of blood, sweat, and tears. The bank became the town's primary expression of community.

By the 1950s, the concept of town began to fade into the suburbs. The bank's branch office went up first either within or adjacent to the malls that came out of California to usurp the town and become decentralized hubs of most activity. The new youth spend all of the weekend time hanging out at these malls. They used to go to church picnics.

Like the church picnic, the mall has an intergenerational quality. This is evidenced by the elderly who sit on the benches and people-watch in order to pass time and relieve their loneliness and boredom. As long as their roles remain passive, they are not considered bothersome. Of course, it's okay if the elderly interact with each other during the mallwalks early in the morning before the stores open. So, where is America heading, where is community?

"That's it," thought Christian. "I can't stand the suspense another minute. While all of this prose is certainly attempting to corral the themes of community building, identity crisis, the decaying of America, and a mish-mash of a hundred other ideas, none of it explains the 'Eyespell Experiment' or 'off-world observer.' "

His father's manuscript smacked of its own identity crisis. While interesting in spots, the text seemed more an expression of anger than an offering of suggestions for improvement. That too was terribly unlike his father, to criticize without giving accompanying recommendations toward progress.

Just as Christian was about to get up from his chair to seek out his father, demanding answers, the study door swung open. Not surprisingly, it was Phillip. "So, you think you have read enough. I suppose you have, and I suppose it's time that I answer your questions."

"What you have read was written by me during a period of tremendous inner turmoil in my life. In fact, it was written around the time depicted in that old photograph that made me cry. That far away look on my face that I know you've often wondered about, was a look of longing, a look of longing for the unequaled pastel beauty of my home, my home planet, the planet Eyespell."

Christian was frozen to his chair by his father's words. And, yet, there was a piece of him that was not surprised. He recovered quickly and darted back with, "Well, I guess that explains 'off-world observer.'" With perfect hindsight, Christian had been sure of the meaning and implications of the phrase the moment he had first read it in his father's manuscript. His logic had simply gotten the best of him as he searched for a less dramatic, but more easily accepted, explanation.

Phillip sat in the castered oak chair, rolled up to the large desk and removed a notebook from one of the hidden panels. He handed the notebook to Christian explaining, "This contains the technical details of the Eyespell Experiment as best I can recall them. Read the notebook carefully. We can discuss it in detail tomorrow. It's quite late." Without saying anything further, Phillip reached inside Christian's mind and soothed the apprehension that was festering. Christian could feel his father's familiar presence within his thoughts and left the room now content to wait until tomorrow for further discussion.

Phillip tipped back in his desk chair and stared out the clerestory window of the study. He looked past the twisted branches of the huge oak tree into the night sky where, at this hour, the fourth moon of Eyespell would be rising. His thoughts flashed back.

* * * * * * * * *

He began to think about the days right around his twentieth Earth-birthday when he was making plans to kill himself or, as he now knows, when he was making plans for re-entry. Thinking about that time always produced a strange sensation. Back then Phillip was never sure whether Eyespell was just an imagined memory or a different reality. He had the opposite sensation of Antonio and the others because at the time Earth, not Eyespell, was his present moment. He had not experienced re-entry. In any event, over time Eyespell had become an integral part of who he was. He remembered Eyespell as a place before birth. The memories of Eyespell were vivid, but somehow out of sequence; they did not follow a linear time frame and they were incomplete. They did not seem real but rather the outcome of an overactive imagination. He would sometimes joke with himself and call these feelings, "Eyespell-plane vibrational leakage."

Anyway, in 1992, and approaching his twentieth birthday, Phillip was going to college in the Southeast, a public university in Boca Raton, Florida, to be specific. Boca, near the tip of the Devil's Triangle, was a place susceptible to negative "vibes" in Phillip's opinion. The university, for example, was an administrative and political mess. There had been a shooting, a suicide, and lots of psycho-junk in the air. Phillip was very vibe sensitive. More often than not he acted based on how things felt on an abstractly intuitive level. The bottom line, however, was that it didn't much matter to Phillip that he was in a place that felt negative to him, he was intent on killing himself anyway. In fact, he had plans for a double suicide; he and his girlfriend, Melissa Commings, were going to do it together.

They finally decided on the method, and both knew it had to be soon. Their birthdays were only a few days away and each had a driving need to be done with life at twenty. Immediately before the agreed upon time of suicide, Phillip, for all intents and purposes, simply disappeared. Unable to sleep, he went for a long walk. He did not bother to take any money or identification with him. He walked for hours. It is unclear exactly what happened at this point. He was deep in a walking meditation and evidently wandered into a crosswalk against the signal. He was hit by a car at an intersection near the interstate, and was pronounced DOA at the hospital.

Phillip remembered hovering several feet above his physical body, looking down at himself. He was fascinated, but not concerned. The brown eyes of his body were rolled up and glazed over and he had a horrible bump on his forehead. Otherwise, he looked just fine. His blonde hair was reasonably neat and he had trimmed his beard just that morning. He was wearing pastel plaid shorts, a seafoam green Polo shirt and tan Birkenstocks. Best of all, he had on clean underwear! He could almost hear his mother's voice admonishing him, "Phillip, make sure you have on clean underwear. What if you're in an accident and they have to take you to the hospital? Wouldn't you be embarrassed if your underwear was dirty?"

Phillip started to laugh but, at just that instant, he felt himself being pulled upward. He was somewhat startled as he began moving swiftly away from his lifeless body lying on the gurney in the hospital emergency room. He thought he heard someone named Kathryn call to him and he thought he saw a soft pink planet with a beautiful blue sun. He saw Melissa with three strangers about their own age, a girl and two guys. It was as if he knew them all.

Then there was a blinding flash with an accompanying sensation of falling up a tunnel. He found himself moving rapidly toward a white light at the end of the tunnel. Although this experience should have been frightening, it was not. In fact, the feeling was quite the opposite, extremely mellow and peaceful. All motion stopped as suddenly as it had begun a few moments before. Phillip lay suspended in an aura of white light and felt totally one with the universe.

Still immersed in the light, he saw a small dark figure jump from a thorn tree and race across the browned grass, arms flailing wildly, apparently trying to get the attention of the rest of the tribe. Hands cupped around his mouth for amplification, he was screaming, "Kambudi! Kambudi! Kambudi, kami alla goda!"

Following the shouts of this diminutive figure heralding a special event, Phillip received the message: "Mystic Management." His attention was piqued as he crossed the unseen barrier. Then it was all gone. "Kambudi, kami alla goda," the "Coming of the Spirit."

The floating sensation and the light were interrupted as if by a loudly ringing telephone. His conscious thoughts flashed back to the body, lying dead he supposed, in the emergency room. He felt instantly yanked back through the tunnel and came crashing inside his head. He barely caught a glimpse of himself as he re-entered his body.

Every part of him hurt. While nothing was broken, his body had done quite a dance with the asphalt and concrete at the intersection. He had absolutely no idea who he was, where he had been, or what had happened to him. He had two distinct thoughts: there was a God and he had no intention of killing himself. He was at peace like never before.

A doctor came rushing over to what she assumed to be the dead body of a young man who had been hit by a car near the interstate. He was muttering, "Mystic Management, Mystic Management is the way." It immediately became clear that even though he had been declared DOA, he was not dead now. His heart was beating out of his chest and he was gasping for breath. Phillip was, most definitely, alive but not aware. He slipped almost immediately into a coma and remained unreachable for almost three weeks. Even when he became conscious, for another two weeks he had no recollection of who he was. By the time he rediscovered his identity as Phillip Hansen, the semester at college was over and Melissa had killed herself right on schedule. He deduced that at the time of her suicide he was in the hospital emergency room. He thought that she no doubt had assumed he had chickened out and, being a headstrong girl, she went about the business of her death without him.

He had one nagging recollection that ran though his consciousness like a melody one can't help but repeat over and over and over: "Mystic Management...Mystic Management...Mystic Management." This overshadowed even the trauma of his accident and Melissa's death which were paramount in his thoughts

Phillip finished college and, in spite of his completed major in psychology, opted for a short course to prepare him for the Series Seven Examination for stock brokering. He passed the exam and took a job and moved to the Washington, D. C., area in 1994, two years after his accident in Florida.

His memory was still sketchy in spots and he was suffering from panic attacks when he got to D. C. In fact, Phillip was reasonably sure that he was losing his mind. He kept a diary; he was intent on cataloging his madness for posterity. While working in the world of business, he continued his education in psychology, eventually receiving his Ph.D. Over the years, Phillip Hansen had moved from successful stockbroker to renowned psychologist.

* * * * * * * *

He had not thought about his "diary of madness" for years. The new development with Christian finding the old manuscripts rekindled a rash of memories. Phillip reached behind one of the secret desk panels, and produced a badly creased clasped envelope containing three or four steno pads filled with scribblings from what seemed like a different lifetime.

Since Christian and his mounting questions had been put off until morning, it seemed like a good time to skim through the old diary. It would be interesting to review it for the first time as a seasoned clinical psychologist. Moreover, Phillip thought it important to recapture some of the intense feelings he had had while struggling to come to grips with his Eyespellian identity. He felt he would be able to better answer his son's questions if he himself again became immersed in the events of that earlier time, "the time of madness" as he referred to it.

He pulled the spiral pads out of the envelope and, with a certain apprehension, searched for the early entries. With little difficulty he found what he was looking for, descriptions of the first hints of his horrible anxiety. He had

had panic attacks coupled with exceedingly strange dreams and what seemed like memories that initially led him to believe he was going mad.

The first entry Phillip selected was dated February 28th, or the 23rd. The writing was pretty shaky, so he couldn't be sure. He knew the diary would be difficult to decipher in spots. He wanted to throw his psyche back in time and put as much present moment energy as possible into his task.

February 28

> In the *Book of Matthew*, it is written: "…do not be anxious about tomorrow, for tomorrow will be anxious for itself. Let the day's own trouble be sufficient for the day."

> While I see the wisdom in that, I am constantly plagued by the nagging events surrounding my accident. I am especially concerned about the dreams and partial memories I have been having ever since I first glimpsed that incredible pink planet as I moved through the tunnel. I still mourn Melissa's death and I still see people and places that are both perfectly familiar and strange, all at the same time. The odd phrase "Mystic Management" still flows in my semi-consciousness. I fear that I am going crazy. I worry very much about tomorrow.

Phillip absent mindedly swiveled his chair around; the bottom of the seat bumped solidly against the side of the desk cavity. It didn't take much effort to put his thoughts back to those personally troubled times. He realized, literally with a jolt, that he still missed Melissa. He read the next entry in the diary.

March 3

> If only I could have reached Melissa before she killed herself. While I would not have been able to explain it logically, I could

have shared some undefined hope with her. I could have given her reason to go on living; I could have convinced her of a future, our future together. In the months right after the accident, I was in close touch with something; something that gave me the courage to go on. I felt close to God. And now, I'm not so sure.

Phillip got up from the chair and began to pace back and forth parallel to the bookshelves lining the study wall. He was thrown back in time to the doubt-filled Phillip Hansen who wrote the diary entry of March 3rd. He remembered, as if it were yesterday, the circumstances of that first horrible panic attack. He read the next diary entry holding the notebook at a distance lest he again feel the anxiety captured in those pages.

March 4

Although my anxieties began before I moved to the D. C. area and before I met Jo, I had my first serious panic attack last November. November 18, 1994, to be precise. It is the most horrible memory of my life. That lunch at that little Persian diner at Bailey's Crossroads, Virginia, will be lodged in my brain forever. I'll never forget how I came flying out of the diner, light-headed, clutching at my Adam's apple, unable to swallow. I was sure that I was dying. I honestly thought that I had contracted some rare Middle-Eastern disease, a disease that attacks the throat with absolutely no warning.

I was such a fool. Now I know better. I am simply going crazy; I am losing my mind. It's been months and little has improved. I am beginning to feel more and more like I did in Florida; I think I want to die.

Phillip could hardly stand it. His memories became so vivid, he thought he was going to have a panic attack right then and there. He could feel both the panic and the despair of the young man he had been. What upset him the most, however, was reliving the feelings of utter and desperate confusion. At the time, Phillip had had no idea what was happening to him. There was no logical explanation, and this was disturbing to a very intelligent person.

As Phillip continued to pace, other memories of that frightful day at Bailey's Crossroads moved into his conscious realm. He could see himself outside the diner, alternately spread over the hood of his car, face to the metal, and then madly walking around, still clutching at his throat. He remembered that he had felt totally insane.

In spite of his embarrassment at stumbling and crashing out of the diner that day, Phillip had been glad that he was not alone. He smiled and shook his head as he thought about how horrible his ordeal must have been for Jo. She was there with him that infamous day at the diner. By this time, Jo had come into Phillip's life. It was only much later that she had explained her role as his protector chosen by the Universe. If she had not consoled him, assuring him he was not crazy, it is hard to say what would have become of him. They married the following April.

Phillip finished out his thoughts of that first attack. The ordeal did not end with lunch. About twenty minutes after the first onslaught of panic, everything started over, only it was worse. He recalled how he could actually feel the blood rushing through the veins in his arms. It was absolutely terrifying. He thought death was imminent.

Engrossed in these thoughts, Phillip again bumped the chair hard against his desk as he relived the ride to Alexandria hospital, and the events in the emergency room. He was in a hospital again, the first time since Florida. This time he was not labeled DOA and there was no peacefulness, no tunnel, no white light. Phillip was indisputably alive, and suffering.

After checking him over, the doctor told Phillip that he was fine physically. He explained that he had had an attack of what's called "globus hystericus."

He then proceeded to tell him about a little old lady who had been in just the other day with the same thing. "The poor woman was so frightened," he could hear the doctor saying as clearly as if he were still there, "that I just sat here and held her hand for about twenty minutes and talked to her, tears streaming down her cheeks the whole time."

Phillip threw the steno pad across the room with renewed anger as he thought about that stupid doctor and the story about the little old lady. How insensitive and fear producing. What came next was absolutely incredible. The doctor actually told Phillip that he needed to talk to somebody, a therapist. Now that really made him mad. There he was, dying, and the doctor had told him to see a shrink. He did not understand, or at least he was not prepared for, what the medical man was saying. He interpreted the doctor's message to be that he, Phillip Hansen, was crazy. Phillip remembered that he had been so overwhelmed, that he had simply gone home and pretty much stayed there for the next four years. He became a classic agoraphobic, terrified to leave the house. He was capable of going only a few places. He could not walk around the block, go to the store, to a movie, and certainly not out to lunch. Most days he could go to work and come right home again, but only with the aid of valium. His fears continued to multiply and the greatest fear of all, going insane, seemed to become more of a reality.

Phillip's chair, bumping against the desk again, banged him back to the present. He was startled by his ability to recreate the past scenario with such detailed and strong feeling. He recalled his absolute stubbornness, his refusal to see a therapist in spite of suffering anxiety and suspicions of insanity. His reluctance to deal with his own issues in spite of his education and training as a psychologist, was perhaps the most peculiar aspect of the time of madness. The battle went on for years. Phillip read another of his diary entries.

September 25

I had to make an emergency visit to the mental health clinic early this morning, about 2:30 A.M., if I had to guess. Things are becoming unbearable. It hits out of nowhere, for no apparent reason. I had to work pretty late tonight. I was sitting there alone, eating a stale chocolate chip cookie. I remember mindlessly staring at the remnants of a cup of coffee, a half-empty glass of water, three open and scattered packs of gum, and a messy pouch of pipe tobacco, all of which I utilized to soothe me in my times of stress and potential panic.

And then there was that dull plastic, safety-topped container of small yellow pills: valium, 5 mg. I was fondling the container and reading the label: "TAKE AS NEEDED." And at the bottom, in that bright day-glow color, it said: "THIS PRESCRIPTION CAN BE REFILLED ONLY BY AUTHORITY OF YOUR PHYSICIAN." With horror, I noticed that the container was empty.

I was instantly surrounded by that feeling that, without warning, I might stop breathing, hyperventilate, pass out, lose control, begin yelling and running around aimlessly and afraid like a crazy person...like a crazy person...like a crazy person. I am absolutely terrified that I am losing my mind. I really feel as if I am going to go off the edge at any moment. Dying along the interstate in Florida would have been much easier and, certainly, a whole lot faster.

The fear had always been so real, thought Phillip. It had been much more terrifying than he had imagined anything could be. To make matters worse, during this same period the intermittent memories of Eyespell had begun to increase. Phillip had simply added his delusions of being an alien to the mounting proof of his escalating madness. One thing fed upon another and the anxiety worsened. Phillip scanned another diary entry.

October 1

> My anxiety isn't getting any better. Why do I feel like this? My stomach is twitching; my throat is tightening. My throat, what about my throat? I can't swallow! It's happening again…it's been five seconds, ten, fifteen!!! Oh my god! My head is coming off, bursting. I am losing perspective, reeling. I am in a panic! I am afraid! No. There is nothing logically wrong. If only I had five magic beans, I would be Jack.

Sometime in the third year of his ordeal, and with the constant urging of Jo, Phillip had agreed to see a therapist on a regular basis. He was just too exhausted to continue on his own and, surely, the magic beans he craved could be purchased at seventy-five dollars a session!

Phillip tipped further back in his chair and propped his socked feet on the desk. He remembered his therapy well. "For my first seventy-five dollars," he thought, "I learned that anxiety could not be ignored and that I would have to assume total responsibility for getting in touch with my feelings." He was not impressed, then or now. Ultimately there had been some talk about self-concept and the notion that the brain could not solve problems of the heart or the soul. It was hypothesized that there was an imaginary steel plate in Phillip's throat separating his brain from the rest of him. At that time Phillip was not an integrated person and he was incapable of truly feeling what was going on in his life.

Phillip remembered that, no matter how hard he had pressed the issue, the therapist would not concede that he was, indeed, crazy. Evidently, the therapist knew something Phillip didn't know.

After about six months and one thousand eight hundred dollars of what Phillip considered psychological drivel, the magic cure had finally entered the scenario of his therapy. He had been introduced to his inner child. And through that child, Phillip had gotten in touch with both his fears and his Eyespellian heritage. The imaginary steel plate had been removed from Phillip's throat and he had begun to accept the possibility of the pink planet as part of his reality. Although he never did mention the pink planet to his therapist

Throughout this entire ordeal, Jo was his rock. Her presence soothed him on a moment-to-moment basis and once again Phillip Hansen did not commit suicide.

Phillip had been with his diary and with his thoughts throughout the night. It was mid-morning when Christian knocked on the study door. He poked his head in and asked, "Does this mean that I am half Eyespellian?"

Phillip smiled. He felt like his much younger self, the Phillip who was bathed in the white light at the end of that tunnel where there were no restrictions of either time or space. Probably for the first time Phillip had a clear vision of Mystic Management and he knew it would ultimately come to be through the efforts of his son, Christian.

CHAPTER 13

▼

THE GATHERING OF LIGHT (EYESPELL)

Three days had passed, the third moon of Eyespell was rising in the evening sky, and the predetermined time for the Full-Round had come. The Council Chamber was full, the Eldersix were in the center circle, and the entire population of Eyespell was in mind-link preparing to conduct the planetary business of survival and preservation of the light-skew. The light-skew had been in tact since the first recorded Full-Round over ten thousand years ago. The meeting of the Full-Round was typically a celebration of the light-skew, not an attempt to preserve it. The encroaching and ever more powerful force of the dark-skew was threatening Eyespell's very existence. The question was whether or not Eyespell could gather enough light to overcome the seemingly inevitable darkness.

This was the first time that loss of the light-skew was actually a possibility. It was the first time that movement toward homeostasis, balance of light and dark, had become an Eyespellian reality. Since the return of

Kathryn and "the four," evidence of homeostasis was undeniable. Eyespell was put on notice that there would be unprecedented and unwanted change. Until now light versus dark, and good versus evil had only been hypothetical abstractions carried down by the Elders in the recounting of legends. The concepts of juxtaposition of light and dark and homeostasis were the subjects of scary midnight stories shared by teenagers while on pilgrimage in the desert during no-moon.

Daniel addressed the Full-Round. "Because of the seriousness of our situation there will be no opening ceremony and no display of lights. All of our light energy must be conserved for the business at hand. Eyespell is changing and not in a manner that is desired or apparently within our control. We are moving into unknown territory. This is a frightening prospect. While fear of the unknown symbolizes an inner conflict Earthlings frequently find themselves immersed in, such conflict and fear has been virtually non-existent on Eyespell. I'll share with you a short story Kathryn brought back from Earth dealing with this fear of the unknown. Perhaps it will give us a starting place, and its humor might lighten our spirits." Daniel read the piece into the minds of Eyespell.

Never Call A Kid A Dirty Kookamonga

I discovered the Kookamonga Effect in 1975. My son was sitting on the sidewalk in front of the house peacefully dismantling a bearded iris. He was about five years old at the time. Another youngster approached and, for no apparent reason, began calling my son names that reflected poorly upon his heritage and alluded to acts disgraceful and abusive committed by both himself and his reputed parents.

Somewhat annoyed by the harsh and polluted consonant sounds, my son pulled slightly harder at the iris. Distraught at being ignored, the other youngster started to walk away. However, in a last-ditch, over-the-shoulder effort he yelled, "And besides that, you're a dirty kookamonga!" My son leapt from the sidewalk screaming, "I am not," and punched the other kid right on the top of the head.

I am ashamed to admit it, but evidently "dirty kookamonga" was the only unfamiliar phrase in the long list of insults thrown my son's way. Now, why do you suppose my son did not simply ask the other kid what a dirty kookamonga was? Why did he deem it necessary to react in anger and hit the other kid on top of the head with his fist?

And so my discovery of the Kookamonga Effect. The Kookamonga Effect is the inability to constructively deal with the unknown. We do not seem to have effective coping behaviors for handling anything unfamiliar.

When we are young enough and objectively ignorant enough, we might show curiosity rather than hostility toward foreign circumstances. However, by the time we learn even a few things, as we become more socialized, our innate coping mechanisms begin to deteriorate dramatically. We choose to distrust that which is not familiar and we develop a compulsive need to maintain the status quo.

We are plagued throughout our lives with this tendency toward non-acceptance of the unknown and aversion to change. Picture that same child twenty years later as a young executive. He is sitting behind his desk instead of on the sidewalk. He is peacefully dismantling a wooden elephant puzzle instead of a bearded iris. Someone says something annoying. He pulls harder at the elephant's leg. Someone says something not only annoying, but unfamiliar, something that he simply does not understand, something absolutely unknown to him.

The child on the sidewalk awakens within the man and, in a fit
of anger, he smashes his fist right on top of the desk.

Daniel began, "So the story makes us smile; that can only be a good
thing. Imagine. We have embraced an Earth story, a story from the place
of the dark-skew, and we have not yet gone up in a puff of dark smoke."
There was laughter throughout the council chamber.

Daniel continued, "So what can we learn from this prose? It reinforces
things we already know. First and foremost we cannot respond to Earth-
plane vibrational leakage in anger, regardless of how negative the impact
might be on our planet. We may not hit Earth on top of the head with our
fist." Again laughter rang throughout the chamber and the planet. "See
how well we're doing; we're laughing, not punching. Excellent! Our task is
to constructively deal with the unknown; we need to understand and deal
with the effects of homeostasis on our planet. Exactly how will balance
affect the light-skew and the cell-matrix? So far the impact of the leakage
has been disruption in nature and in the states of mind of those closest to
the Eyespell Experiment. We have experienced thunderstorms, earthquakes, dissension, anger, and sarcasm. None of these outcomes are desirable. The question is, do we have coping strategies for dealing with these
new and undesired realities? Are we capable of changing or have we, like
the Earth child in our story, developed a compulsive need to maintain the
status quo?"

Daniel gave Leo the floor. "The intent of this unique Full-Round is to
develop strategies for reversing the effects of the leakage brought on by the
outcome of the Eyespell Experiment. If that is not possible, we hope to at
least mitigate its effects, and understand the implications of light-balance
for Eyespell. Indeed, the key is for us to understand and embrace balance."

Rebecca followed up with, "The movement toward homeostasis must
be slowed enough to prevent the pendulum of light from initially swing-
ing too far into the dark zone, the dark-skew. It is the dark-skew that
maintains the vibrations of sickness, conflict, chaos, ignorance, isolation,

lethargy, hatred, and poverty. Some of these factors, potentially lethal to our way of life, already have been felt on Eyespell. The green-light corridor seems particularly sensitive. I am unable to maintain our natural environment as we have known it. The nature of Eyespell is shifting dramatically even as we speak."

Rebecca's words trailed off. Eyespell continued to display a disharmonious and hostile natural environment, a side of nature totally unfamiliar to Eyespellians. The planetary cell-matrix seemed to be breaking apart in spots as small stress cracks in the planet's surface widened to giant fissures. In these early days of homeostasis, anomalous natural occurrences became more and more frequent. Rebecca hoped to harness the collective energy of the Full-Round to keep the planet from regressing to a totally primitive natural state.

Eyespell's natural beauty was unparalleled in all of creation. From outer space the pastel planet shone against a galaxy of star clusters. Its vast desert sands glowed a soft pink against the rays of a blue sun and these same sand oceans reflected a soft blue, and sometimes a deep aquamarine, in the light of a yellow sun. A myriad of colors converged on the hillsides and mountains, leaving trails of pastel rainbows. What the daylight did not dazzle by two suns, the night sky outlined under the colored lights of four moons.

And then there was the aliveness of the planetary cell-matrix itself. The cell-matrix was united with the color affinity of each Eyespellian, individually, and all Eyespellians, collectively. All of this culminated in a shimmering and ever-changing aura of thought-colors superimposed upon the sun-colored sands, rainbow mountains and moonlit horizons. This fusion of mind and nature produced hues in infinite harmony, defying descriptive labels. Even a brief glimpse of Eyespell from space was, in and of itself, mystical and compelling.

As Eyespell moved on its new and dangerous path there remained, in the heart of every Eyespellian, the hope that something this beautiful in the universe would not simply disappear. However, as an ancient nature continued to awaken, the fate of the planet was none too clear. There were dreadful thunderstorms with lightning strikes, dangerously high tides, ground tremors, landslides, and a host of other natural disturbances. The most dramatic upheaval occurred in the desert out from Elasia. It rained so heavily there that flash floods flowed over the Blue Desert sands and into the crater-like Valley of the Bluenoon. In the immediate aftermath, only the tower tip stood out of the water, needle like, at the center of a huge lake. The holy place was now inaccessible in the traditional manner.

Those gathered in the amphitheater began a desperate response to the planetary condition. The earlier decision to conserve light energy was reversed. It was quickly recognized that to preserve and hoard the light energy was inappropriate and a subtle way of feeding into the dark-skew. Rather the light corridors were opened in a majestic attempt to accentuate the light-skew. This light show was perhaps more glorious than any before. The Elders and others in the Council Chamber wore the monk's garb, and it was pronounced a holy time. Eyespellians everywhere were in touch with the vibration of the three hundred thirty-seven in the gathering of light.

Under the laser-like lights the immediate task became clear: to slow nature down, seeking a return to the light-skew. Rebecca, centered in the twenty-seventh ring and at absolute-middle within the chamber, held the emerald crystal of nature cupped in her hands high above her head with the point of the pyramid facing down. The remainder of the three hundred thirty-seven, and, in turn, the entire populace of Eyespell, including those souls in the birth/death transition, color-visioned in consonance with the green hues of Rebecca's crystal.

Never before had a single color-strand achieved such potency in the dimension of Eyespellian reality-creating. A globe of light instantly began to emanate outward from Rebecca's cupped hands. The globe slowly turned, elongated, and reformed as a larger sphere. It increased its physical dimension while in constant cyclical motion. Within minutes, the entire amphitheater was in the globe's penetrating light. Within hours, all of Elasia and the closest desert areas were enveloped in the emerald green.

After three days, the entire planet and its aura, including the four moons, were within the crystal's one-color of nature.

The erratic behavior of a nature gone wild slowed. The pull toward homeostasis, while not stopped, was delayed, slowed. The process for maintaining the light-skew was continued. While the cell-matrix of the planet continued to change and even fragment in pockets of time and place, the extreme natural disasters of the dark-skew were for the present averted. Eyespell continued its planetary healing process under the guidance of the emerald vibration for approximately the next forty Earth years.

Time is not linear on Eyespell; it is a multi-dimensional measurement. Describing an instant versus an eternity becomes tricky business when trying to measure people's actions against places and events. For example, during the nature-healing, the Elders maintained their vigil in the twenty-seventh ring of the council chamber for the entire forty years. From a time-linear perspective this would be an impossible strategy whereas in non-linear time it is just one of many possibilities.

During the Elders' emerald immersion, Eyespellians everywhere attended to the cell-matrix and consciously "thought" energy toward healing the environment, calming nature, and ensuring the permanence of the light-skew. This movement toward the dark-skew in the world of nature was only the first sign of light-skew disruption. The physical fabric of the planet was one thing, its psychological and spiritual well-being were quite another.

Leo was asked to work closely with Kathryn and the four returnees as a first step in dealing with the psychological impact of Earth-plane vibrational leakage. He took them to a protected oasis deep in the Blue Desert. With the possible exception of Pete, they were still the locus of Earth-plane vibrational leakage and the starting point of most light-skew disturbances. Close and constant check on Kathryn, Antonio, Melissa, Nancy, and Pete was necessary in order to keep a pulse on the planet's mental condition. When one of them behaved uncharacteristically of Eyespell, Leo telepathically alerted the other Elders and they would, in turn, divert a quantum of Elder-energy to momentarily still the vibrational leakage. It would do little good to abate the scourges of nature if the people of Eyespell were to suffer a global psychosis.

An amazing thing happened during this time of turmoil. As the emerald sphere expanded its dimensional boundaries and enveloped all the Eyespellian domain, continual and soaring energy releases were detected, releases something like sunspots. At the apex of one of these energy releases, Myana and Gracina reached with their spirits into the universe far beyond Eyespell. As their soaring spirits were returning from the vastness, they brushed past the aura of Earth. For an instant of an instant they sensed a familiar life-force, the life-force of an Eyespellian. There could be only one conclusion, Phillip, the missing Eyespellian, was alive and on Earth!

With intense feelings of exhileration, hope, unconditional love, compassion, and oneness Myana and Gracina put their energies together in attempting to contact Phillip on the planet Earth. They were almost immediately successful in their task. They identified themselves to the Cosmos as "Elders of the Lght" and then, using their crystals as transmitters, called out to the mind of Phillip Hansen. They hoped to reach him while his mind was quiet in meditation or sleep. Within a matter of hours, they sensed a response clearly of Phillip's vibration. And, within a few hours after that, they sensed a second, and unexpected, response, a response clearly Eyespellian but not of Phillip.

They pressed toward the Council Chamber with the astonishing news. There was not one Eyespellian on planet Earth, but two!

CHAPTER 14

▼

THE EYESPELL CONNECTION
(EYESPELL AND EARTH)

It was Earth-year 2032; Phillip was approaching his sixtieth birthday. It had been two years since that evening in Waterford, Virginia, when he had shared his Eyespellian identity with his son, Christian. Dreams and memories of Eyespell were continuing and with a renewed intensity.

The first dreams of another time and place had come spontaneously to Phillip in 1992, shortly after his accident along the interstate in Florida. Through those initial dreams, memories of Eyespell gradually evolved. His first truly irrefutable belief in Eyespell and his Eyespellian identity, however, had come to him through conversations with his inner child during therapy several years later. His dreams, memories, and inner child all contributed to his recognition of the realities of the higher self, and Eyespell ultimately became a significant part of that higher reality. Even though Phillip gradually sensed everything about Eyespell to be true, there was actually no tangible proof of it. In rare moments, now even in 2032, he still had nagging doubts left over from the time of madness.

As always, Jo was there to help him through these moments of doubt. While the evidence of Eyespell was no more tangible for her than for him, her arguments in favor of a higher reality were convincing. Jo would often meditate with Phillip, sharing the vibrations of her higher self with him. After such a meditation, he was always sure about Eyespell's existence and his strong tie to the pink planet he could vision floating in the galaxies of his mind. His faith was always restored.

2032 was different. The renewed dreams about Eyespell were unlike the old memories. The new conversations were not simply from within and they did not have that elusive quality of the higher self. This time the voice was from without, from somewhere, someone, outside himself.

For the first time since the tunnel experience forty some years ago, Phillip unexpectedly heard a mysterious woman's voice call to him. She identified herself as "Gracina of the Light." With every fiber of his being, he knew that someone from his home, Eyespell, was making contact with him.

Realizing the magnitude of this fact, Phillip called Christian on the phone. He left messages both at home and at work. He was busting to ask him to fly from Rochester, New York, where he lived with his family, to Virginia as soon as possible. Christian laughed when he heard the obvious urgency in his father's messages. He returned the call immediately and said, "I know about the Eyespell connection; I too heard 'Gracina of the Light.' I already have my plane ticket and was just going to call to tell you I'll be arriving at Dulles International at three o'clock tomorrow afternoon."

Phillip hung up the phone and in his excitement dashed for the study. He felt compelled to meditate. He now had confirmation from another Earth-bound soul that Eyespell existed. While he had always relied on Jo to help him maintain his faith, he was absolutely high with this new validation from yet another. As he approached the study door it dawned on him in speeded-up time that he had just swept past her in the hallway. Her laughter was just catching up with his brain and her voice trailed off in his head, "And I suppose you'll be off to Eyespell, Dr. Hansen!"

He yelled out the study door, "Do you wanna come?"

"It's too far and I don't have a thing to wear," was the tongue-in-cheek reply.

Although Phillip had made his way to the study intending to reconnect with Gracina through meditation, he was too hyper to deal with anything demanding such focused attention. His brain was filled with mind chatter and could not be quieted. He learned years ago that the soul would quiet the mind of its own accord when the time was right. Nonetheless, he felt like a little kid anticipating his new toy, still wrapped and just sitting under the Christmas tree.

He kicked back onto the study sofa and thought about conversations he had had with his inner child during the 1990s. Most of the early talks hinted that Eyespell was more than part of a passing vision, a vision most probably related to his near-death experience. The child within revealed, at any given time, only that which Phillip was capable of assimilating. More often than not, this inner child pushed the outer man to his limits of understanding.

Phillip recalled that during the time of madness, things Eyespellian were both comforting and confusing to him. The comfort came during periods of meditation when he would become one with the child envisioning Eyespell through the child and the higher self. During these meditations, as the memories of Eyespell unfolded, the predominant feeling was one of extreme peacefulness. It was a lot like the feeling of being immersed in that white light at the end of the tunnel. His anxieties were momentarily soothed and the possibility of ever having another panic attack seemed remote. "God was in his heaven and all was right with the world."

Confusion always came directly on the heels of such comforting peace. Phillip's logical side always tried to make sense out of the Eyespell insights, feelings, and memories revealed in meditation. He tried to understand things that should have been allowed to stand on their own merit. When in this logical mode, he was left hopelessly incapable of proving his feelings or convincing himself that Eyespell was anything more than delusion and simply part of his ensuing madness.

Phillip's concern for his mental stability became even more intensified when visions of Eyespell began to occur during full consciousness. Sometimes, when he was caught up in the beauty of a natural setting, for example, he would spontaneously recollect something about Eyespell. His mind might be peacefully immersed in the beauty of a scene and the child would slyly throw in a vision or two; he would catch Phillip "unawares." Much later, Phillip came to call these times of spontaneous revelation, "child-chatter."

Phillip recalled one child-chatter evening in particular. He had left his office for the small parking lot by way of a path. There was no sidewalk, only pine needles, mulch, and leaves set between old railroad ties. The path was framed by thick ground cover, a couple of big trees above, and, at one end, a bunch of piled up coral rock that had a man-made waterfall in mind.

It was dark by the time he started along the path and there was a bit more than a drizzle coming down. A large spotlight nailed to the biggest tree illuminated the slanting rain. About halfway into his journey, Phillip sensed a single movement, a single frame taken by the reflex of an eye. There was a breath inhaled that captured some different reality, something just out of sight. That fraction of an instant pierced his very center and then it was gone, and Phillip was almost one step further along the pathway.

He looked back, somewhat perplexed, curious, almost onto something. And then, with another reflex of an eye, Phillip envisioned himself standing in the middle of a cool afternoon desert, basking in the light of two suns. And in yet another reflex, with a blue sun still in after-image, Phillip found himself staring at four glorious moons and a galaxy of unfamiliar stars in spiraling array. And then all of it was gone and, again, he was almost one step further along the pathway.

This is how Eyespell had been revealed, in puzzle form, with small pieces of memory set in place to become part of Phillip's consciousness. It is no wonder that he sometimes questioned his sanity.

Phillip's mind returned to the study and 2032 as he stretched his body slowly and deliberately like a cat, one stretched-out foot barely touching the far end of the sofa. He got to thinking about how the time of madness had seemed to last forever. The anxieties started in 1992 and remained the focal point of his life into the first part of the twenty-first Century.

It was 2000 and Phillip had insisted on moving with Jo and two-year-old Christian back to Florida where all the craziness began. They rented out the old Waterford house and headed for Boca Raton. He hoped to find his answers in this place from his past. He had taken a job as Visiting Professor of Psychology with a small private college.

The return to Florida and the beginning of the new millennium had marked a period of intensive inner searching. Phillip had made great strides in his personal awareness during this time and had all but dispelled the madness. Somewhere in all of this he finally began to acknowledge and internalize his own expertise as a therapist and teacher. Even though convinced he was not going crazy, Phillip still faced an interesting psychological dilemma—he continued having lucid visions of Eyespell. His inner quest intensified. He was prepared to follow his feelings and acknowledge them as truth, especially his feelings about Eyespell.

Phillip turned on his side and this time stretched an arm over his head and around the curved arm of the couch. He sighed a long sigh. It was already two in the morning. The return to Florida to find his answers had been, he remembered, the beginning of a difficult period. His mind wondered off again, this time to that one momentous day when things Earthly and things Eyespellian had finally begun to fall consciously together.

"It must have been over thirty years ago by now," thought Phillip. "I remember that day as if it were yesterday. I wasn't exactly depressed, I was just a little off to the side, experiencing that not-quite-here feeling. I remember watching myself from somewhere else that morning; I remember watching and wondering what was real, what was relevant."

Phillip stretched forward as if to get closer to his reverie, "There was the weather; it was beautiful and surrounded me. There were the birds whistling and chattering at the feeder and the orchids blossoming in the lanai. There was the little brown mouse who wandered by each morning to eat yesterday's hibiscus flowers then-fallen and scattered among the deco bark and round chattahoochie stepping stones. And, of course, there was The Moe, the fluffy white family cat who mindlessly watched the whole scene from between the vertical blind slats and the frame of the sliding glass door. It was clear to me that all of this was relevant."

Phillip sat up and planted both feet squarely on the study floor, elbows on his knees and hands clasped around the top of his head, "I remember leaving The Moe by the window. I got in my car and headed for work. My certainties about what might be relevant began to fade almost immediately. I noticed that I was still tired from yesterday's work, my finances were in a shambles, Jo was unhappy about being in Florida, and the anti-Christ, guised in the garb of the terrible twos, had moved into Christian's body. By the time I reached my office, I was less cognizant of that same beautiful weather, a golden rain tree, the huge banyan, and the small lake, beyond and to my left. It was no longer clear to me what was relevant."

Phillip stood up and began to pace in front of the couch deep in thought, "By the time I walked into my office and opened the desk drawer to collect my notes for that morning's lectures, I was totally uncentered. I was separated from the very things in nature that just a little while earlier I knew to be relevant. I remember desperately trying to center myself and grasp the meaning of what I did for a living.

Phillip stopped his pacing and stood at the window, transfixed by his thoughts, "I needed to sit under the trees by the lake and feel the day, the blossoms, the creatures, the Earth. I needed to be like an Ancient One, elbows in the grass, sharing with my students. I needed to transcend the moment in a myriad of colors, feelings, and emotions. I needed to be mystical."

Phillip spun around and facing his imagined self on the sofa almost yelled, "And there it was! My Eyespellian identity had been fully recognized for the very first time. Yes, there it was; that which I called the renaissance in my soul."

Phillip crossed his arms and hung one hand over each shoulder as if hugging himself, "Indeed, the renaissance in my soul is still the creation of my own reality from past, present, and future memories. It is my ability to transcend self-image and present circumstance moving to a higher plane. This renaissance in my soul explains why I sometimes feel the monastery walls at my back when working in the garden. The sweat on my brow belongs, perhaps, to a medieval, or perhaps Eyespellian, monk. Sometimes, the sound of raindrops beating down on the brim of a baseball cap or ice clinking in a glass jerks me into an unconscious awareness. At other times, scenes in old movies or pictures of distant places bring back bittersweet memories of experiences that I've never consciously had. And that is the renaissance in my soul that I discovered one day at a small Florida college right around the turn of the century."

Phillip, still hugging himself, stretched his neck like a turtle popping his head out from under his shell and peered at the couch to make sure his imagined self was still paying attention. In a sudden gesture he let go of his shoulders, shook his head and buried his face in his hands as he recalled what he had actually done that day even in the light of his incredible self-discovery. He had let his logic get the best of him, and he had actually taught his classes in their classrooms. Phillip winced as he could hear his own voice droning on in lecture as if he were there right now. He was able to recapture the feeling of utter despair that had surged up when he first realized that he had chosen the wrong reality once again. He had chosen the collective aloneness of a sterile classroom. He had bypassed the oneness of nature; he had forfeited the connectedness with Eyespell in the face of logic. He had given up being mystical; he did not choose a piece of the Eyespell puzzle that day.

Phillip literally jumped onto the sofa and came crashing down on his imaginary self, ecstatic that he never made that infamous error of logic over connectedness again. From the turn of the century forward, Phillip had made the "Eyespell teachings" his secret reality, and had followed them. And now, some thirty years later, Eyespell is reality—reality confirmed by his son.

Phillip was still too excited to meditate and by now too overtired to sleep. Dropping back onto the study sofa his head filled with positive and exciting thoughts, he had a sense of childlike hopefulness. Keenly aware of the feeling continuing to well up inside of him, he thought to himself, "I was not always so optimistic and hopeful; hope was a hard-learned lesson for me." Phillip stretched out flat on the study couch and began to drift off in spite of his excitement. "Christian should be here in just a few hours; I can hardly wait. I think we're in for a magnificent adventure." Phillip smiled at his childlike presence of mind. "I love who I am now. I am so full of hope. I'll never forget that day thirty years ago in the ice cream parlor when I learned about the choice between hope and despair. Christian was just a tot and I recall my state of mind so vividly. I remember as if it were yesterday…"

> Christian and I were in the ice cream parlor having lunch. A young father came in with his much younger son also of about two, two and one-half, tops. The little one was somewhat duck like in his almost-people walk. He was following his giant dad, eyes bug-like as only a small child's can be in anticipation of an ice cream treat.
>
> As they were leaving, I noticed that the child's face was particularly beautiful in his joy and innocence. And then, I thought to myself: "How cruel life is, young one. Someday you will watch a

child such as yourself and, like me now grown, you will think what a cruel joke life is."

In those instantly chosen thoughts, the child's eyes, buggy with excitement, suddenly appeared to be sunken with desperation and lost hope. That moment was one of the singularly most unpleasant of my entire life. Imagine, with a thought, a mood, the instantaneous loss of hope, I was able to turn the pure innocence and excitement of a child into menacing darkness in my mind, the rose into flowerless and painful thorns. I was able to turn lunch into the rubble of my life.

I remember that across the table from me, Christian's lips began to move and I almost simultaneously heard him say, "i-cream," pointing toward the counter. I think the request startled me...I didn't know there was any ice cream left...

Phillip fell asleep still thinking about that long ago day's lesson in the ice cream parlor. His last thought before dozing off was, "There is hope in despair and despair in hope. The choice is in our control, in our thoughts, and all in that reflex of an eye."

After falling into a shallow sleep, Phillip saw Gracina's face in a dream and remembered her as one of the Eldersix of Eyespell. It had been forty years since his twentieth birthday and the Eyespell puzzle was nearing completion.

The alarm went off and startled Phillip toward the morning coffee that he could smell brewing in the kitchen. Jo was sitting at the kitchen table doing the daily crossword puzzle.

"You're just in time," she said with a big smile and a big hug. "What was the name of the movie that won the academy award in 2011? It's on the tip of my tongue, but I just can't get it. It was about that business guy from Pakistan who was supposed to save the world. Remember, we watched the DVD and you and Christian spent the next two days arguing about the plausibility of the plot. And if memory serves me correctly you lost that argument to a thirteen-year-old."

"Yes, yes, I remember that one well. But I have the same problem you do, I remember everything except the title. You know, the memories of Eyespell have started again."

"Yes, and Christian will be along this afternoon and the two of you will be heading off to some holy place to meditate together."

"How could you possibly know all that?" Phillip asked.

"While you may be from Eyespell and different, my husband, I too have my dreams and my memories and my meditations. When "Gracina of the Light" called to you, I heard her from within my head. Think hard, what's the name of that fool movie?"

Phillip thought that Jo was probably the only woman on the planet that he could be married to, managing to be one step behind her most of the time. "Since you seem to know more about what's happening than I do, any thoughts on where Christian and I are supposed to go or what, exactly, we're supposed to do?"

"I thought you'd never ask. I have it all in writing for you. Last evening I had quite a long session with my spirit guides. And I can't wait to see Christian, it's been too long."

Phillip finished his coffee, took the papers Jo had prepared for him, and went out into the garden to study them. The aroma of wet honeysuckle was still fresh in the air. It had to be Phillip's favorite smell and reason enough to settle in the Virginia countryside.

He squeezed behind the table of the big redwood glider with the bright green-and-white canopy and cushions. He pulled his wire-rimmed glasses out of his shirt pocket and began to read the beautifully handwritten papers. Phillip was fascinated. A slight breeze came up before he realized that what Jo had given him to read was inscribed in a handwriting unrecognized by him on a sort of metallic paper that did not move with the wind. This "paper" was not of Earth! Another piece of the puzzle came to rest in its proper alignment. This paper and its message were of Eyespell and manifested here through "channel." Phillip began to read.

> Gracina of the Light put these thoughts and instructions into the cosmic mind. I have picked them up and, in turn, pass them along to you, Jo Hansen. It has been long since we last spoke, my lady. It would appear that your husband and your son have important work to accomplish on the Earth plane. Their destinies are at hand and, indeed, the destiny of your entire planet. And that of the planet Eyespell...

Phillip continued to read, his mind virtually reeling with the limitless possibilities.

> Dressed in the plain brown garb of the monk, make your way to the red rock country surrounding Sedona, Arizona. Specifically, go to the base of that which is called Cathedral Rock where the vibration is female and the color is yellow. Be there at full moon in full meditation and await our vibration. Bring only your son.

Phillip put the metallic-like pages in his pocket and made his way back to the house. He had no inkling where he might locate monk's clothing and he was not all too sure he liked the idea. He chuckled to himself, realizing that this was no time to let logic or practicality get the best of him. He had had little sleep the night before and decided a good nap would be in order before picking Christian up at the airport. He figured if he left the house at two-fifteen or so, he would have plenty of time to meet the three o'clock flight.

Phillip awakened to the familiar sound of a car pulling into the gravel driveway. Just as he was thinking about getting annoyed at such an unexpected intrusion, he realized that it was already five-thirty and it was his car pulling up with Jo at the wheel and Christian beside her. He rushed outside to meet them.

"Good grief, Jo, why didn't you wake me?" He smiled and worked his way around to giving them both big hugs. "I've got too much to do to be getting senile and oversleeping, missing people at airports."

Christian was truly glad to see his father. "Well, where do you suspect we are off to, Dad?"

"According to your mother's spirit guides, we have to make our way to Sedona, Arizona, red rock country, land of the positive vortexes. We are supposed to arrive at Cathedral Rock on the night of the full moon wearing, of all things, monk's garb. How's that for mystery?"

Christian did not seem surprised. He unzipped his soft-sided suitcase and pulled out two monk's robes in the drabbest brown one could imagine. "Will these do?"

Phillip just shook his head. "Now how in the heck…why?"

"It was really strange. After we spoke on the phone yesterday, I fell sound asleep. I had a dream that Mom was inscribing a very important note, a channeled note. I didn't consciously remember anything about it. But, when I got up this morning to get ready to go to the airport, I had a strong intuitive feeling that I should leave early and stop to see a monk at the monastery near town. It was funny. He met me at the entrance as if he knew I'd be coming. He introduced himself as Brother Andre, handed me two robes, and gave me his blessings. He was crying; tears of joy, he said."

Phillip Hansen was sure of one thing. They were not in this alone. "We have three days to get to Sedona for the full moon. We should leave for Phoenix day after tomorrow."

"There is one other thing, Dad, the crystal. We need to wait here for it to come our way. Brother Andre told me that we could expect a large, beautiful golden crystal in the shape of a double pyramid, pointed on both ends. He said just to wait for its arrival."

Neither Christian nor his father made a habit of arguing with the Cosmos. They were content to wait for the anticipated crystal the monk had said would arrive. They had a great dinner, a garlic pasta dish Jo was famous for, and spent the rest of the evening speculating about the "Eyespell Connection," as Christian called it.

The next afternoon at about four-thirty, a small van pulled into the Waterford driveway. A stocky man of about seventy-five worked his way laboriously out from behind the wheel. He slid the side door open and removed a package from the back seat. He finally reached the front door and used the knocker instead of the doorbell. Phillip answered the door.

"My heavens! Jo! Christian! It's John Beechmont. John, how are you? We haven't laid eyes on you in ages. Come in, come in, sit down. What in the world brings you to our doorstep this glorious day?"

"Phillip, you have always been a mystery. I think you are waiting for this." He produced the package he had taken from the back seat.

Phillip took the package and opened it carefully. Wrapped in a silken scarf was a huge, opaque, golden topaz cut into a double pyramid, pointed on each end. The stone was flawless. Phillip looked at the crystal and then back at the man who had handed it to him. "And where on Earth did you find such a treasure?"

"In a vault at the Smithsonian. This stone has never been on display. It was brought to me by an old man of at least a hundred years. Let's see, it must have been right around the turn of the century; yes, thirty-two years ago. He showed up in the gallery right around closing one Friday afternoon. He insisted on seeing me privately in my office. He took the crystal from an old leather pouch tied at his waist. Of course, I could only guess its enormous value and was shocked to see it in the possession of this old man.

He looked me straight in the eye and said that this crystal had been 'manifested' for a man named Phillip Hansen, and that I should give it to him in the year 2032. He said I would know the exact time.

I was enthralled, staring at the flawless stone. When I looked up, it was as if the old man had simply vanished into thin air. I searched for a good fifteen minutes and he was nowhere to be found. I even called security.

I met you for the first time almost five years after that incident and here I am. Last night I had a dream about the old man. He told me to bring you the crystal today. Understand its value, Phillip; I could have retired simply by selling that crystal the day after it came into my possession. Use it well and God bless you."

John stayed for a quick cup of tea with the three Hansens, then, worked his way back behind the wheel of the van and was gone by five-thirty. As he left, he was crying; tears of joy.

Christian hurried to the phone and called the airline, making reservations for the next day. He and his father were scheduled to arrive in Phoenix at three-thirty. This would put them in Sedona hopefully no later than five-thirty by the time they retrieved their luggage and rented a car.

The flight to Phoenix was uneventful as was the drive to Sedona. Upon arrival in town it was simple to find an area vortex map depicting the exact location of Cathedral Rock. Actually finding the place, however, was accomplished only after paying out thirty dollars to a local and following her down an obscure dirt road to a small parking area adjacent to the site. By that time it was dusk and the full moon would be rising in, what would prove to be, a clear-as-glass night sky.

Father and son donned their monk's robes, feeling odd to say the least, and gathered up the beautiful golden crystal. Through a second channeled message to Jo the previous evening, it was made clear that they were to wear nothing but the monk's robes and sandals, bringing nothing but the crystal. This message was manifested, like the first, on that same metallic Eyespellian material.

They made their way down a small embankment and across a dry streambed. The climb to Cathedral Rock was gradual and, while there was no specific pathway, the route was easy to follow. After about ten or fifteen minutes, they were at the base of the rock. There were outcropped ledges of red sandstone all along the perimeter. They skirted the ledges wherever possible, and climbed them only if the walk around and up seemed too long. In any event, they never had to climb more than six or eight feet before reaching the next rocky plateau. The red sandstone rocks falling and breaking under their sandaled footsteps was almost musical. The vibrations of this place were filling their consciousness. Energy sur-rounded them. The full moon was hanging in the sky as if awaiting its next direction from the conductor of the Cosmos.

Finally, the two "monks" reached the solid tower of rock protruding from the desert floor. They looked up wondering where they might possibly go from there. Further climbing was more than either of them was prepared to do. Then Phillip remembered, "In full moon and full meditation," and he intuitively knew they had arrived at their destination. He shared this with Christian and they sat cross-legged at the base of the tower. They simultane-ously broke into a long, single-toned chant and achieved a deep meditative state within minutes. Bathed in the aura of Cathedral Rock, father and son shared the same cosmic space as if they were one mind. Phillip and Christian Hansen had achieved total telepathy link.

While in this state of oneness, they were hailed by Gracina and escorted in "vision" by Leo to the Valley of the Bluenoon. The tower in the middle of the crater-like valley on Eyespell was almost identical in shape and pro-portion to the center spire of Cathedral Rock. With the vision of the twin towers, the two pilgrims immediately understood the connection between this holy place on the Earth and that holy place on Eyespell.

Phillip placed the golden topaz against the heels of his pressed-together palms and stretched his arms high above his head as if in an offering to a higher power. The two Earth-bound Eyespellians were lifted out-of-body to the pinnacle of Cathedral Rock.

At first light, father and son "awakened" from their meditation, still cross-legged at the base of the spire. Without speaking, they made their way down and back across the streambed to the parked car. Christian was the first to consciously realize that they had been communicating the entire time. They were still in telepathy link with each other and with Eyespell. The "Eyespell Connection" had become a reality.

▼

CHAPTER 15

THE MYSTIC MANAGER (EYESPELL AND EARTH)

It had been three weeks since Christian returned home to Rochester, New York from Sedona. He was sitting on the back patio waiting for the noise of the distant freight train to clear the air and the sound of the dusk-crickets to return. He could barely hear the droning sounds of the TV set pouring through the open window between kids' tub-splashing squeals and the growls of their mother being a huge water monster. Smiling he thought to himself, "My world is totally different now. A month ago life seemed comparatively simple. There is no question that my life began to change with the revelations about Eyespell as they were uncovered a couple of years ago. Those old manuscripts of Dad's and the leather-bound notebook describing scattered details of the Eyespell Experiment were indeed fascinating. However, prior to Arizona the idea of being half-Eyespellian could be taken with a grain of salt. Now I am forced to consider the literal truth of the matter. This growing reality places everything I do in a new light. There is more to be done in this life of mine than I had ever suspected."

Christian, now thirty-four, was an upper-middle manager with Used Water Works, Inc., whose primary business was water recycling. The corporation was environmentally aware, socially responsible and on the cutting edge of a technology central to planetary growth and survival into the 22nd Century. Its vision statement was simple and to the point, "Used water works for mankind." Christian was headed for the upper echelon of the company. He was already successful by any American corporate standard, and on the career path he had first envisioned for himself when only a college sophomore.

With the Eyespell connection now a reality, Christian's life took new and unexpected turns. He could communicate with his father at will, just by thinking. He was in steady contact with Eyespell, primarily through lucid dreams. He, more often than not, knew exactly what the people around him were thinking. His ability to predict complex business trends increased markedly. That upper-management position he hoped for would be in the offing, not in a few years but by the end of the fiscal year. He would become President and Chief Executive Officer of Used Water Works. Christian had a mission, a new sense of purpose, a forthright insistence upon changing things, making them better. He had always thought of himself as a visionary, and he was extremely comfortable in this new role.

He recalled from his father's old manuscript several statements about a new model of how things should be, a new paradigm. There were powerful statements about how the old paradigm kills, how Earth must change in order to survive. He sometimes imagined himself as spokesperson for just such a new paradigm, and felt that he would achieve, and use, a position of corporate power to "save the world!" To say he felt a certainty of purpose would be understatement. The whole scenario reminded him of that movie that won best picture in 2011, the one about the Pakistani business leader. He never could remember the name of it, but its leadership concept was huge.

Christian was still on the back patio as dusk turned to darkness. The TV was still droning on with no audience and the tub squeals had turned to before-bed quiet time. He was writing a few remarks on the inside front page of his dream journal, "The first inklings of my new calling came to me in dreams that began almost immediately after my experience at Cathedral Rock. The dreams were most often didactic, dreams with a message. The messages were often hidden in typical dream confusion and dream magic. I sometimes felt as though I were reviewing bits and pieces of someone else's dream. Parts of dreams seemed as though they belonged elsewhere. Other times there were long narrative interludes without any visuals at all as if someone were whispering a story inside my head. Other times I would dream lucidly, actually interacting with the dream plot at a conscious level. My dreaming would go back and forth among the elements of narrative, typical dream stuff, and conscious interaction. Because of all this dream confusion I felt the need to meticulously record each dream in this journal. I wanted to study them and be able to interpret them carefully. I at times was not quite sure where the lessons began or ended. In any case, I wanted to share each dream with Dad in exacting detail since our newly developed telepathy skills are sometime fraught with all kinds of mental static."

With darkness imminent Christian put the journal down and thought about that first dream of less than three weeks ago. He had read this journal entry so many times and had pondered each word to the point where he could review it by heart. The first dream was of particular interest, capturing all the mixed elements from simple narration to conscious interaction. He recorded it in three distinct parts for easier interpretation; the dream images and messages did not flow logically, shifting from place to place and subject to subject. This dream was dated May 15, 2032, and was entitled *Myth Building*. The beginning narration seemed out of context, except perhaps as a warning for Christian not to get a swelled head with all the notoriety that was likely to accompany the pursuit of his new mission. As he sat in the dark, eyes closed, he could picture his steady black-ink-handwriting against the buff-colored and light-blue-lined pages of his journal. He sat back enveloped in the newly fallen darkness and reviewed that first dream in every detail.

The First Dream—Myth Building
(May 15, 2032)
Part I

I dreamed about a man who daydreamed a lot about being famous. He had the silly habit of daydreaming just before bed. A great deal of dream time and dream energy was spent wondering how he would actually handle his new-found notoriety. He wondered just how clever he would be on the talk shows. He could picture the host of the show laughing the way they do when they've been had and they're "hading" you back. The man wondered about the money. How much would he have? He dreamed about everything he could buy and every place he could go.

The thought of spending the summer at an A-frame in the mountains was wonderful. However he started to worry about logical things, spoiling the whole adventure he had only begun to create. He worried about the consequences of being gone to the mountains all summer. He thought, "Who will take care of the two cockatiels, Woody and Cheeks? What about Lucky, the lost parrot who landed in the mahogany tree out front last spring? And then there were the three cats. Who would mow the lawn and weed the shrubbery beds? Good grief, the fish tank would probably have to be drained. What if there was a bad storm, who'd secure the house? And, besides that, who'd take care of the pool? And, what's the use having a pool anyway if I'm going to be gone all summer?" By the time the man finished with this logic, the daydream of being famous just wasn't worth

it. Overwhelmed by the details, the man picked himself up, went
to bed, and had a night dream about a mystic manager.

Part II

In a dream-workplace there was a mystic manager who exempli-
fied kindness and generosity. This corporate environment was
psychologically healthy, an environment flowing with feelings of
common purpose and community. This was an extraordinary and
unorthodox corporation. Its existence was prophetic and signaled
a paradigm shift. There was emphasis on long-term goals versus
short-term profits, sustainability versus maximized profits, teams
and individuals working toward common goals versus quick profits, ethical and legal action versus legal-loophole-profits, socially
responsible behavior versus irresponsible profits, loyalty to
employees versus downsizing-profits, and unparalleled service to
customers versus buyer-beware-profits. There was nothing new in
concept here. It was the collective implementation of all these
ideas within one corporation that was exceptional and paradigm-
shifting. The mystic manager re-established, remade, remodeled
the old notions. The rigidity of the chain of command was
replaced by the flexibility of teamwork and group-centered leadership all directed toward sustainable communities. The fabric of
economic society was challenged.

There was a globalness about this time and place of the mystic
manager. The outwardly small changes in this corporation would
stretch to their potential, explode, and re-create themselves into
massive and permanent shifts impacting the total business environment. Each thing, each change, each small shift was recognized as part of the larger whole. And, ultimately, what happened
in this business environment reflected in education, reflected in

government, and, reflected in the society as a whole. The Mystic Management was the new frontier of community building.

Business was the springboard to other areas. Business technology was being used to plan, direct, organize, and evaluate the community of humankind, the consummate organization. Business textbooks began to map out entire sections on Community Building Strategy. The mystic manager understood that what happens in one person reflects in another person, and another person, and another person. The mystic manager understood that community could be built by capturing and molding just one fuzzy piece of the human hologram.

Part III

The dream stuff stretched and I had that terrifying falling sensation. I came down hard on a linoleum floor next to an old maple kitchen table. I grazed the table as I fell and a small book landed in my lap: *The Mystic Manager, Qualities and Characteristics.* I had become a part of the dream; I was no longer a passive observer.

Still amidst that stretchy dream stuff, I opened the book. The dedication was simple: "Toward an effort to move from the traditional business world's concept of the P*R*O*F*I*T of exploitation, to the new business community's concept of the P*R*O*P*H*E*T of sustainability. Toward the acceptance, dissemination and implementation of a Mystic Management on the Earth."

I was stimulated by the juxtaposition of "profit" and "prophet." I recognized this as the crux of the new paradigm; this was the shift toward the new model of sustainability. With the book still open to the dedication I thought about what this might mean. Maybe a Mystic Management would look at nature in a new way. Maybe a tree could be appreciated for its value as a living thing rather than its value as a replaceable resource. Maybe the mystic manager leaves the tree alone and develops a new technology altogether. Maybe the Mystic Management goes beyond sustainability toward a new dimension of physical reality creating.

At this point myriad thoughts whispered through my head as if spoken through the very fibers of my imagination. "Imagine such a shift of vision," said the soft female voice. "Imagine a conversion of energy from the economics of industrialization to the synergy of mind, body, and spirit linked in a global conscious system. Imagine the ultimate information system beginning as a single strand of cosmic stuff pushing against imagination to create the reality of a collective togetherness, a collective conscious. Imagine such a reality for the Earth." The inner whisper trailed off and my consciousness again focused on the Mystic Management.

I could sense that the leadership of a Mystic Management would set the systems and sub-systems of all things into a totally compatible order. This would represent a shift to a management for sustainability where, for example, economic systems would operate in harmony with environmental systems. It would be a movement from the false magic of the myth of inexhaustibility to the mature reality of nurturing for perpetuity. A mystic leadership would seek the constant harvest, the long-term solutions.

Christian focused away from the dream journal pages running through his head. The night air had turned chilly and he abandoned the patio for the comfort of his favorite living room chair, stopping on his way to tuck in the kids. His thoughts were still with that first dream, "That dream with its hints of the Mystic Management sure had a dramatic impact on me. I knew immediately that I would need to pursue the dream of a Mystic Management. I would somehow need to make that dream a reality." He envisioned himself as the Mystic Manager, and Used Water Works as the corporation. Together they would become the role models for society, a society poised and ready for positive and dramatic change.

Christian was thinking he ought to give his Dad a call to discuss this Mystic Management business in detail. Phillip's voice immediately popped into his head, "Why use the phone, son."

"Good grief, Dad, you startled me," thought Christian. "I am definitely not used to this mind-link think stuff. Have you been listening in the whole time?"

"Of course not. Your telepathy link opened just this minute. Anyway, what's up?"

"I've been reviewing that first dream again and I think it's time to do something with that Mystic Management stuff. I have a very strong feeling that it's time for me to take action, to become the mystic manager, if you will."

"Well," said Phillip, "perhaps we should get together and develop a blueprint. I know your mother is anxious to see you and the family. I don't have anything going on for the next few days, the weather is great and we're really in the mood for a drive. If we leave here tomorrow morning around ten o'clock, we can be on your doorstep by six-thirty or so. Ask Sally what she thinks of our coming."

Without getting up from his chair, Christian yelled in the direction of the kitchen, "Sally! Sally! I've got Dad inside my head and he wants to know if it would be okay if he and Mom came tomorrow for a few days? Dad and I need to do some brainstorming."

Sally stuck her head around the corner so she could eyeball Christian and said, "The kids will be thrilled; I think it's a great idea. I suppose using the phone so your mom and I could get in on the conversation would too common for you Eyespellian types." Before Sally stopped laughing the phone rang. She and Jo finalized the plans while Christian and Phillip finished up with their Mystic Management business for the evening.

Christian went to bed that evening with that sugar plum feeling. He could hardly wait for his parents' arrival the next evening. He finally fell asleep hoping for a prophetic dream to add to the materials that he and Phillip would be synthesizing in less than twenty-four hours. Christian was not disappointed. He awoke about four in the morning to carefully record the dream he labeled *Systemic Change*.

The Second Dream—Systemic Change
(June 6, 2032)

My garden was in serious trouble. Several of my favorite plants were being attacked by insects. The insects were sucking the life out of the flowers, bushes and trees. I immediately referred to my gardening encyclopedia and under the heading of "systemic insecticide," I read, "…systemic insecticides are those that are applied to the leaves or soil, are absorbed and circulated within the plant, killing harmful sucking pests."

How interesting I thought, "With the application of a systemic, the plant itself becomes the cure for its own disease. The insects, detecting no change, feed themselves into oblivion."

The dream stuff stretched and I turned from the gardening book and instantly found myself, bigger-than-life-size, atop the Used Water Works headquarters building with a huge sprinkling can filled with some unknown and powerful-smelling concoction. I carefully angled the can slightly backward and toward myself so as to not accidentally sprinkle the rooftop. As I gingerly approached one edge of the building's roof, I leaned out a little, looked down, and saw what must have been a one-storey-high, brown-glassed bottle.

The bottle was lying on its side, cap off and label up. An ever so slight breeze brought that same powerful sprinkling can odor from the uncapped neck of the bottle to my nostrils. I stretched a little further in order to read the label. Across the top, in heavy black print, I could make out the words: "Systemic Change."

Before proceeding, I carefully scrutinized the rest of the label. There was a warning printed in red script on the very bottom, "Harmful or fatal if absorbed through the left side of the brain; keep away from all logic." The middle portion of the label contained what I was looking for, instructions on what to do atop a corporate building with a very large sprinkling can of Systemic Change.

Momentarily distracted, I looked up. In that fraction of a second, the dream stuff changed again and I found myself normal size, sitting under a tree, and in a very lucid conversation about organizational and societal change with someone who identified herself as the Mystic Manager.

She said: "A major error in dealing with problems of organizational change is to disregard the systemic properties of the organization and to confuse individual change with modifications in organizational variables."

I gently squeezed the end of my chin between by thumb and the side of my pointer-finger and said in my most academic tone, "I think I know what you are getting at. If the insects recognized that the plant was different once treated with the systemic insecticide, they simply would not eat it. They could continue to live on the plant, to coexist with the plant; they would merely have to stop sucking the life out of it!"

As I looked up to get a reaction to my brilliant insight, the dream stuff shifted suddenly and I again stretched bigger than life, finding myself, sprinkling can in hand, back atop the headquarters building. I tipped the can, soaking the rooftop, sides, interior, and grounds of the corporate headquarters with "Systemic Change." I then held the can high over my head and soaked myself in a shower of that same "concepticide."

By the time Christian finished recording his dream he was ecstatic and wanted to shake the whole family awake to share his excitement. He barely managed to contain himself as he ran from the bedroom and silently slid across the shiny kitchen floor in his bare socks. "I wish Dad was here now."

"I am," came the soft reply.

"There you've gone and done it again; you've scared me half to death. I still don't get what, exactly, turns this telepathy thing on or off. Anyway, what can I possibly do to calm my speeding mind until you get here? I just had the most amazingly prophetic dream. I've just soaked myself and corporate headquarters in something called Systemic Change Concepticide."

"Now there's a turn of a word. It sounds like something an Eyespellian would say." Phillip laughed aloud, "Concepticide, how horribly clever. I'm sure you'll share all the details with me, but I already know what it is we have to do."

Christian plopped down on a large pillow adorning the family room floor and just blurted out, "And what's that, oh brilliant one?"

"We simply have to figure out what's in that concepticide. See you tomorrow, actually later today. I've got another forty-five minutes of sleep coming and I'm going to grab it before it gets away. Speaking of getting away, to calm your mind just let it wander, don't try to tame it. What would you do if you were appointed Mystic Manager of the World starting tomorrow? Good night and I love you."

"You too, see you for dinner." Christian clasped his hands behind his head and thought, "Mystic Manager of the World, let me see…"

All manner of things came to Christian as he let his mind wander in search of Mystic Management puzzle pieces. There was the role of Used Water Works. Christian was certain that under a Mystic Management leadership it would become the ultimate cutting edge company and transcend current technology introducing a new era of environmentally perfect wastewater reclamation. World concern about water shortages and water pollution would come to an end. The world water well would become unpoisoned, and a new non-economics would evolve around an unlimited water resource. His vision was that this new system and its accompanying social implications would trigger community building as a focal point on the planet Earth. The availability and utilization of recycled water resources would be the take-off point of a new economic paradigm compatible with the planet and its peoples; recycled water would literally be Earth's concepticide.

Although the critical puzzle pieces would revolve around the tenets of a Mystic Management, tenets that he and his father had not yet fleshed out, Christian imagined that his campaign for a Mystic Management needed to get underway immediately. He pictured conducting meetings and issuing company-wide memoranda to inform every employee of U.W.W., from Chairman of the Board to janitor, about the new paradigm. He imagined a flurry of activity and open discussions of issues of creativity, sustainability, and the constant harvest. All ideas would be solicited to assure the success of this new long-term world-view. He would be so bold as to openly solicit ideas to save the planet. And he would even recommend that a two-day period be set aside for all employees in the corporation to brainstorm, brainstorm, brainstorm. He would prescribe a forum where the organization hierarchy was irrelevant, a forum where all ideas were welcome and necessary to the process. His intent would be to make sure that every employee be empowered in the new Mystic Management. Community building and compassion for the entire world would begin with U.W.W.

Christian imagined awesome results. So many people, ideas, and energy focused behind his positive leadership would spark like a laser, a laser warming up to project a piece of the human hologram. The dream stuff that he had been faithfully recording would begin to stretch into the real world and corporate America would be on the pathway to community building. The Mystic Management would be projected onto the fabric of society.

Christian pictured himself sharing and communicating his vision of Mystic Management for the remainder of his life lest it fall by the wayside as fad with little or no long-term durability. He would become the exemplary model of the new management. He would gradually widen his sphere of influence by giving talks to community organizations, church groups, colleges and universities, and corporate groups around the country. He would in every way possible bring the concept of Mystic Management into the public eye. He even hoped to do a talk show or two only unlike the poor fellow in his dream he would not let his new-found notoriety spoil the daydream. And what a daydream it was, a virtual storm within his brain. He had to laugh at his unbridled idealism. What was even funnier is that he believed it!

Still on the floor pillow Christian dozed off into another dream, a dream symbolizing his mounting passion for the Mystic Management. He took on an increased certainty of purpose that in itself was mystical.

The Third Dream—Colors of the Hologram
(June 6, 2032)

The mystic manager was lying in an open field gazing into the pale blue backdrop sky. She saw the red, white, and blue, the streets paved with gold, the yellow brick road; the *Scarlet Letter,* the graying of America, black power, purple mountains' majesty and amber waves of grain.

She saw the colors of America come into focus as her vision expanded beyond the borders of a manifest destiny. She saw the colors of America in an instantaneous panorama as she *looked to the sky from the Earth.*

Christian awakened and, as was his habit, immediately recorded his dream. This dream reminded him of a passage in his father's old attic manuscript. The excerpt was entitled "Planetaryvision." It began: "And in the real world, a man *looked to the Earth from the sky* and he saw the colors of the whole Earth in an instantaneous panorama from outer space." The reference was to an American astronaut reflecting upon his feelings from space during an Apollo Mission. "Community already exists," thought Christian, "We just have to be able to see it." He dropped back to sleep, pen still in hand.

Christian had taken the day off from work intent on gathering all of his materials and thoughts for his father's arrival. Six-thirty finally came and his parents pulled in the driveway right on schedule. Making few bones about their desire to get on with their work, Christian and Phillip were almost immediately dismissed with some healthy kidding and finger shaking by Jo, Sally, and the kids. Sally said, "We're going out to dinner and to a movie; you two get to go to the study with no dinner. Because we love you, we might bring something back for you. If you really get to starving, there's plenty of good stuff in the fridge." Within minutes Christian and Phillip were busy trying to figure out what was in that bottle of Systemic Change Concepticide.

They decided to begin their Mystic Management work in the study. It was a very peaceful room on the second floor. It overlooked a steep back yard hill going up perhaps two stories higher than the house itself. You could almost reach out the window and touch the hemlocks, pines, and spruces that climbed the steep bank, as if holding branches so as not to fall backwards into the yard below. Inside, the furnishings were organic, made exclusively from naturally fallen pine logs hewn into intricate and unique designs. There were cushions to ease the body and many pastel fabrics and drawings placed around the room to ease the mind. There was a ficus tree in one corner trying to reach the heights of the cathedral ceiling, its huge beams, matte-finished steel plates and lag bolts holding up the whole thing. On a table near the ficus was a small dish fountain, bringing into the room the sound of the out-of-doors.

Phillip and Christian sat at the round table near the window overlooking the hill and yard. Phillip reached into his briefcase pulling out a stack of materials and placed them gently on the table. Christian went over to the desk, grabbed a different stack of papers and his dream journal and added them to the already substantial pile on the table. "Well that looks like everything," said Christian, "my dream journal and notes, your old manuscripts, journals, and other writings. Where do we start?"

Phillip reached into his briefcase again, this time bringing out a silken pouch. "Let's begin with a brief meditation." Carefully opening the pouch Phillip said, "This is the topaz we used at Cathedral Rock. Perhaps if we get things started our Eyespellian colleagues will help." Phillip gently placed the golden topaz double-pyramid on its side in the center of the table. Both he and Christian sat in silent meditation for several minutes. The entire room seemed to take on the golden glow of the topaz as the two men let their spirits wander the galaxies toward Eyespell.

Christian spoke first, "Are we ready to begin?"

Phillip nodded an enthusiastic, "Yes."

Both men heard a resounding "yes" within their psyches. They were in link with each other and with Eyespell. Their inner voices said, "Begin your work and we will interject where appropriate. As is the Eyespellian way, your creative thoughts are most important and we would not presume to dictate their exact direction." This psychic conference call left both Christian and Phillip mesmerized for several minutes before they were able to consciously attend to the task at hand, to define the tenets of the Mystic Management.

Phillip smiled and said, "Just about the time I think I'm used to these Eyespellian faculties, they take on new and interesting dimensions. I really had to laugh last night when you found yourself confused about how to turn your telepathy link on and off. Believe me, I am barely one step ahead of you. I didn't honestly expect a direct link with Eyespell this evening. Somehow I thought Cathedral Rock was a unique experience perhaps to be followed up by some later visit to the same site. Just for the sake of comfort, and to accomplish our task, let's use the spoken word along with our telepathy link."

The inner voice, now recognized as Leo, once again interjected, "Greetings to both of you. You have no idea how typically Eyespellian you are, Phillip. We more often than not do the same thing here; we love a good spoken conversation in spite of telepathic capabilities."

"Leo, yes of course, hello," said Phillip. "I am just this minute remembering that you were my teacher on Eyespell! I loved those lessons in the desert. I can't say I recall exactly what they were, but I remember loving all of it. I would be willing to bet some of it had to do with Mystic Management."

Christian kiddingly said, "All of that was before my time, I don't remember a thing."

"You'd be amazed what your soul remembers," played in Christian's head as if sung into his consciousness by a church choir, by several people.

"Wow, how many are on this 'call', Leo?"

"A bunch of us, now get to work, you two," said Leo with near laughter in his tone.

"Dad, the one thing that impresses me the most about our contact with Eyespell is how good the interactions always feel. There is never an unkind word or thought. I never feel chastised, criticized, or in any way made to feel uncomfortable or stupid."

"That's true. In my time of madness I remember thinking I was going completely crazy, yet my contact with Eyespellian images were always soothing and kind, they always abated my feelings of despair and panic. I'm not sure I ever pieced it together quite so clearly or consciously before. The bottom line is that my dignity has never been violated by anything Eyespellian, whether we're talking about our experience at Cathedral Rock or just holding the rose quartz specimen from my curio cabinet and thinking about the pink planet."

"Maybe that's the starting place for finding out what's in that systemic concepticide. One major ingredient must have to do with respect, dignity, compassion, and kindness. In any management scheme there should be no room for disrespecting others, belittling anyone, or being unkind. It seems to me that any unkindness would likely come back to haunt the perpetrator in the long run. Certainly if not in this life, then in the next. I've always believed that 'what goes around comes around,' it's a karma thing."

Leo piped in, "I can't believe how close you have come to a Mystic Management tenet we hold dear. We call it 'Karmic Kindness: What goes around comes around *and kindness is the only way*'. You've hit it exactly on the head. There are six Mystic Management principles and Karmic Kindness is number four."

"Dad, do you want to record this or would you like me to?"

"You do it, your dream journal is far prettier than this beat up old leather one." Phillip looked across the table at his son. He felt great hope for Earth's future.

"Okay then, principle number four, Karmic Kindness, what goes around comes around and kindness is the only way. I have a really nagging question, how do you suppose we could ever presume to convince managers, supervisors, leaders, or business types at any level to be kind?"

"We can't dictate kindness if that's what you mean, but we can, you can, provide the example. Remember your dream, it just takes one piece of the human hologram to create that which you seek. And already we have six pieces, you, me, Sally, Jo and your children. Let's get the message out there and see what happens."

"If I might add something here," said Leo, "on Eyespell thoughts and light create reality. That's what we're all about and that's what you're all about. The Eyespell Experiment was no accident. The energy of the two of you on Earth adds unique possibilities. Look at the example you might provide; don't forget, you are of Eyespell."

"Well then, let's open our minds and get creative," said Christian.

"Creative, now there's a word that keeps popping up," added Phillip.

Christian immediately expanded on the idea. "Last night when I let my mind wander, trying to quiet my excitement a little, the significance of creativity kept coming into my thoughts. In my imaginary mystic managing, creativity held a place of critical importance. Not only were all ideas welcome, but necessary. And that meant all ideas, all the time, and from everybody willing to contribute. In fact, as I pictured the new Used Water Works paradigm under my direction, a primary trait in everything we did was creativity."

"What I like about what you're saying is that there is an implied community aspect to the creativity you propose. It seems as though everyone is involved in some way in the process of management. It seems to be a collaborative effort."

Leo interrupted, "Not surprisingly you've done it again, you've hit another Mystic Management principle right on. The principle is Collaborative Creativity, and is the first tenet. It promotes a management style that examines all ideas. Everybody's ideas are welcome all the time."

Christian, wincing a little, said, "As a manager in the real world, hypotheticals aside, I balk at this notion the more I think about it. It's a wonderful idea in theory, but I'm afraid it could put us out of business in practice. While kindness might have personal costs and demand psychological realignment, this creativity notion could become so time consuming that productivity would suffer beyond salvation. After all, time is money and this process could easily get out of hand. I even thought in my mind wanderings of last evening about having a two-day brainstorming session. That was only two days, and the cost would probably be prohibitive. How could you possibly make creativity work all the time and involve all people?"

Both Christian and Phillip sat silent listening to lots of mind chatter that they were unable to interpret in any meaningful way. Finally Leo spoke, "You've certainly set off a debate here. Everybody has an opinion;

it's quite lively and delightful. We have tremendous latitude here on Eyespell on the issue of creativity and how much time it might take; we do not have an economic system based on tradeoffs among limited or scarce resources. We do not juxtapose time and dollars against performance. In fact, it would be fair to say we don't consider the economics of anything, ever. We do not have money and we do have unlimited time within which to accomplish anything we desire. We literally combine thought and light to produce whatever physical reality we want."

"And I thought I was creative," quipped Christian.

Phillip sat squinting as if in bright sunlight, shaking his head slowly up and down deeply in thought. He finally said, "We can't give up on this collaborative creativity idea. It's too important; I think we need to put the concept out there. We need to encourage everyone to incorporate their natural creativity into their work at all times. While I may be Eyespellian, I've spent sixty years on this planet and if I've learned nothing else it's to go as far as you can with an idea. I've learned to 'push the envelope' as my colleagues are so fond of saying. This is where new paradigms live, at the edge and away from that which is logical and practical based on current practice. Significant change begins as a matter of faith, not logic. We certainly don't want to put you out of business, Christian, but what can we do short of that? You can and should brainstorm about how to best enliven and incorporate Collaborative Creativity into daily work. What would have to be different to allow this concept into your daily business routine?"

"I think I see what you mean," said Christian, "do what you can. Don't say 'no' to an idea, rather say 'yes, we can accomplish the maximum possible within our constraints.' If I can't afford two days of creativity go for two minutes or whatever is allowable given the constraints. We need to learn to trade off more effectively. If a value is placed on creativity and, therefore, the ideas of every person in the organization, then there is the starting place, something to begin with. If creativity has little or no value, it will never be considered part of the optimum mix of viable alternatives. This is exciting."

"So, how can we write it down?" asked Phillip. "Try this. 'The first tenet of Mystic Management is Collaborative Creativity, which means placing a value on creativity and welcoming creative ideas from all members of the organization. Collaborative Creativity acknowledges and supports creativity within appropriate time and dollar constraints, and those constraints are never to allow the time for creativity to fall to zero.' "

"It sounds a little clumsy, but I've got it down in my journal. So, what's next? So far our Systemic Change Concepticide has two ingredients, Karmic Kindness and Collaborative Creativity. And now we should add a teaspoonful of, of what?"

"Perhaps a teaspoonful of smart alec?" chimed in Leo.

"He's always been a problem child," said Phillip laughing aloud.

"And you, Phillip, the perfect child. Do you realize you are about forty years late for dinner? I believe you were supposed to be home in 1992." Everyone had a healthy laugh. Leo continued, "I find your conclusion extremely interesting. I cannot remember ever having to compromise or settle for a portion of anything. We are accustomed to reaching consensus and then creating what we've decided upon. While you are trying to define Mystic Management for the Earth, I need to think about new strategies for solving the problems evolving on Eyespell as a result of our intimate contact with you through the Eyespell Experiment"

"We don't understand, what problems?" said Christian and Phillip simultaneously.

"I honestly don't mean to put you off, but I think we should concentrate right now on finishing up the Mystic Management principles. I can assure you that both of you are and will continue to be in the thick of Eyespellian matters, now and in the future." Leo reached inside their minds and calmed their curiosity in much the same way Phillip had calmed Christian and others close to him over the years. Christian and Phillip were left with the understanding that all would unfold as necessary.

Christian's reaction was immediate, "I trust you enough, Leo, to let things unfold in their natural course. How often is there trust among individuals in organizations today? How often is there a mutual respect for the unique talents and abilities of every member of the organization? There needs to be a shared management and group-centered leadership. In my experience, position means power and power means autocratic direction-giving often with total disregard for the welfare and needs of the individuals being directed. Too often there is lip service paid to the idea of empowerment; it looks good on paper and makes for a good vision statement. The reality of empowering others, however, is far too threatening for most executives. It signals to them loss of control, loss of power, and most assuredly a perceived loss of profits. They feel that people are our most important resource as long as the idea isn't carried too far, as long as people aren't actually empowered. I'm afraid there's too much ego in our leaders."

"Turn that around," suggested Phillip. "Balance the ego between the executives and other employees. Reduce the hierarchy and see what you get."

"Exactly," said Leo. "It's the Mystic Management tenet we call Ego Empowerment. It speaks to our rule by consensus. The orientation is mutually-directed rather than self-or other-directed. It is the second tenet."

"I hate playing the devil's advocate," said Christian, "but here again I see a problem. I don't think you'd get much open disagreement with the idea of empowering employees. There's a lot of conversation out there about the benefits and virtues of empowered employees. Besides it sounds silly to be against it, you would sound like a tyrant, an autocratic dictator, a typical corporate manager, I'm afraid. So everybody says they're for empowerment. The human is the most important resource, right? Look at companies that embrace a management strategy of customer service, continuous improvement, and employee empowerment. Customer service is costly, but essential. Continuous improvement saves money and improves quality. Employee empowerment is costly, time consuming, and threatening to the autocrats. The typical outcome is to dump that part of the system. What you are left with is customer service and continuous improvement in a downsized, autocratic, stress-producing, inhumane system. 'Do more with less' is not the same as empowering employees. This is a deadly paradigm."

"So Christian, tell us how you really feel," said Phillip.

"Good grief, I sound as crazed as some of those old manuscripts lying there on the table. I'm beginning to sound like you did forty years ago, Dad."

"It's nice to know we get worked up about the same things. So, what are you going to write down in that journal of yours?"

"Let's see, the second tenet of the Mystic Management is Ego Empowerment, the honest ability to respect and value the unique talents of every person in the organization. Ego Empowerment demands a legitimate shared management and group-centered leadership. Delegation is not synonymous with downsize."

"We're not doing too badly," said Phillip. "So far the only concept that will put you out of business is unbridled creativity. A little less downsizing is perhaps expensive but still within the range of sustainability and reasonable profits, if not a profit maximizing strategy. I think corporations simply need a little encouragement from a self-confident leadership."

"Yes, indeed. Self-confidence would go a long way in reducing dependency on authority, power, or any potential misuse of position. I think it's up to top management, all management for that matter; actually it's up to everybody in the organization to go the extra step to encourage others. Giving others encouragement is a wonderful way to dispel one's own insecurities. And of course it's a positive circle: giving, encouragement, feelings of security, more giving, more encouragement, more security, and on and on. It would be like Karmic Kindness on steroids. Does anyone have a name for it?"

"I do," said Leo. "We call it Gentle Generosity."

"Okay then, that bottle of Systemic Change Concepticide so far has four ingredients. Let me recap, no pun intended." Phillip hung his head in mock shame at his horrible joke. "All right, all right, I'm sorry."

"You know, Phillip, a terrible joke like that sent via mind link can cause our whole planet to mind-crash. You should really be more considerate," chuckled Leo.

"Anyway, the four we've discovered so far include: Collaborative Creativity, Ego Empowerment, Gentle Generosity and Karmic Kindness. Leo, we are assuming that the order in which we've come up with the principles has not posed a problem. Are we giving each tenet its proper due?"

"Absolutely, the order of discovery is no problem. It's the process that's important. There are two others yet to describe."

"Got it," said Christian. "It always fascinates me how good ideas are so interrelated. It's as if everything were just one thing. It's the whole systems/sub-systems thing."

"And there you have captured the sixth principle, Systems Sensitivity. All things are, indeed, interconnected and what happens in one part ultimately affects all other parts. What were you thinking, Phillip?" asked Leo.

"Oh, just that that's how change occurs. Progress, whether it be technological, psychological, or spiritual for that matter, is one thing linked to another in an infinite series, an infinite continuum, a circle. No matter where you impact the circle all of it vibrates. It might be like taking past, present, and future and hooking them together. One would always lead to the other in some non-linear expression of oneness."

"Your Eyespellian nature has not dwindled a bit," interjected Leo.

"Okay, I'm writing this down," said Christian. "Collaborative Creativity, Ego Empowerment, Gentle Generosity, Karmic Kindness, Systems Sensitivity, and one more. I fear we are doing this the hard way, but we are doing it. Is this the way, Leo?"

"Any way that gets the job done is the way. There is no rule suggesting that there is one best way to do anything. There might be a thousand ways, all valuable. How do you feel about what's going on, Christian?"

"I feel fine, we are getting there. In fact I feel great and appreciate that you are not simply dictating the Mystic Management principles and expecting me to follow them with none of my personal energy invested. You seem to have great tolerance for multiple styles. I sense here the last principle we are looking for. And what do we call it, Leo?"

"Inclusive Integrity, there is no one best style that covers all situations all the time. What's important is achieving the goal."

Phillip popped in, "So how does our complete list of ingredients read?"

"Try this," said Christian putting the finishing touches on his journal entry. "The six tenets of the Mystic Management are: (1) Collaborative Creativity, (2) Ego Empowerment, (3) Gentle Generosity, (4) Karmic Kindness, (5) Inclusive Integrity, and (6) Systems Sensitivity."

The glow from the golden topaz faded and the study returned to its more earthly hue. "They're gone," said Phillip, "Let's raid the refrigerator."

CHAPTER 16

$$\blacktriangledown$$

JOE SENT ME (EYESPELL)

Antonio awoke with a start. He was having another nightmare about the Earth-time. His Earth experience had proved to be the most psychologically difficult of the Eyespellian re-entrants. He still carried with him in vivid detail the Earth memories and feelings that had led to his suicide, his giving up in the walnut grove. His time on Eyespell did little to dissipate his feelings of despair. The feelings of hopelessness that Antonio had felt on Earth had returned with renewed intensity six months after re-entry. The feelings were manifesting even in his physical appearance. Some days, Antonio looked almost like the gaunt field worker who had died on Earth in 1992. All of this was an extension of the internal Earth-plane vibrational leakage initiated by the Earth-time memories.

Antonio's nightmares on Eyespell created havoc with the planet cell-matrix. When he dreamed about the harshness of his Earth experience, it caused the typical environmental breakdowns. There were unexpected and severe thunder and lightning storms, small cracks in the planet's surface, minor landslides, and so on. These manifestations of Earth-plane vibrational leakage sometimes occurred within a range of several miles from Antonio's physical presence

It was imperative to find a way to psychologically soothe Antonio. Due to the character of the Earth vibration causing the discomfort, typical Eyespellian techniques simply did not work. Mind-link therapy proved almost useless. It was hypothesized that a more Earth-based psychotherapy was necessary, fight fire with fire. This was a unique problem for Eyespell demanding a unique solution. It was unclear which of the Elders should handle it, under which crystal charge might such an Earth-type therapy be most successful?

It was finally decided that Antonio would best benefit from the combined vibrations of three of the Elders. The Elders with the crystal charges for unconditional love, oneness and energy directed their energies toward Antonio. Myana with the pink crystal of love, Gracina the clear crystal of oneness, and Matthew the red crystal of energy began to work with Antonio's vibrations. Antonio's need peaked during the forty-year vigil when the Eldersix were already in constant mind-link trying to maintain the light-skew of the planet as a whole. This made the task more complex than it normally would have been. Fortunately a crystal charge could be focused toward more than a single purpose at a time. Antonio's pain and the planet's pain were, indeed, interconnected and Antonio's healing was first and foremost a labor of unconditional love.

Antonio was summoned to the Council Chamber and, by an unprecedented decision, was invited physically into the twenty-seventh ring with the Elders. The risk of mixed vibrations fragmenting the crystal charge was balanced by the seriousness of Antonio's condition. He was seated on a large velvety pillow and instructed to sit spine straight, cross-legged in the traditional meditative position.

Myana stood facing Antonio and pointed the pink tourmaline crystal's saber-light at his heart area. Gracina stood at his back and to the left pointing the white light at his head. Matthew also stood at his back, equidistant to the right of Gracina and directed the red rays of his crystal, like guy wires, touching Antonio's shoulders and knees. The three elders formed a double pyramid of light around Antonio with one light point to the north and the other light point to the south. Antonio was literally suspended in the aura of pyramid-light.

The Elders did not probe Antonio's mind, but rather let him fall asleep within the healing rays of the three crystals. They maintained the light around Antonio and meditated affirming, "Antonio's Earth-time nightmares are healed by his mind's own inner workings, finding the necessary Earth-bound solution." They repeated the affirmation over and over like a mantra. The Elders maintained their vigil and unobtrusively watched, continuing to repeat the affirmation as Antonio began to dream about his experiences on Earth.

Antonio, in this dream of the Earth-time, was sitting on a small wooden crate in front of a run-down store just off the highway. He was on his lunch break. He was thirsty and hungry and had no money. "Today is Tuesday," he thought. "I get paid on Wednesday and I'll be able to eat well through Friday. Next week will be the same. What I really want is to simply die peacefully against a tree."

Even though they were not in mind-link with Antonio, the vibration of hopelessness projected by Antonio's dream was so intense that the three Elders found tears beginning to form at the corners of their eyes. In Council and still in mind-link, this could be extremely dangerous to the light-skew. However, Myana's unconditional love was so powerful that the tears turned to droplets of joy for the sheer love of Antonio. The Elders continued their vigil over Antonio, careful that their own emotions did not intermingle with his dream.

Antonio's dream continued in the same vein for a long while. His Earth existence had been harsh in almost every respect, from his birth in 1972 to his death in 1992. He did not have a safe or pleasant childhood. While his parents loved him they felt guilty that in their poverty they could do almost nothing for him. All hope for the future was lost with the death of his mother. Antonio was sent to live with relatives. The dream of this

Earth-time was a vivid nightmare reflecting the living nightmare it had been. Image after image of his despair and hopelessness passed through Antonio's brain. Then it happened.

In the dream, Antonio was sitting under a walnut tree several hours before his death on Earth in 1992. An elderly gentleman with hand on cane worked his way to Antonio and sat cross-legged facing him.

"You know the problem, now, don't you son?" He cackled an old man cackle, slapped his knee and said, "Yep, that's it son. Life's a bitch and then you die."

Antonio, unable to raise his head, whispered, "And you bother to come here to mock my death. Why?"

"Well, son, it's simple, you need a new coping strategy. I don't suppose you ever read Dr. Freud, hey?"

Antonio laughed, almost, indicating, "It should be fairly obvious that I've never read anything!"

"Well, there you are then. Let me tell you a story about Dr. Freud and a guy named Joe. When I'm finished you'll be able to figure out why you feel so bad and get rid of all that negative mental baggage. Understand what I'm saying?"

"Not really, I just want to die."

"Well son, that's not exactly true; you're just trying to re-enter."

"Re-enter? Old man, go away and let me die."

"Well now, I can't do that. At least not until I tell you that story I promised. Anyway, this Dr. Freud says that the Ego is the manager of the mind. And I say the Ego watches the world out there from a control booth located directly behind your eyes. This Ego character sees what you see and experiences what you experience. Unfortunately, he has nowhere to hide when you get feeling this bad about things. In fact, in your whole life, when you've been laughed at, rejected, felt confused, ignored, not worthy, and not loved, this Ego fellow has been expected to absorb all the pain and cope. He is expected to continue to manage your life effectively. Get my drift so far, son?"

"No, and you're holding up my death. Go away!"

"I already told you, I can't do that. Here's your problem. There's a relationship between all the hurt in your life and your inability to develop effective coping strategies. That is, strategies that will relieve the pain and allow you to go on with your life. Now, clearly, you've failed in this regard; you want to die. Anyway, not only aren't you coping, but you've also got this bag of psychological junk weighing you down. The bag is so heavy you can't get up. You'll just have to sit under this old walnut tree and die! Unless, unless you use 'Joe'."

"Okay, old man. I can see you're not going to leave me to die until you have your say. And, I must admit, I am curious. Who is Joe?"

"Well now, that's better. Okay then. It's not exactly who Joe is, but what Joe is. It's actually called 'Joe Sent Me,' and it's a coping strategy designed to keep the Ego intact and in touch with your present moment, in touch with what's going on right now. Joe is designed to keep you from psychologically protecting yourself into continued illness."

"What does that mean?"

"Here's the way it works, Antonio. Each time in your Earth-life, your Earth-time, that you could not cope with something in the outside world, your Ego, your 'mind manager,' called on the 'mind team' for help. Now the mind team is composed of two other fellows, the Id and the Superego. One thing is for sure, they are very reliable; they always answer the Ego's call for help."

"But, it's not that simple. The mind team always operates indirectly and secretly. They travel deep within your psyche and make some secret deal, a secret tradeoff, with somebody in there; we're not sure what or who. But the Ego has to live with the final outcome of the deal. The Ego gets instructions about how to behave, how to cope, in order to survive a particularly bad moment in time. Now, mind you, the Ego does not complain. Whatever coping strategy the mind team comes up with is good enough. The alternative is, purely and simply, insanity."

"The trouble really starts after years and years of secret tradeoffs. In your case, Antonio, twenty years of tradeoffs. The bottom line is that you end up stuck with all kinds of neurotic behaviors that were originally designed to help preserve your sanity. The problem is that once the mind team makes a deal or trades something off, it is never traded back, even once a particular coping strategy outlives its usefulness. Take you, for example. While there was a time when your nightmares actually helped preserve your sanity, now they are in the way, no longer useful. Unfortunately, the Ego cannot take the initiative to correct the situation because the Ego never knew what was traded off in the first place."

Antonio interrupted, "I see, I think I know what you mean. Say some kid is being laughed at all the time and it gets pretty painful. The mind team might make a tradeoff and the kid starts wetting the bed instead of feeling the pain and going nuts. Is that it?"

"Exactly, my son, exactly! Now where the problem arises is if that same kid is still wetting the bed twenty years later! There's no way the young adult will figure out the connection between bed wetting and being laughed at as a kid. So, the kid could go through intensive psychotherapy that might take years, or he could use 'Joe Sent Me.'"

"Antonio, you don't need the nightmares any more; you have already achieved re-entry; they're a useless, leftover strategy. I think Joe can help you get rid of those nightmares you are having that are also disrupting the cell-matrix on Eyespell."

"Anyway, this is how Joe works. You don't need to make any conscious connections between your nightmares and anything that happened to you in Earth-time. Just sit back and admit to yourself that all kinds of inappropriate strategies may still be operating within your head as a result of 'psyche tradeoff residue.' "

"Okay, now visualize yourself in a crisis situation. Your Ego jumps up from the chair in the control booth behind your eyes. He starts running around frantically inside your head waving his arms and yelling. You are totally unable to cope. Imagine that you are on the verge of a nervous breakdown. In desperation, the Ego runs as fast as he can toward the back of your head, looking for the mind team, searching for help."

"After much mind ranting and raving, visualize yourself slamming to an abrupt stop against a thick wooden door with a slide opening of prohibition era ilk. See yourself bang on the door as hard as you can with both fists. When they pull back the slide, and they will, just say 'Joe Sent Me.' You will not be allowed in the back room, but they'll ask: 'Yeah, so what, whad'ya want buddy?' Then you hit'em with, 'Joe said the deal's off! Trade back, now!' And, poof! No more nightmares. And that's how Joe works. You don't need to know the specifics. Just keep going back to the door; keep trading back until you start to feel better. And that's it."

Antonio, instantly healed through his dream, leapt up from under the walnut tree, his six-foot-three-inch muscular frame dwarfing the old man. Antonio laughed heartily and asked the old man, "Do you know how to get to Eyespell from here?"

In the Council Chamber, Antonio shifted into a peaceful sleep. Myana, Gracina, and Matthew maintained their watch until Antonio awakened of his own accord. He seemed in tune with the planet's cell-matrix. With Antonio's permission the Elders established a mind-link and the dream exposing the distressing details of Antonio's Earth-time were reviewed in detail. Antonio left the Council Chamber a much more settled Antonio than the young man of just a day ago.

The Eyespell Experiment, while couched in the sense of hopelessness of the youth of America and climaxing in four apparent suicides, never intended to put any of the participants through the seemingly horrible existence Antonio had experienced on Earth. Somehow the Earth fusion had gone awry. Eyespell had no indication that such a dark-skewed life would be in store for any of the Earth-fused souls. In fact, until the link with Antonio's dream no one was aware of his plight. Any hint of such suffering and Kathryn would have had her way, the Eyespell Experiment would simply have been cancelled. An even more puzzling issue, however, was why hadn't Kathryn reported the extreme despair Antonio had been feeling? If the Council had known, perhaps early re-entry might have been possible. They needed to speak with Kathryn to review the Earth-lives of the other participants and find out why she did not disclose Antonio's very real despair while on Earth.

CHAPTER 17

▼

A QUESTION OF TIME (EYESPELL)

The Elders called Kathryn to the Council Chamber. They explained their curiousity about why she had not reported the negative aspects of Antonio's Earth-life in her mind links. Leo began, "Kathryn, as you know, Myana, Gracina, and Matthew have worked closely with Antonio to help relieve some of his vibrational discomfort. In their dream-link review with Antonio, many aspects of his Earth-life that we had been unaware of were brought to our attention. This was especially true with regard to his times of extreme difficulty and hardship. My question is, why don't any of your reports, verbal, written, or mind-linked, speak of the anguish Antonio went through on Earth?"

Kathryn looked bewildered, "I'm not sure what you mean, Leo."

"Let me recount two specific incidents for you. What about his being forced to leave home, and his sometimes going days without adequate nourishment?"

"I know nothing of this. And, certainly, if I did, it would be in my reports along with a suggestion to halt the Eyespell Experiment. As you know, I was not exactly in favor of the idea in the first place. If early re-entry to Eyespell was deemed too risky, I could have rescued Antonio myself on Earth. In fact, I most certainly would have done just that. I could have had him come live with me on the pretense of saving a homeless child that no one wanted. I would not have needed to explain anything Eyespellian to Antonio until the re-entry window appeared. And by then, he would have developed an intuitive sense of Eyespell and our role on Earth."

Leo knew Kathryn was telling the truth in spite of her somewhat edgy attitude. There had never been occasion to suspect any Eyespellian of not telling the truth. And yet, here was this mysterious inconsistency. Did Antonio suffer as he said? How did Kathryn somehow not perceive all that took place?

"Kathryn, I apologize for putting you through this kind of conversation. I do not doubt your integrity; however, something is wrong. None of the written records you have provided, or the mental recollections you've shared about Antonio's Earth-time, parallel his experience as he himself recalls it. While you state that there was some hardship as a field worker and, certainly, much identity crisis, you indicate nothing of a lifetime of severe struggle. It's as if you're describing an altogether different life."

Kathryn thought a few minutes about what Leo was saying and then asked, "May I review Antonio's dream? I would like to see the life he portrays versus the one I have recorded."

Leo was able to accommodate Kathryn's request easily, through an agreed upon mind-link with Matthew. Antonio's dream and the spontaneous evolution of "Joe Sent Me" were examined in every detail by Kathryn.

Finally, she broke mind-link and spoke, "What I just experienced through Matthew may help explain why there is such inconsistency between what I reported and what Antonio actually experienced on Earth. In reviewing Antonio's dream and life through Matthew it seemed it was not the first time I'd seen the negative events. It was as if I remembered them simultaneous to reviewing the dream supposedly for the first time. I suspect our problem is one of Earth-time versus Eyespell-time. Time on Earth, as we know, is linear, whereas time on Eyespell is, well, simply time. When The Eyespell Experiment participants Earth-fused in the red light, and were born on the Earth, they were immersed in linear time for the predetermined twenty years of the experiment. The events of the twenty Earth years appear linear and sequential in the participants' minds. For example, when Antonio recalls his Earth-time, his memory stretches from conception to twenty years. The events in his Earth-life follow a specific sequence from beginning to end."

"I did not Earth-fuse," said Kathryn, "I went to Earth out-of-body and manifested my physical being once there. I did not, however, manifest in linear time. There is no guarantee that my recording or experiencing anything on Earth was represented in a linear fashion. It is possible that I have selected memories and events from Antonio's total soul life, regardless of where or when those events actually happened. Or it could be a matter of what Earth psychologists call selective perception and retention, seeing and hearing only what one wants to see and hear regardless of the reality of a situation. Maybe Antonio's experience was simply too painful for me to assimilate."

Kathryn continued, "While I certainly manifested in linear space, I did not manifest in linear time. So, my memories could be like random selections from a laser disk. Without a specific point of reference, there would be no way to tell past from present from future, or, for that matter, if the event actually existed in time at all, or was only a creation of the imagination."

Leo felt a sudden sense of urgency; he needed to talk to Melissa, Nancy, and Pete. He looked at Kathryn and said, "Maybe you were right all along; maybe we Eyespellians should mind Eyespell and leave the rest of the galaxy alone regardless of our well-meaning motives. In this Experiment we seem to have overlooked a great deal. I hope we have not put our other children through such a difficult Earth-fusion due to our oversights."

Melissa arrived at the Council Chamber already telepathically informed of the concerns. Leo asked her to highlight some of her Earth-time experiences.

"Let me start in reverse, with my twentieth year," began Melissa. "I was in my junior year of college and I was a reporter for the school newspaper. Earth was a strange place in terms of learning; some of the dumbest people on the planet were actually in charge of learning. Forgive me for being judging. I realize it's a characteristic not becoming of an Eyespellian. But, planet Earth is a true contradiction when it comes to education."

Leo interrupted long enough to formally introduce Melissa's presentation to the Council. As she spoke he compared what Melissa was now saying to his notes from Kathryn on the time period being discussed. Again, there was inconsistency. For example, there was no mention in Kathryn's report about Melissa being editor of the school newspaper, or her disdain of the educational process. It was also apparent that Earth-plane vibrational leakage was manifesting in Melissa's subtle enjoyment of her judging attitude about Earth's educators. This became even more obvious as she continued.

" Learning in Earthlings, I noticed, becomes stagnated uncomfortably close to the time formal education begins. It's amazing. I'm certainly not opposed to formal education, although it is an archaic concept, but I think Earthlings would be substantially better off if they got their education without ever confronting an educator."

Melissa began to laugh hysterically at her joke. It took every ounce of self-control for Leo not to ask her to leave the Council Chamber. She was contaminating the light-skew. Again, Myana was able to soothe the imbalance with the comforting vibration of Unconditional Love. Leo was disturbed by his own momentary impatience and recognized, first hand, the true potential danger of this Earth-plane vibrational leakage, which could come from so many directions at once.

Melissa gathered her wits about her and continued, "Anyway, in order to make my point about these dumb educators, I wrote two pieces in the school newspaper. They were great. So great that I almost got expelled, except that those same educators were forced to uphold my First Amendment rights, freedom of speech and freedom of the press. In other words I could say and write whatever I wanted. And I did!"

Melissa, looking totally smug, inappropriately got in Leo's face and continued, "The first piece was absolutely a kick. I called it *The Parable of the Wheel*. Earth folks like to categorize, label, prioritize and rank everything, even teachers; oh excuse me, professors. Teachers teach in the lower grades and professors teach in colleges. See what I mean, they categorize everything. Anyway, the parable was inspired by this type of archaic, academic thinking. Not only was the term teacher relegated to the lower grades, and professor uplifted to the college and university level, but professors were ranked in an academic pecking order. I have to tell you by the way that the Earth term 'pecking order' is derived from observing behavioral patterns of one of Earth's absolutely, bottom-of-the-barrel, dumbest beasts—the chicken! I think it's just great irony that supposedly smart humans, professors, derive their status measure from observation of these dumbest of beasts. I'm sure some professors eat chickens; maybe we should eat professors!"

Melissa lost it again in a totally manic outburst of laughter. This time the Council was prepared, and already had her bathed in the soothing rose ray of unconditional love. However, Melissa was becoming more sarcastic with every recollection. She continued.

"Professors are ranked in four primary categories. There is the Lecturer or Instructor at the bottom, then the Assistant Professor, then Associate Professor, and Full Professor at the tippity top. Well, I thought such a ranking was disgusting. In fact, I thought it was rank."

The Council was hardly able to contain Melissa this time. It was as if she was possessed. Even though she managed to gain enough composure to continue, the Eldersix had her sealed in a vibrational vacuum chamber, taking no chances that this level of leakage might further escape into the planet cell-matrix.

"Wait, wait, listen to this. I wrote *The Parable of the Wheel*, and had it printed right smack-dab on the front page of the school newspaper. Here, mind-link it for yourselves.

The Parable of the Wheel

by

Melissa Commings

In a kingdom called Academia, there lived a populace ascendingly cast into Lecs (Lecturers), Assfessors (Assistant Professors), Socfessors (Associate Professors), and Old Farts (Full Professors). The Old Farts ruled and said it was good. The rest said nothing. And it was good.

A merchant brought a wheel down from the mountain one day for the Old Farts to spin upon. They liked it. They spun upon it most of the day and sometimes, far into the night.

Time and a little more gas passed, and the Old Farts decided it was not good in Academia. They were the only ones spinning. So, to keep the kingdom good, they slowly drew the Socfessors, Assfessors, and Lecs to the spokes and rim of the wheel, keeping only the hub for themselves.

God looked down upon Academia and decreed that it was selfish of the Old Farts to hoard the activity-of-the-hub (known as the hubbub). So, God created a huge wind. In the wind's fury, the wheel began to wobble, and everyone came crashing to the ground, landing on their behinds.

God, in his mercy, allowed the Old Farts to continue to rule Academia from "what" they landed on. And they are continuing to do so to this day.

The Council members and others present had no difficulty in understanding why Melissa was almost expelled. At best her parable was tacky. Again Melissa broke into a laughing fit, this time stomping her feet and slapping her hands almost uncontrollably against the tops of her thighs. Oblivious to her vibrational isolation, Melissa calmed slightly and continued her scenario on education.

"Well, that one really did it. Yes, sir, they were really buzzing in the halls, especially the Old Farts. It's really incredible. Most of them had what is called a "Ph.D." degree, a Doctor of Philosophy, a very big deal in educational circles (how big a deal depending upon where you got your degrees, of course)."

"I hope you're taking notes, Leo," said Melissa, "After all you're Eyespell's equivalent of an Old Fart." Again she began to laugh hysterically. Leo blushed a little. In everyone's recollection this was the first time an Elder had ever been insulted. It took every bit of energy from each light corridor to keep the planet cell-matrix intact. It seemed crucial, however, to allow Melissa to continue.

"Anyway, talk about dumb. Some of those folks running around with Ph.D.s, Doctors of Philosophy, never even took a philosophy course. How can you be a Doctor of Philosophy without a single course, not one credit, in philosophy? What about Doctors of Medicine and Doctors of Law? Do you suppose they don't have courses implied by their degree titles either? Idiots, one and all. Why is it so? Why don't they call it what it is?"

Melissa was actually screaming at this point. The Elders were prepared to remove her from the Council Chamber, out-of-body, to the fourth moon of Eyespell where Myana could concentrate the vibration of unconditional love around Melissa. If she were to continue in this state, surely both she and the light-skew would be permanently damaged. The cell-matrix would probably just break apart and Eyespell with it.

"Just one more story!" screamed Melissa. "Let me tell you about the second article I wrote for the school newspaper and I'll go to the fourth moon of my own accord."

The Council was surprised at her ability to read their thoughts in her manic condition. She was fully aware of their plans to remove her to the fourth moon. They intuitively felt it wise to grant her request and let her continue her story. Melissa sat down, exhausted, ankles crossed with the sides of her feet on the floor, her knees bent and off the ground. She looked more like a broken bunch of sticks than an Eyespellian. In a whisper of a voice, she continued.

"About a month after I wrote *The Parable of the Wheel,* I wrote my second brilliant article condemning academia. I called this one, *Mine's Longer Than Yours; A One Act Play.* It isn't actually a play; well, see for yourselves."

Mine's Longer Than Yours
by
Melissa Commings

The most serious error thwarting ethical educational leadership is that educators take themselves and their credentials much too seriously. They all too often lack the ability to laugh at themselves. It seems that the all-too-serious attitude of the sometimes pipe-smoking, patched-sleeved, academician is counter-productive.

I once read a story about these two newly-introduced professors openly sparring at a meeting about whose credentials were better. In fact, the introductions opened with that nauseating question, "What's your degree in? And where did you go to school? And when did you graduate? With honors?" As the sparring between the two was drawing to a close, the chap who seemed to be losing the battle, in a classic statement, stood upon the conference room table and simply peed all over the other guy. The poor guy so hideously christened started dissolving and cackling something about, "And what methodology did you use to statistically verify the null hypothesis?" The scenario ends with everyone leaving the room careful not to step on the pile of empty clothes, all that remained of a once smart fellow.

This leaves the sanity of educators in question. There is, also, a certain legacy with numerous idiotic concepts that education carries forth. For example, one might consider fertility in ancient Greek drama, chimneys as phallic symbols, or, perhaps, the untold problems Gulliver caused by relieving himself in Lilliput! There are LIFO and FIFO, the twin brothers, raised by wolves, who discovered Rome. There is the marginal utility of a loaf of bread, if you've already eaten one. And, there's the distinction between aggressive and assertive behaviors, both of which will get you in trouble with the arresting officer.

The fact that we actually pay tuition for our own torment is an amazement to me. We pay educators to assign us some of the most boring reading in the world. Over time, we read thousands of pages of it. And then, one of those academic types might whip out an obscure quotation and demand the author, the work, the genre, and ultimately, the relationship of the quotation to the mating behavior of French bread!

What kind of legacy is this to carry forth? The bottom line is that without all that education we probably wouldn't have the critical thinking ability to know the difference. We wouldn't know as we passed through life how bad some of it really was, and how good other parts were, and how desperately education needs changing. The good and the not-so-good in education are all part of who we are and who we are not. It is simply a part of our identity.

Melissa collapsed. She was taken to the fourth moon, and to Myana's charge for a total mind, body, spirit healing. The Council sat quietly for several minutes. Kathryn was stunned by Melissa's perception of America's educational climate. As in Antonio's case however, this perception was nothing she was aware of, nor anything she reported back to Leo.

When Nancy talked with the Council of the Elders, there were, to no one's surprise, discrepancies between her Earth-time experiences and Kathryn's records. In Nancy's case the Earth-plane vibrational leakage was the most severe. Antonio's leakage was focused in despair and for Melissa the focus was sarcasm. Nancy's primary problem was anger and this proved to be the most serious Earth-plane vibrational leakage Eyespell would face. Nancy's anger was neither sporadic nor manic, it was constant and deliberate. It approached evil, a vibration Eyespell was totally unfamiliar with and unprepared for. Nancy got into it right off.

"You know, you Elders, you Eyespellian Elders, are not as unique as you might think. The Earth has its New Age and you better pay attention to the Earth's crystal charge, and the power of that charge to bring Eyespell its due for hoarding the light-skew. There are rituals on the planet Earth, Satanic rituals to name one type, the vibrations of which could cause this planet to crack in two! Eyespellian rainbows would be shredded into ribbons of black suffering. The blue sun would fall from the sky and the planet would be bathed in the hideous warmth of a deadly and silent radiation that would slowly turn skin to scrap heaps of burnt and crusted flesh. You would be forced out-of-body forever."

Nancy smiled an unnatural smile in a face that shifted almost imperceptibly, alternating between striking beauty and intense ugliness. The dome of the Council Chamber began to give off quick, sharp, cracking sounds as a warning that it might shatter into trillions of bits of molecular dust if the vibrational onslaught were to continue.

The Elders, taking Nancy's essence with them, moved out-of-body to the furthest reaches of the Pinar Galaxy. They came to rest on the outermost edge of the Domeshodar, a menacing black hole. Legend had it that the ancient Eyespellians, in the time of creation of the light-skew, cast out all evil, throwing it into this galactic hole.

The negative vibration near the perimeter of this place was too great for any Eyespellian to endure for very long. Daniel, keeper of the Yellow Crystal of Knowledge and Head of the Council, recognized the acute danger here on the fringe of Eyespell's galaxy. To save the other Elders and his beloved planet from the rapidly encroaching grip of the dark-skew, he grabbed Nancy's essence and dove into the center of the Domeshodar.

Shaken by this powerfully negative experience the remaining five Elders materialized once again in the twenty-seventh ring of the Council Chamber to continue the business of saving Eyespell. They formed a prayer circle around the perimeter of the central ring, trying to recreate the spirit of the sixth and lost elder. They did not move for thirty-three days.

The cell-matrix of the planet was breaking apart as the Earth-plane vibrational leakage sparked by Nancy's outburst in the Council Chamber wrought tinges of evil upon Eyespell. Pockets of devastation were swift and final, like the powerful and sometimes instantaneous lava and pyroclastic flows down the side of a mighty and exploding volcano. Eyespellians fled the planet surface out-of-body, and stayed suspended in cavities of safe space high in the planet's aura hoping it would be possible to return.

Four hundred twenty-six physical bodies were lost in the destruction. The physical presences of these Eyespellians could be re-manifested, but only at a great energy cost in times already draining the light-skew. When the time was right Matthew, Keeper of Energy and the red-light corridor along with those in his charge, would play the instrumental role in the re-manifestation of the lost bodies.

There was great demand on the Council's energies in many areas at once. There was the constant vigil of protecting the light-skew of the planet in general, the repairing of substantial breaks in the cell-matrix, and the healing of those with extreme vibrational discomfort, such as Antonio and Melissa. There was the maintenance of the prayer circle. There was a new link with Phillip and Christian on the planet Earth. And there were

Nancy and Daniel; in all likelihood they were gone forever. The Eldersix were now five.

At noon on the last day of the five Elders' thirty-three day vigil, a beautiful clear diamond cut in the form of a double pyramid manifested at the exact center of the prayer circle. The crystal appeared to be floating about seven feet above the floor of the chamber giving off a pure yellow light. Over the next several hours the form of an Eyespellian manifested around the crystal. The full figure stood holding the diamond crystal high above his head with one point of the pyramid resting on and balanced within the center of the heels of his cupped hands. The Council acknowledged this being as the new Keeper of the Yellow-Light Corridor. Peter emerged from the yellow aura. He was the fourth Eyespellian to have returned and was, indeed, the same entity who had donned a Raider's cap on the Earth less than one year before.

He spoke to the Council, "Greetings. I now keep the charge of the yellow-light corridor. I am soul-son of Daniel and take his place here by his choice. He must stay out-of-body to cleanse his spirit of the Domeshodar, a task of interminable duration. I know of Earth and I know of Eyespell."

The clear diamond crystal on its rope of yellow light lay glistening against Peter's chest. With Peter in the center ring The Council was again whole and would resume its vigil over Eyespell and now under Leo's direction as newly appointed Head of the Eldersix. Before the thirty-three day vigil ended, another crystal manifested at the exact center of the council chamber, this time a golden topaz identical to the one in Phillip's charge on Earth.

CHAPTER 18

▼

THE CAMPAIGN TRAIL (EARTH)

Christian was running for a U. S. Senate seat in New York State. And he was sure to win. The world vision was changing. There was movement away from a nationalistic, monocultural perspective to a multicultural perspective. There was the positive impact of Mystic Management and what Christian's father called, "planetaryvision." Planetaryvision is the broad vision of the world as the interconnected whole, not only in physical attributes, but in peoples and cultures. Distinct individual differences become a celebration.

It was 2038, six years since Christian, Phillip, and their Eyespellian colleagues had first formulated the Mystic Management principles for Earth. Christian's success as CEO of Used Water Works was nothing less than spectacular. He was charismatic in his ability to preach and practice the six tenets he first scribbled down in his journal; he truly "walked the talk." While he had not previously thought about politics, his involvement did seem an appropriate step in deploying Mystic Management on a wider scale. His nomination acceptance speech focused on the commitment he had made to uphold and spread the Mystic Management tenets...wordwide.

"Ladies and Gentlemen, it takes but one fragment of the hologram to reconstruct the total image. We are here today to gather fragments of community to project through our laser. So let's focus our thinking on the history of American ideals. Let's focus on that combination of myth and milieu that defines our reality as Americans. We Americans have a predisposition to the frontier mindset and we have a propensity for forging into the virgin land!"

The crowd cheered Christian's opening words.

He continued, "That is, Americans have a propensity for forging into the virgin land, and very nearly destroying everything in our path on the way to achieving our high-minded goals! The themes of timelessness, sacredness, and rebirth through nature have taken many forms in the art, literature, politics, and business philosophies of America. But somewhere in our desire for greatness we became corrupt! The purity we seek can be delivered to posterity only if an unadulterated tie with nature can be maintained. And somewhere in the past while seeking this purity, we instead delivered corruptness as the untamed and limitless expanse of the American wilderness of the nineteenth century offered itself as a sacrificial ground for our unbridled greed!"

The crowd stood and clapped in unanimous approval. After several moments, Christian continued.

"What happened after industry ate up the land? Where is the sustained nature? Now the land is polluted; we have fouled our own nest. We must become one with our environment, instead of haphazardly dominating it. We must celebrate the new frontier with new community achieved through Mystic Management and a mystic leadership. And I offer you the promise of both. Thank you."

While Christian was speaking his words in New York, his father was presenting a paper at a National Education Association convention in Washington, D.C., also spreading the word.

Phillip opened his talk, "It is imperative that we, once and for all, liberate education. Traditional education kills creativity and domesticates students. In order to be viable, education must be dialogical; there must be the exchange of opinions and ideas among all involved in the process. Effective education must also reflect community and empower the individuals within that community to think for themselves."

Phillip skillfully led his audience from creativity to group-centered learning, and ultimately to the principles of Mystic Management applied in the educational context. While there was healthy debate, there was surprisingly little substantive disagreement with Phillip's message.

Christian and Phillip served as Earth's key role models for the Mystic Management. They continued to spread the new paradigm through a variety of venues. With the help of those on Eyespell, they worked at giving the Earth a shove in the right direction. It had been six years and the Mystic Management was still only a molecule adrift among all other Earth vibrations. It was imperative for that molecule to permanently bond to the fabric of the Earth's social matrix.

The Earth needed to openly embrace the principles of Mystic Management to establish the basis for a new cell-matrix, bonding Earth and her inhabitants. The single most important characteristics underlying the possibility of Earth achieving this cell-matrix were compassion and unconditional self-love. Christian and Phillip were in constant touch with Eyespell and, recognizing unconditional love as a primary Eyespellian trait, they sought much council in the development of such from Myana. She provided extensive and interesting insights.

"Let me try to explain it this way," began Myana, "While one must love oneself before one can truly love others, on Earth it has been easier to love those at a distance, those we have little contact with and no responsibility for. Loving in the abstract is less challenging than loving in a first hand, personal way. Consequently, those of Earth have serious problems with unconditional self-love. Self-love, for and on Earth, would be achievable only by starting outward from a global perspective, working inward to the self. Unconditional self-love is the innermost circle of the system, the smallest sub-system, the most personal. It is the locomotive roundhouse connecting meaning and identity in the physical world, the psychological world, and the spiritual world. In this context, unconditional self-love is also the outermost circle of the system and the most global. It is the fabric that spirals in and out of all living molecules; it is the building block of the planetary cell-matrix."

Phillip interjected, "Planet Earth, through its Mystic Management, is beginning to spiral outward into the transcultural and inward into a self-assured identity. The outward is the easier task. It seems that the further an Earth being moves away from self, the easier it becomes to love unconditionally. Love for its own sake has never been simple to achieve within the typical Earth vibration. Unconditional love is of the light-skew."

"Yes," said Myana. "On Earth, it appears that one can, without expectation and unconditionally take up more easily the cause of an unknown child in a third world country than the cause of a child across town; the cause of a distant relative's child than the cause of a sister's child; the cause of a sister than the cause of one's own child; and most difficult of all, the cause of one's own inner child. It seems that the closer to self one gets the more conditional the love; the more likely there are rules and expectations. "I will do this if you won't do that." "I'll help if you promise to...or not to...""

Christian added, "One effect of the dark-skew is that it causes most people on Earth to be secretly terrified that something awful lurks inside them, something that might surface at any moment. For most people, internalization of the dark-skew leads to vibrations such as fear, anger, hurt, pain, anxiety, guilt, worry, depression, and other symptoms of lost identity and poor self-concept. These inner feelings whether manifested in any action or not, certainly make unconditional love a trying task. Trust me, I know. It's only recently that I sense my Eyespellian heritage. While I've been fortunate to have Mom and Dad as coaches, I've not always been so sure of myself or so able to love unconditionally."

Phillip was pensive. After a few moments he looked up and said, "Living on the Earth is like living in a vibrational cesspool. The trick is to survive life within the cesspool without becoming an integral part of its contents. The time of madness was my deepest immersion in the dark-skew—I was in the deepest part of the cesspool. If it wasn't for your mother, Christian, I don't know what would have become of me. Unfortunately, the dark-skew has its share of followers. There are those who are, indeed, willingly an integral part of the cesspool. Many on Earth vehemently oppose the concepts of Mystic Management. In fact, I came across a pamphlet just yesterday launching devastating attacks against the new paradigm."

"Was that the one called *Mystic Nonsense*?" asked Christian.

"Yes, where did you see it?"

"It has been widely distributed, believe me. That pamphlet is quite a piece of propaganda. I hope these types of opposition don't slow the fruition of our efforts. In this case the vibration smacks of mixed-message humor and black satire. It's just clever enough to confuse those who may be on the fence. What's really disconcerting is that I am personally attacked. My Mystic Management message is heralded as Pollyanna nonsense that will cost people their livelihoods, and maybe ultimately even their lives. In their claim to actually believe in a number of the basic positive tenets of Mystic Management the mixed message is insidious."

"A loving message is deemed a dangerous thing to some people," Myana softly stated. "Could you mind-scan the pamphlet for me? I am curious to know what you're up against."

"Allow me," said Phillip. He carefully scanned *Mystic Nonsense* for Myana to review.

Mystic Management or Mystic Nonsense?
(Easter, 2038)

Brethren, I believe that forces of good and evil battle all around us.
I further believe that positive thoughts draw good vibrations and

negative thoughts draw evil vibrations. And, most importantly, I believe that each of us has the responsibility for the vibrations we create and the energies those vibrations potentially unleash into our shared lifespace. Yes, brethren, that is what I believe.

The most significant concept I will ever share with you is this: I believe that internal disharmony is the most subtle and wide-spread form of evil. I believe that individual internal disharmony is the springboard from which mild dissatisfaction can escalate toward severe warring among the peoples of this planet.

And, I believe this new Mystic Management philosophy you've all been hearing about has the potential to create just such disharmony. I believe it is a bunch of nonsense, down-right stupid, silly, not fit for a child's brain! It will cost you your jobs and your lifestyles just for starters. It is quick to tell you what to give up, but not so quick to replace your loss with anything but a bunch of well-sounding words! So let's laugh it off.

As you know, I am the founder of the Church Of The Sixteen Intertwining Minds and Foot. I'm sure that doesn't sound any dumber than Mystic Management, now does it? And, as the Foot, I speak the truth, out-of-mouth, or is that, out-of-body; oh so sorry. This pamphlet, *Mystic Management or Mystic Nonsense*, is one in a series the Church presents to bring fundamental truths to light where there has been tremendous discussion and dissent, such as in this Mystic Management business. Perhaps you have read some of our other publications:

#17 *Has Early Retirement Worked For Christ?*

#22 *The Virgin Mary On Birth Control*

#86 *Is There Masturbation After Death And, If So, Does It Still Cause Blindness?*

#64 *Animals Of The Old Testament*

#93 *The Father, Son, And Holy Spirit: Team Management or Chaos?*

#51 *Speaking In One Tongue At A Time*

#45 *How The Seven Deadly Sins Can Make You Happy And Rich*

#15 *Bush Talk: An Interview With Moses.*

Brethren, for every moment that you may have laughed at our nonsense, for every one of those moments, internal disharmony was prevented. For every one of those moments, there was no negative vibration and, in some small way, we were delivered from evil, amen! Now this Mystic Management stuff causes a lot of heavy thinking and therefore, a lot of potential disharmony, and very little laughing, amen! For example, we are forced to think about things that might produce guilt. And then, even if we end up doing the right thing, whatever that may be, we do it out of that guilt. This costs us a great deal of mental energy and ultimate disharmony. Why should the right thing feel so bad? And before long, nobody is happy, nobody is laughing. We all sit around wishing we could bring the old ways back. And how often have each of us thought that?

Now, these insights that I am privy to, brethren, did not come to me easily. You have, no doubt, heard of the *Akashic Records*. These are the recorded history of the Collective Unconscious. They contain everything that has ever happened to every soul in all of their lifetimes. This is a very large book and is kept in heaven.

When Christian Hansen chose to go to sleep to dream about a mystic manager, I went to heaven to find out the real story. And guess what I found? It isn't called a Mystic Management at all. In the *Akashic Records*, the mystic manager is found in the annals of the Star Light, Star Bright School of Management Thought. Before you know it they'll be telling us that all the mystic manager has to do is wish it, and, poof, there it is! My, my, how convenient. What shall I create today? Kind of stupid don't you think?

Myana said, "Little can be done to counteract the vibrational impact of the pamphlet. It operates in the realm of half-truths and deception. Indeed, the great truth in what your opposition says is that 'the subtlest form of evil is internal disharmony.' And he creates it so well and indeed, such disharmony would block unconditional self-love. It is amazing how one thing always seems to eventually connect to everything else. The circle must be pure or it ultimately contaminates itself."

Despite efforts to the contrary the concepts of the Mystic Management flourished and the next year, 2039, saw the Earth moving toward the light-skew. It had been seven years since that transforming night at Cathedral Rock when Earth and Eyespell connected. It had been forty-seven years since the re-entry window had moved past the Earth plane and left Phillip Hansen on an alien world. The events on Earth and on Eyespell during those forty-seven years put the two planets in undeniable vibrational crossover. Earth-plane vibrational leakage was threatening to destroy Eyespell and the Mystic Management was promising to save Earth.

There was one irrefutable connection between the two planets, one thing that was of Earth and of Eyespell, and that was the manifestation of the golden topaz pyramids. There was an Order higher and more powerful than either planet bent on saving them both. And that Higher Order was the Creative Life Force, the One Infinite Creator, the Logos, God, the Goddess, whatever term one chooses to use. It was time to meet again at the Valley of the Bluenoon and at Cathedral Rock. Phillip, Christian, Leo, and Pete began making preparations.

CHAPTER 19

▼

IN THE MEADOW
(EYESPELL AND EARTH)

By the light of Earth's July full moon, and for the second time in seven years in monk's garb, Phillip and Christian made their way up the flank of Cathedral Rock. Once at the base of the central spire, they sat cross-legged, facing each other with knees touching. They immediately achieved a deep meditative state as they held the golden topaz between them, supported by the tips of their twenty fingers.

By the light of Eyespell's third full moon of Oneness, Peter and Leo made their way to the tower of rock in the center of the Valley of the Bluenoon. Once at the base of the spire, they sat cross-legged, facing each other, with knees touching. They immediately achieved a deep meditative state as they held the golden topaz between them, supported by the tips of their twenty fingers.

At Cathedral Rock, the golden crystal's light expanded to embrace both father and son within a chamber of yellow light and at the Valley of the

Bluenoon, the golden crystal's light expanded to embrace both Peter, Keeper of the Yellow Sun, and Leo, Keeper of the Blue Sun within a chamber of yellow light.

The topaz light continued to expand in the two holy places as the four remained in deep meditative states. Within a short time Earth and Eyespell achieved connection through an interstellar corridor of space and time and the four pilgrims, two on Earth and two on Eyespell, began to travel, as if sucked through a powerful vacuum tube, at faster-than-light speed from opposite directions toward a place exactly between the vibrations of the two planets.

As their minds reached outward, they saw the likeness of a million-faceted mirrored ball spinning against the dance floor of infinite space. The colors of the universe reflected in the silver ball's mirrors. As if on cue, the dance-floor-ball exploded into a trillion dots of cosmic color reforming into a beam of brilliant yellow-white light stretching far ahead of the four travelers. Their journey continued along the beam as if falling through a tunnel toward an incredible white light. Phillip immediately recognized this as the same tunnel and light of his near-death experience over forty-seven years ago.

Within what seemed mere seconds from the onset of their journey, the four pilgrims in simple monk's garb spilled out from the tunnel experience onto the soft carpet of a lush green alpine-like meadow. There were two mountain streams, pencil thin as viewed in the larger perspective of the surrounding meadow. They were flowing down the gentle slopes from opposite directions, cascading over the moss-covered, rounded boulders. The melodic sound of water making its way over the rounded rocks soothed and invigorated. The wind almost imperceptibly sang in the uppermost reaches of the stately trees at the meadow's perimeter.

The four pilgrims stood on a ledge of neatly layered rock just above the point where the two streams merged. The crystal clear waters cascaded gently into a shimmering pool below them. Still awestruck by their journey and the beauty of their reached destination, no one moved or spoke.

After several minutes, the four embraced and cried soft tears of joy. It was as if Eyespell and Earth had joined like the streams meeting above the pool as the four pilgrims embracd two separate worlds.

The beautiful yellow-white light intensified and countless golden light specks drenched the meadow and its visitors like a spring morning's shower. Bathed in this light shower, the four pilgrims felt a peacefulness and the sense of being loved unconditionally beyond description within the boundaries of language. The feeling even surpassed Myana's light charge of the pink crystal on Eyespell.

A figure of light manifested before them and picked up the two golden topaz crystals, reshaping them into a single perfect sphere. The sphere was placed close by in a small moss-covered cave of rock, not much larger than the sphere itself. Just above the cave the two streams, having separated, merged again and danced over the ledge of rock in a small waterfall, shielding the cave entrance and the golden sphere behind a shimmering veil of water.

The figure of light sat among the four and spoke these words into their consciousness, "Welcome into the love and the light. The golden sphere is the symbol of the perfect manifestation of Divine Order. It represents the coming of the spirit. The energy and essence of the four of you together in this place makes it possible for you to carry the vibrations of the meadow a thousand-fold to Earth and a thousand-fold to Eyespell."

"Earth and Eyespell come together in this meadow like the two streams. And, like the two streams, they emerge as one. The continued evolution of both planets is assured, as they merge. Eyespell will be of the light and Earth will be of the water. Light and water are of Eyespell and Earth." The figure of light touched their souls once again, leaving them bathed in the spirit.

Peter, Leo, Phillip and Christian stayed in this holy meadow between Eyespell and Earth for one hundred days. The destinies of Earth and Eyespell were forever connected. The vision was light for Eyespell and water for Earth.

CHAPTER 20

▼

RETURN TO THE DOMSHODAR (EYESPELL)

Eyespell's cell-matrix began to stabilize and the planet once again moved in harmony with the light-skew, only this time a light-skew not so fragile as to be destructively intolerant of vibrations unlike itself. Eyespell underwent major psychological adjustment, an attitude adjustment if you will, necessitating that Earth-plane vibrational leakage be embraced rather than avoided. Eyespell began to create a new reality, a reality meshing the vibrations of Earth and Eyespell.

It became increasingly more evident to each Eyespellian that the danger lie hidden not in Earth-plane vibrational leakage per se but in how it was perceived. Earth vibrations never had the capability of destroying Eyespell, only Eyespellians were capable of destroying the planet and its light-skew through their own manifested terror of homeostasis. The fear of Earth-plane vibrational leakage and its consequential negative impact was an Eyespellian-created reality. With the dispelling of this apprehension and acceptance of Earth-plane vibrations, balance between the dark-skew and the light-skew began to create a more comfortable and inclusive reality.

When Peter and Leo returned from the meadow this philosophy of inclusiveness was brought to bear on the planet's dilemma. The message of the golden sphere shaped by the Being of Light demanded a melding of Earth and Eyespell that would set both worlds on new and stirring paths through the cosmos. Through mind-link Leo visioned this new course for Eyespell. Detailed visualizations of the meeting in the meadow with the four pilgrims and their encounter with the Being of Light touched each Eyespellian. It did not take long for Earth-plane vibrational leakage to be appropriately reduced to the category of "different" rather than "dangerous," something to embrace rather than shrink from.

Under Leo and Peter's direction the Elders held several Full-Rounds introducing and expanding upon this new "Philosophy of Opposites" until it became part and parcel of Eyespell's collective consciousness and planetary cell-matrix. This philosophy was integrated with the Mystic Management, its teachings falling under the principle of Inclusive Integrity. The Philosophy of Opposites specifically added the element of surprise to Eyespellian reality creating. Prior to this time Eyespell was tolerant of all things Eyespellian. It was a loving and inclusive planet within its own framework. Eyespell was capable, willing, and even eager to give of itself to the universe (and thus the Eyespell Experiment). It was a compassionate planet. Eyespell did not however consider receiving back from the universe except from some defined Power even more of the light-skew than Eyespell itself. So embracing opposites such as Earth-plane vibrational leakage was initially no easy task for the Eyespellian consciousness.

Ultimately, however, the vibrations of Earth were so completely absorbed that they manifested as a new and darker color of the Eyespellian rainbow. This new assemblage of colors in the deep indigo to purple to violet shades was absorbed, at least for the moment, as part of the blue-light corridor, Leo's crystal charge. The pastel beauty of the planet was actually enhanced with the addition of this planned, understood, and appropriate contrast. So then, the encounter with the Being of Light and the insights gleaned through His compassion and love were deemed so extraordinary that a new page entitled "Meadow Spirit" was added to *The Book of Dreams*. What happened in the meadow was nothing less than a crossroads in Eyespellian evolution.

The Mystic Management espoused, valued, and celebrated differences as never before. With this adjusted psyche and acceptance of even extreme opposites, Eyespell was for the first time truly secure in a multifaceted Universe, a dynamic giving and taking universe. Acknowledgment of Earth as a sister planet on its own pathway of the light-skew gave Eyespellians the ability to effectively deal with and dispel all fear of the dark-skew. As comfort with Earth vibrations increased and work with the new color configurations amplified, what just a while ago was dubbed Earth-plane vibrational leakage was the basis not only for new colors in the Eyespellian rainbow, but the basis for the formation of an entirely new light corridor. The first hint of this phenomenon was the appearance in the Eyespellian consciousness of a glorious deep purple amethyst crystal on a rope of light. This was unprecedented and magnificent.

Antonio, Melissa, and Peter with their Earth-fused memories were tremendous assets in the conversion to balance and the expansion of the light-skew. It was still strange to think that Peter, now one of the Eldersix, had been Pete, N.Y.C. juvenile delinquent. However, it was just this type of fusion that made the psychological shift possible on Eyespell. Probably the most valuable and difficult lesson for Eyespell, and a prime reason for its continued vision of embracing differences, was the loss of Nancy and Daniel in the Domeshodar. All were convinced that such a loss could have been averted with their new, more balanced vision. Perhaps, with the new joining of Earth and Eyespell even this grievous loss might yet have a positive resolution. With Daniel somewhere off world and out-of-body for an indefinite period cleansing his spirit of the Domeshodar, and Nancy still deep in the Domeshodar, there certainly existed a formidable challenge.

But just maybe the Domeshodar might be a far less threatening place with Earth-plane vibrational leakage as an ally.

****

In celebration of his one-hundred-fifth birthday and having completed his role in the Earth's transition to a Mystic Management, Phillip Hansen in the Earth-year 2077 manifested permanently to Eyespell. He would have been unable to maintain his life-force on planet Earth for much longer and he was not yet ready to end his current incarnation. A new re-entry window was created for him on Eyespell and on Earth Phillip died peacefully in his sleep. It would have been difficult to leave Jo and Christian behind were it not for his telepathy link. They were literally never more than a thought away.

The missing Eyespellian finally returned home eighty-five years after the original re-entry window had closed on the Eyespell Experiment. He found himself naked under the fourth and most beautiful moon of Eyespell. The moon shone a bright pink across the white desert sands as if in his honor. Phillip's over-one-hundred-year-old Earthling frame had already tightened into the pleasant anatomy of the typical Eyespellian. He was again one with the planetary cell-matrix and he could feel it in every molecule of his being.

A light breeze swept over his limbs and carried a barely perceptible voice between its undulating currents, "I'm coming, I'm coming, I'm coming." Phillip instantly sensed the voice as Leo's. He looked up and caught a glimpse of Leo almost bounding over the evening-lit sands with a small bundle between his hands.

He stopped just short of Phillip, almost running him down in his excitement. He threw the bundle in the air and grasped him in a crushing bear hug, "You are the fifth one back! Eighty-five years late, but back nonetheless. I believe I've just thrown your clothes away. I think I'm excited." The sands shifted ever so slightly under their feet as the cell-matrix positively and excitedly responded to the long overdue reunion.

Phillip gathered up the bundle, spilled out the contents, and got dressed. With pure mischief in his eyes he said, "This may be the first time I've ever seen an Elder leaping through the sand. With eighty-five years to plan it, you would think you could have hit my re-entry a little closer."

"Yes, you would think. But, alas my son, just like the first time, you were the problem, not me. I about had a fit when I reached the re-entry point and you weren't there! My agitation probably caused a thunderstorm or two. I think I even used a little profanity, something I learned from you during your Earth time. I was exactly where I was supposed to be; three dunes to the north. But you landed here. Just a flicker of a thought about the tunnel that broke your telepathy link last time, and wham, you were three dunes off on re-entry. That'll make an Elder leap!"

Phillip could barely stop laughing at Leo's feigned indignation. Finally he managed to say, "It feels so good here. I haven't laughed so hard in over a hundred years. The only comparable feelings on Earth are my love for Jo and Christian. I am even now in touch with them. I have obviously avoided any re-entry trauma; everything seems in perfect working order."

"Wonderful. Bring your mind-friends and join us for the party. Everything is set."

"So where is this party?"

"Exactly three dunes to the north where I believe you were supposed to be in the first place."

Phillip's homecoming to Eyespell was nothing less than spectacular. There was light bending just-for-the-fun-of-it, rainbow making, and other games of the light-skew. The initial bouts of Earth-plane vibrational leakage bent on destroying Eyespell were gone and the planet cell-matrix felt whole with the return of this adventurer.

Phillip took up residence in Elasia and almost immediately turned his psychic attention to issues of Eyespell's expanded blue-light corridor and what might be done about the still uncertain destinies of Daniel and

Nancy. Perhaps his prolonged stay on Earth would allow him to intervene
in a way impossible for any other Eyespellian. Phillip and Leo spent much
time together hypothesizing about what might be done and when. They
often discussed the beautiful golden sphere left in the meadow assuring
Eyespell and Earth's joint destinies. They wondered if another visit to this
meadow might hold the clue. They shared their thoughts openly and there
were exciting debates as to where the place of the yellow light might actually be in physical space, assuming, of course, that it had a physical reality.
And that was the subject of even more exciting debate, was the meadow a
real place? Things were quite normal on Eyespell; debate was lively and
time was of no consequence.

And then it happened. In the midst of particularly lively planetary ban-
tering about the exact whereabouts of the meadow, the deep amethyst
crystal recently brought into Eyespellian awareness manifested in physical
reality. It materialized hanging from its rope of light around the neck of
none other than Phillip Hansen. The Eldersix instantly became the
Elderseven with Phillip taking charge of the newly formed Purple Light
Corridor. This was Kambudi, the coming of the spirit.

A Full-Round was immediately called and for the first time on Eyespell
a Full-Round opened with the laser show from seven light corridors coming from seven crystals in the twenty-seventh ring of the council chamber.
And with this opening came other new things to Eyespell. The three hundred thirty-seven in the council chamber became three hundred thirty-
eight. The planetary cell-matrix physically expanded to host a beautiful
purple desert with its shifting sands of color in every hue of purple. A fifth
and violet moon appeared in the night sky. And most amazing of all, new
souls arrived on Eyespell as purple points of light. In-body their cheeks
shone ever so subtly the beautiful purple tones of the spirit. The whole
had become greater than the sum of its parts. There was, indeed, a cosmic
synergy on Eyespell. The spirit of Eyespell filled the Pinar galaxy.

Phillip took up his crystal charge and led his new soul mates into the purple desert for their first pilgrimage. They totaled two hundred twelve. Their

robes were a deep purple and on each sleeve was the insignia of two planets in overlapping arcs, one distinctly blue and one distinctly pink with the overlap a plum purple tone. The symbolism was of Earth and of Eyespell.

This first pilgrimage was both celebratory and solemn in its purpose. The celebration was one of new souls, a new light corridor, and the leadership of a new Elder. The immensity of this level of change on Eyespell was staggering even to the Eyespellian imagination. This was the first time the reality of Eyespell seemed to be coming from outside of itself. Albeit positive and of the light-skew Eyespell until now, had been a closed system. Eyespellian reality had been predictable, it was, after all, created by consensus. This new reality, this expansion, was different. While possibly lurking somewhere deep in the unconscious mind of Eyespellians the manifestations of recent days did not appear to be controlled by them. The created reality of the purple light corridor was not one of consensus but one of surprise. The physical manifestation of the amethyst crystal light charge was a cosmic surprise. While Eyespellians were always pleased with their creations, they were not surprised by them. Moreover, the expansion of the planet's size and the fifth moon in the night sky seemed beyond the reality creating abilities of mere Eyespellians or, at least they had never consciously thought to create anything of such magnitude. In any event, with the arrival of the souls of the purple light corridor on planet Eyespell all doubt about whether there was outside influence was erased. Eyespellians were certain this was not their creation. This was of the One Infinite Creator, this was of God.

This pilgrimage of the two hundred twelve to the purple desert was not the typical Eyespellian pilgrimage. The Elder leading such a happening always had an absolute certainty of purpose and direction. Phillip was infant in his role as the Seventh Elder of Eyespell. He was not even clear where, exactly, out from Elasia the purple desert was. It was even less clear what, exactly, it would be like in its topography or its vibration. For all practical purposes, except for a brief light show at the last Full-Round, no one on Eyespell had any experience with the purple light corridor. In spite of this uncharacteristic backdrop there was no fear of the unknown on Eyespell, simply quiet, focused, and yet childlike expectation.

After five walking days travel north and past the Valley of the Blue Noon the party of two hundred twelve found themselves at the fringe of the purple desert. As they stood looking out for the first time over the multi-purple-hued dunes, dark colored sands washed over their feet in small waves of greeting. The colors in their cheeks sparkled in consonance with the gently tumbling grains of sand as they fell back into the desert. Phillip removed his crystal from its pouch and held it high above his head as the two hundred twelve introduced themselves to their new landscape. The party moved a short distance onto the purple sands and gathered into a prayer circle. This was a circle of joy, celebration, and welcomed new beginnings. It was in stark contrast to the circle of foreboding Leo hastily formed to protect the Eyespell Experiment returnees from the first tremors of Earth-plane vibrational leakage in what seemed just a moment ago. Phillip stood at the center of the circle and with his amethyst crystal pointed toward the heavens, opened the purple light corridor and formally presented this new place to all of Eyespell. The purple vibration was now officially part of Eyespellian reality. After much rejoicing the corridor was closed and the pilgrims set about the more solemn aspect of their first pilgrimage into the purple desert.

Phillip addressed the children of the purple skew. "It has been a wonderful celebration of new life on Eyespell, both symbolically and literally. We are of the spirit. When I was on planet Earth and moved through the tunnel of near death I saw a tribesman running and yelling, 'Kambudi! Kambudi! Kambudi, kami alla goda!' The experience was profound. Even though it seemed totally disconnected from my conscious thoughts I somehow knew that the tribesman was announcing the 'coming of the spirit.' I could feel his excitement. I thought the circle of my thoughts was closed in the meadow when the Being of Light used those same words. I thought I understood that the coming of the spirit meant that the Being of Light would connect Earth and Eyespell in this cosmic dance. I had no inkling of this time and this place. I had no inkling of the destiny I feel for us. I know that through the power of this light corridor, the purple light corridor, we can retrieve Daniel from out-of-body and save Nancy from the depths of the Domshodar. We can make Eyespell truly whole again."

Each pilgrim spoke softly into Phillip's mind, "Let us begin."

Phillip knew intuitively to journey further due north into the heart of the purple desert and there he would find the place they sought to begin their work. This time he moved with the absolute certainty of an Elder leading a holy pilgrimage. The monks put up their beautiful purple robes and donned the brown garb of serious business on Eyespell. They moved across the purple sands chanting and drenched in the light of the violet full moon.

By daybreak they came upon a succession of steep dunes leading upward like a giant stairway. At the top of the seventeenth dune the desert sands gave way to a concave carved bowl of lavender stone. The bowl sloped down to a huge entrance to a cave. Phillip knew this to be the place they were seeking. He led the pilgrims into the mouth of the cave. The vibration was reminiscent of the Valley of the Blue Noon as this too was a holy place. Where the valley of the Blue Noon stretched out from the landscape the Cave of Purple Dawn, as it came to be called, leapt into the desert floor. The inside of the cave was lit as if by an invisible candle and shone mirror-like crystals of all shades of amethyst lining its walls and ceiling.

The pilgrims moved to its innermost sanctum and formed a tight 'ball of monk' part in-body and part out-of-body to become one with each other and the Purple Dawn surroundings. At the very core of the ball Phillip pressed his crystal to his solar plexus and the two hundred twelve monks began to spin slowly in place in a counterclockwise direction. The purple light corridor burst open creating an intense stream of deep purple, almost black, light from the Cave of the Purple Dawn to the Domshodar. The energy force produced by this incredible burst of spirit pierced the blackness of the hole and snatched Nancy's essence returning it filled with purple light to Eyespell. Nancy became one again with her body and awoke as if from a long sleep. She found herself in the cave surrounded by the absolute love of her soul mates. She all but glowed a deep purple.

Phillip was the first to speak. "Nancy, do you know where you are?"

Her reply was quick. "Know where I am? Of course, and you, Phillip, I see you finally made it home." Her broad smile and loving eyes did not speak of a woman whose vibrations, not that long ago, threatened to destroy an entire planet. She hugged Phillip for a long time and in due course made physical contact with each Eyespellian in the cave and mental contact with the entire planet of Eyespellians. She remembered nothing of the Domshodar except that she had been there. The pilgrims, now numbering two hundred thirteen, left the cave.

Phillip's incredible excitement about Nancy's return was only slightly dampened by the failure to bring Daniel back to Eyespell. He thought to himself, "I'm sure we will succeed next time."

"What do you mean next time?" The booming voice reverberated around the cave's opening and seemed to bounce off the concave floor mightily into everyone's head.

Phillip and the others looked around but in the glare of the yellow sun high over the desert could not see anyone. Nonetheless Phillip could feel the strong vibrations that went with the ever so strong voice. And then, from out of the shadow of a giant bristle cone tree growing out of the rock, stepped a tall, very black man. Around his neck from a rope of light hung a pitch black smoky quartz crystal. All of Eyespell recognized the vibration of this man, it was Daniel. The Elderseven were now Eight.

"Yes, I am Daniel and you have brought me home Phillip Hansen, or should I say Elder Phillip Hansen?"

Phillip was unable to speak. He approached Daniel and put his hands around the black crystal hanging at his chest. He was astounded at what he felt.

Daniel laughed a booming laugh. "Curious isn't it? Mine is the crystal of no light, no corridor. I need no corridor, all of Eyespell's light corridors are my no-light-skew. I am the black pigment in the white paint. Mine is the crystal charge that will give Eyespell its ultimate balance and ultimate protection. I complete the circle from Gracina's white light corridor to this, the no light corridor. There is so much power in my blackness that I manage this charge alone. I will remain the only one like me on Eyespell. My return is the ultimate gift of the two things Eyespell has ever feared, Earth-plane vibrational leakage and the Domshodar."

Phillip hugged Daniel and all of Eyespell welcomed him home. The only thing Phillip managed to say was, "So what do you think of this purple desert?" All had a good laugh at Phillip the Elder's inability to verbally express his incredible amazement at the events in the purple desert and the Cave of the Purple Dawn.

It wasn't long before Eyespell got back down to the business of debating the all-illusive whereabouts of the meadow. But they had time.

CHAPTER 21

▼

THE ELDER-NINE (EARTH)

Earth's new vision took on physical as well as psychological expression. Within a mere quarter of a century after Phillip and Christian returned to Earth from the meadow, the Mystic Management had permeated almost every major corporation, government agency and educational institution across the planet. Subsequent to his father's return to Eyespell, Christian Hansen, by then seventy-nine, carried on the work of the Mystic Management and was instrumental in the planet's sustained movement toward the light-skew. After his Senate win in New York Christian vigorously supported the direction of corporations like U.W.W., ultimately returning to private life as a consultant to organizations throughout the world. His objective was to infuse the Mystic Management philosophy on a local and a global level.

Jo Hansen, now one-hundred-four-years of age, stubbornly insisted upon remaining on the Earth plane. She said that she had much left to do and her time to manifest elsewhere had not yet come. Whenever Christian became too insistent upon her leaving the Earth plane for, perhaps Eyespell, Jo was quick to remind her son of his own almost octogenarian status. On Earth, unlike on Eyespell, there was not yet general acknowledgment of the existence of a sister planet moving in concert with a cosmic plan. While the acceptance of divine help had always been within the scope of the Earth psyche, the concept of extraterrestrials helping the Earth move toward the light-skew was not a part of most peoples' thinking.

Nonetheless, capitalizing on Christian Hansen's Eyespellian heritage the Elders used sustained mind-link to bring the Mystic Management teachings of the Council directly to the Earth-plane. These times of sustained link were dubbed Earth Summits. They were planned gatherings drawing large crowds and typically "awakened" many already enlightened souls on planet Earth. The continual movement toward the light-skew was greatly enhanced by these sessions and was most noticeable in the slow metamorphosis toward a planetary cell-matrix. The connection between the aliveness of the planet and its inhabitants was undeniably apparent. For the first time people of Earth noticed the relationship between feelings and physical reality. It became obvious that the planet's physical/geological well being was tied to its inhabitants' psychological well being. A harmony espoused by the lofty ideals of a Mystic Management seemed appropriate for keeping the Earth intact. Compassionate community-building was central to the Earth's conscious move toward sustainability and the focus of this newly recognized relationship between people and planet.

****

By 2063, the conflicts between disciplines such as economics and ecology dissipated as the Constant Harvest Philosophy replaced the myth of inexhaustability. This fresh direction for Earth evolved through its water conservation technology, the benchmark for which was set by Christian's early leadership in Used Water Works. U.W.W. was instrumental in developing crystalline city-structures that evolved out of their visionary water resource technologies. And with the advent of the first crystalline cities, the basis for current economic thought became almost instantly out-moded. New strategies were in order, strategies steadfastly bound to the long-term survival of planet Earth.

The groundwork for this transformation had existed since the late twentieth century beginning with the biosphere experiments in the New Mexico desert. U.W.W.'s conception of crystal-like city structures that combined technology for water conservation, the new economics, Mystic Management, and an environmentally alive cityscape would become the new paradigm of sustainability and was the crossroads in Earth evolution much like the advent of the Purple Light Corridor was the crossroads that permanently shifted Eyespell's consciousness.

The first crystalline structure was built in the Owens Valley, California, in 2074. It was based on the hexagonal properties of the quartz crystal replicated in huge double pyramids. Each was some two thousand feet across and ten stories high at its mid-point. The first crystal city contained twenty-seven clustered pyramids and three thousand thirty-nine perma-nent inhabitants including Phillip and Jo Hansen.

The inhabitants lived, played and worked within these environments. There was a natural evolution from fragmentation to community. The energy of the structure itself was healing and the relationships among peo-ple and between the people and the planet could be felt from every corner of the pyramid city. Within this city and among its inhabitants commu-nity eventually advanced to within a whisper of telepathy, mind-link, and cell-matrix as experienced on Eyespell. And this first city became the tem-plate for all cities on Earth throughout the next millennia.

The water recycling technology of U.W.W. formed the most critical infrastructure for these new cities. All water was captured, rejuvenated, and prepared for reuse. It was possible to capture ninety percent of the water on the first complete cycle alone. In economic terms, that meant if all of California used 35 million acre-feet of water per year, after the first year of recycling, some 31.5 million acre-feet of water could be available for reuse. Maintaining the same level of productivity in the second year would demand only 3.5 million acre-feet of "new" water. These statistics ultimately had a dramatic impact on productivity and gross national product. Perhaps even more important, the process allowed for tremendous population density increase at no additional long-term costs.

Integral to this new vision the various landscapes outside of the structures were restored to their natural wetland, woodland, desert, forest, or other pristine state. There was no reason to further ravage the land in the name of progress. Over the next years crystal structures were erected on sites where the natural landscape had been previously destroyed, such as current city locations or places where the natural aquifers had collapsed due to over-pumping, mining, or other man-made disasters.

The new cities provided agricultural, industry, government, education, and leisure. There, of course, was no restriction of movement between cities nor any reason to remain confined within a crystal structure. The physical face of civilization on planet Earth was dramatically and positively altered. The waters of the Earth flowed freely as the water molecule itself encompassed Earth's vision and became the first step in reality creating. The planetary cell-matrix for Earth was strengthening as boundaries and ownership were weakening in the face of the new communities directed by the Law of One.

In a future century, the light of Eyespell and the water of Earth, might create yet another mystic paradigm. Someday extraterrestrial brothers would retrieve the golden sphere in the meadow. Today as Christian Hansen stood at the apex of his pyramid abode watching the sun slowly rise over the desert, a brilliant clear crystal on its rope of light manifested around his neck. The Eldereight became Nine in a definitive cosmic gesture of planets joined.

About the Author

Dr. John Cicero lives in Northern California with his wife Christina. He is a professor at the local community college teaching courses in management and computer applications. His son Michael and his daughter-in-law Jessica are physical therapists also living in Northern California. John has over thirty years of blended work experiences including college professor and administrator; middle manager for a Fortune 500 company; consultant to business, education and government; sole proprietor; artist; and psychotherapist. He has his Ph.D. and M.B.A. degrees from Syracuse University and his A.B. from the University of Rochester. Primary avocations include rock, mineral, and gem collecting; landscape gardening; and day hiking.